THE SHADOW QUEEN

BY

SLOANE MURPHY

The Shadow Queen
The Shadow Queen #1
Part of The Seven Realms Saga

Published by Hudson Indie Ink
www.hudsonindieink.com

The Shadow Queen/Sloane Murphy – 1st ed.
ISBN-13 - 978-1-915118-07-3

To the Queens of my Bubble.

This one is for you

ONE

THEN

Have you ever had a moment that you know is going to define the very fiber of who you are as a person? The one moment that will shape who you are and how your whole life plays out? I watch what's happening before me in slow motion, and I know this is my moment.

The moment that's going to get me killed.

I scream in fury as my mother hits me, simply because my father was displeased with my tone at breakfast. I can't say I've ever been that close to my mom—I'm not sure she would have had children if my father hadn't required an heir. To be honest, I'm still not sure why they had me since they already had Ares. Besides selling me off to further their reach, which isn't beyond the Realms of my reality, it really makes little sense.

"It is not becoming of a princess to speak with such feral language!" she screams as she hits me again, her claws tearing through my cheek. My blood splatters against her face. She roars again as if the blood spatter is my fault, and it's all I can do to keep a lid on everything I want to say.

I know better than to talk back. I also know that if I do talk back, my mother won't be the one in here punishing me.

She hits me again, striking me across the chest with brutal force. The lid on my rage flies off. I can't control it as a heat unlike any I've ever known rips from me.

My mother's mouth makes an 'o' shape. It's as if she never thought there could be consequences for beating her child. She disintegrates in front of me, and my heart stops. This is going to change everything.

Holy shit, what have I done?

I fall to the ground, hitting my knees hard as I try to work out what the fuck just happened. I look down at my hands and they're shaking, but other than that, they look just like they always have.

I just killed my mom…

I'm pretty sure I'm going into shock because I can't feel anything. Even the sting of my cheek where her claws slashed me is gone. I'm so fucking numb.

How is this even possible?

Ares, rushes into the room, taking in the scorch marks on the walls and the one on the floor where Mom was standing.

"It's going to be okay, Morgan." My brother strides over to where I've fallen and gives me a quick look over to make sure I'm physically okay. I'm pretty sure he knows as well as I do that I'm not. I'm far from it, really.

He crouches in front of me, inspecting my face. I glance up to find his bright green eyes, as reassuring as always, staring back down at me. He's going to fix this. That's what Ares does. I fuck up, and he fixes it. He's been my savior more times than I can count—it's literally my entire life story.

"We need to keep this between the two of us, okay? I will deal with Dad, but you can never, ever speak of this. Or your power." He holds my chin tight while he looks me in the eyes, making sure I understand him. I nod against his grasp, and he releases me, his face softening once more. The soft expression on Ares' face is all it takes to break the dam holding back the tidal wave of emotions welling up inside of me over what I've done. My whole body shakes as I sob. He drops to the ground and pulls me into his lap, cradling me against his chest like a child.

"What did I do?" I cry, turning into his face and giving into the waves of emotion. He simply holds me until the tears subside. I manage to slow my breathing, focusing on deep inhales followed by controlled exhales, forcing myself to stop losing my shit.

"You have Shadow Fire," he says softly, and the awe in his tone rubs me just the wrong way. It's like I'm not the monster who just obliterated our mother. "There's no way you could have known what would happen. But if Dad ever found out…"

"He'd kill me," I whisper, and Ares nods. His dark hair, the same raven-sheened color as mine, falls into his eyes, and he looks all the more serious for it.

"He would. You having Shadow Fire makes you more powerful than him, and we both know how well he takes threats of opposition. You have to promise me that you'll keep this a secret just between us."

I nod but bite down on my bottom lip, worrying over how that could even be possible. "What will we say about Mom?"

"I'll think of something," he says before closing his eyes. In a blink, he glamours the room so none of the scorch marks show. "That will have to do until I can come up with a reason for us to redecorate. Are you okay?"

"I think so," I say shakily as he helps me to my feet. The weight of guilt presses down upon me, and I wrap my arms around my middle, trying desperately to keep myself together. "I'm a monster."

"You are not a monster; we were born of monsters. That doesn't make you one. You were defending yourself. I could hear her wailing from down the hall. I was coming here to step in as soon as I heard." He pulls me into his arms and holds me tight. Ares is the only safe space I've ever known in the life of darkness we were born into. "I've got you," he murmurs as he holds me, "you know I'll always have your back."

"And I'll have yours," I whisper as I cling to him. The soothing sound of his heartbeat under my ear lulls me into a momentary peace, but the panic comes back full force with a heart-stopping realization. I pull back, my heart beating erratically once more as I ask, "What if someone heard?"

"There was no one around. You know Mom sends the staff away during our lessons," he says, the bite in his tone is as hard as a bite from a Hellhound. "I was coming here to tell you that Father is sending me away on my quarter-century tour of the Realm. Since I know he won't allow you to come with me, I got you a gift. Something to help keep you safe while I can't."

Thank the hells for big brothers because nothing else in this Realm is worth a fucking thing. "You didn't have to get me anything."

"Morgan, I love you, and I know for a fact that The Carver will be here while I'm gone. So just let me do this, okay?" He hugs me tightly again before leading me from the room, while I try not to freak out about The Carver being here while Ares isn't. I take a deep breath and try to shove away the fear because falling apart right now won't help anyone.

"Where are we going?" I ask, struggling to walk without stumbling. Apparently using Shadow Fire is fucking exhausting. My muscles ache against the strain of staying upright, focusing on my forced breathing, and walking all at once.

"You'll see." He smiles back at me and offers his hand again, so I take it. He leads me through the palace, winding through the halls of a place that is more like a house of horrors than a home, until we reach the stables. The black, winged horses that are housed here screech as we enter. Smokey, my Dàgaan, whinnies as I near him, so I reach through the metal bars and pet his nose. I swear he almost smiles as my skin connects with his snout and he feeds on my life force the tiniest bit. Not everyone can make a connection like the one I have with Smokey, but unless someone takes his head, he'll live as long as I do.

Ares gives me a minute to say hello before pulling me toward the back of the stables. "This is your gift," he says before opening the last door in the stable. I peek around the corner and squeal before clamping a hand over my mouth so I don't scare the precious little babies.

"You got me Hellhounds?" I gasp, unable to take my eyes off of the black little balls of sleek fur and squish, fire eyes blinking owlishly in our direction.

"I did. They were only born a few days ago and won't stay this size for long. In a week, they'll be much bigger and will have established their pack hierarchy. I couldn't think of a more fitting present for a princess," he says, walking past me and winking before sitting down next to the group of pups.

I move forward and fall to my knees in front of them, cooing as one climbs to his feet, already looking more fierce than the others. He wobbles toward me, and I scoop him up into my arms. "Aren't you just precious?"

At my words, he stretches up and bites my nose. I can't help but laugh.

"He's going to be a handful." Ares chuckles before stroking another one of the pups who snuggles against his leg.

"I think you're right." I lift the little guy away from me, looking him in his bright orange eyes and smiling. "I think I'll call you Kaos."

The pup yips, smoke curling from his nostrils, and I glance up to see Ares grinning at me. "I think he likes it."

"Me too."

We sit with the pups for a little while until a roar shakes the walls of the stables. "I guess Dad is angry," I sigh, climbing to my feet. Ares joins me as we dust ourselves down from the hay the pack is curled up on.

Ares sighs before giving me a tight smile. "What else is new? We should go face whatever horrors await us. Just remember, not a word of what happened or of your power. I'll work with you on techniques to keep it hidden and under control, but I need you to keep this between us. Promise me, Morgan. I can't lose you; I don't even want to think of what this place would make me without you here."

I take his hand and squeeze it again. "I swear I'm not going anywhere, and neither are you."

TWO

NOW

"Morgan, come on. It's been ages since we had anything fun to do around here. Literally all you do is train with Ares, fly the Dàgaan or wander aimlessly around with me. All you have to do is say yes… Say yes for me!" Amelia, my fire-haired friend, pleads as she waltzes through my closet.

She's not wrong. The palace isn't exactly known for being a fun house. Plus training, with or without Ares, takes a good chunk of my time. Fun isn't something we have in large doses around here. Except today, my father announced a royal ball will take place in a few months. It will officially announce to the Realm that I am its princess.

Yet I have little doubt that my father intends to use me as a bargaining chip to expand his power and reach in some shape or form.

Awesome.

"You might think differently if you were the one on the pedestal," I sigh. "Sitting up there like a prized possession isn't exactly my idea of fun. Do you honestly think my father is going to let me mingle, dance, or have any sort of fun at all? Everyone already knows I fucking exist. This ball is just a powerplay for him. He's such a dick."

"Your dad has a stick up his ass," she laughs, and I snort along with her. "Anyway, that's half the fun of a ball. You'll at least get to dance with all of your potential suitors, right? We can sneak off from there and have our own fun."

"And face my father's wrath as a result." I drop down onto my bed like the petulant Demon princess that I am and stroke the dark fur of my Hellhound and protector, Kaos. "I don't care that I just had my birthday, I am still not old enough to be sold off to further my father's stupid alliances."

"Morgan, you're only one hundred years old. You're literally still a kid—he's not going to marry you off tonight. That would be barbaric, even for him."

"Have you met my father?" She giggles as she continues wandering through the expanse of my closet. Despite the fact I've told her for years that she can take whatever she wants, apparently being the chef's daughter doesn't give her reason to use the clothing in there.

"Your father is an ass," she yells, but I can barely hear her. I freaking hate that closet. It's too big, and it's a literal maze. But she's not wrong, my father *is* an ass, though that might just be the understatement of the century.

My father—known as the Demon King to those who both love and fear him—is the reason for my nightmares, both waking and in slumber. I'd like to say life got better for me in the fifty years since my mother died, but that would be a severe overstatement. After Mom's 'disappearance,' my father became more cruel, more ruthless, and if possible, more bloodthirsty.

Made worse by his friend, now known here as The Carver, thanks to his handiwork in the throne room. My father has taken to putting on shows for his toxic, vapid sycophants. They lap up any attention he deems to throw their way, all whilst fearing his wrath more than anything else in existence.

"But he also knows how to throw a party, *and* all of the other High Families are coming. Let me live vicariously through you!" Amelia practically bounces back into the room, a red dress hanging in front of her, attached by the hanger behind her neck. She prances around the room, and I can't help but laugh.

"We both know that when my father asks for something from me, I don't really have a choice in the matter, so I'll be going. I'm just going to be freaking miserable the entire time. Plus, the only reason the High Born families are coming is because the royals from the other Realms are coming. It's another chance for my father to show off what a good broodmare I am." Kaos snorts at my words, smoke curling from his nose as the flames in his eyes flash.

"Hey, maybe there will be a cute prince that you can run away with. Escape this hell-hole," she says as she drops down onto the bed on the other side of Kaos. He growls low in his throat, so I scratch between his ears and he settles.

"I don't think anything will ever get me out of here," I tell her, "but I guess I should at least start thinking about what to wear to the ball, even if it is a few months away."

"Yes! Please let me help. You know I'm a genius with hair."

"Maybe I'll go in my other form and terrify them all rather than being a pretty little doll on display for the Prince Parade." I smirk, and she grins back at me.

"That would definitely be one way to piss off your dad."

"We both know I live for it," I offer with a sardonic grin. Amelia smiles back, though she shakes her head at me slightly, and I sigh. "For real though, maybe it won't be so bad. Maybe I can run away and escape from all of this. Nothing can be worse than being here, right?"

"I doubt it," she sighs as she lies down. "Though, if you escape, please say you'll take me with you? Or that you'll marry me off to Ares?"

"I love my brother, and I love you, but absolutely not." I shake my head, laughing softly.

"We both know I don't love your brother, but we also know he'd keep me safe and out of the clutches of the assholes here. I mean, and it helps that he's dreamy as hell. Even if I don't like how much he bows down to your dad."

"Am—" I start, but she cuts me off.

"I know, I know. He does it to keep you off the guy's radar as much as possible, but you know… Fight back a little. He could be a total dreamboat of a prince, Morgan. He has the hair, the eyes, the freaking jaw. I just need him to be the rebel too."

"Maybe you should keep dreaming." I look up to find Ares standing in the doorway, leaning against the door jamb with a smirk firmly on his face. I can't help but laugh as Amelia blushes so hard I think she might pass out from heat exhaustion. "Father summoned you, Morgan. I figured I'd come get you rather than one of his handsy lapdogs."

"Thanks." I smile at him, jumping to my feet. I look back at Amelia who looks like she wants a hole to open up under her feet. "I'll see you later, Amelia?"

"Yeah, if I've resurrected by then," she answers, covering her face with a pillow.

"Bye, Amelia," Ares chuckles, and she lifts a hand to wave without removing the pillow.

"Lead the way," I say to him as he steps aside, leaving me space to move around him and lead the way from the room. "Hopefully not to my demise."

I sit on my throne upon the dais. My father sits to my right, and Ares is to his right. Kaos lounges at my feet. The point of the summons was apparently for me to officially start my 'royal training'. Which as far as I can tell so far, 'training' just means sitting through these hells awful parades of depravity from people hoping to curry favor with my father. That or pay off a debt owed to him.

So far he's added four girls to his harem, and I really do mean girls. They can't be any older than I am. Holding down the vomit during that despicable display was agonizing. How Ares sits through this with a mask of indifference is beyond me. I do what I've done since the day I killed my mother, lock away every single emotion inside of me so I seem like the ice cold bitch everyone accuses me of being.

They don't know me, and they don't want to, so I'm

not going to bother showing them who I truly am.

I hate this room. The living statues of my father's victims dotted around the space are a stark reminder of exactly what he's capable of when he's pissed off. I avoid looking at them as much as I can. Their eyes have the uncanny ability to follow you across the room no matter which way you're moving, and I can't take the pleading hiding just behind the glassy surfaces of the statues' eyes. I'm not sure how to undo what my father has done; and until I learn more about my own abilities, I won't ever have a clue. Which is exactly why my father hasn't encouraged me to train with any of my powers. He doesn't want anyone to be more powerful than him. Ares is almost more powerful, the way he can make people see what he wants them to is just the beginning of what he's capable of, but he's also the golden child. I'm the rebellious asshole daughter who hates his way of life.

Between the living statues and the black on black decor of the entire space, even with the hints of gold, it just feels cold and dead in here. If I had my way, the high ceilings would be light and airy instead of filled with a dark mist that can descend on the Demons gathered below and suck the life-force from their bodies. It's the mist that makes my father as feared as he is. It's the one thing, other than Shadow Fire, that can truly kill a Demon—so of course he has control of it.

Though my father would rather encase someone in stone and torture them for eternity than truly kill them.

He's a freaking delight.

I've had about as much as I can take of my father's power show when the sound of chains clinking together and dragging over the marble floor catches my attention. My breath hitches when I see a boy, no older than I am, shackled at his neck, wrists, and ankles being dragged into the room by a man I assume is his father. They look too alike to be anything other than father and son.

The boy looks lost, afraid, and fucking broken.

I hate what my father has turned this place into. I've heard stories about the Shadow Realm while my grandmother ruled and suffice to say that this was a very different place. I just hope that when Ares ascends to the throne he changes shit up because none of this is okay.

None of it.

The smell of burned skin makes me want to gag. I guess they're using salted iron chains. Classy. Not barbaric at all. And I bet they're coated in healing salve, just enough so that it hurts like fucking hell, but won't break the skin enough so that he dies from the wound. Raging assholes, the lot of them. He stumbles toward us behind his father, who simply grins at mine.

"I see you've come to pay your debts, Airon." My father laughs, and the sound booms through the throne room, and

I realize exactly what this is. This guy's just another slave being sold to my father to resolve some debt owed. My stomach rolls as pity overwhelms me. I can't stand any more of this today. It's vile and completely unnecessary.

The man pushes the boy to his knees, and the crunch of his bones as he hits the ground makes me wince, so I pull my icy mask back into place. If I show any weakness right now, this boy won't be the only one in chains. I glance over at Ares, who doesn't even look at the boy. He stares at a spot on the back wall.

"He looks weak," my father sneers down at him, and the boy casts his gaze to the floor. My father sneers, instantly deeming the boy as less than. I've seen that look before.

"He looks weaker than he is. But I'm sure he'll meet your needs, whatever they may be," Airon practically sings as he metaphorically kisses my father's ass. Though I'm sure he'd do it literally too, given half the chance.

This place makes me want to hurl. If this is what being a royal is about, I'm tapping out.

"I'm sure he will," my father says, interrupting my train of thought. I glance up to see Airon gazing over my body. I want to sneer, but I know better. "You should be more careful with your things, Airon. Soon you'll run out of bartering chips."

Airon drops the chains, and the boy flinches at the

sound. I can see him shaking, a fight or flight response pounding through his veins. I wish he would because at least then he would have tried, not just given into this awful fate his father is selling him into. At the same time, I don't want him to cause a scene because I know that the punishment will be worse than the momentary success of making that kind of choice for himself.

My father snaps his fingers and his head lapdog, Tenarious, appears and grips the boy by his hair, yanking him to his feet. The boy hisses at the pain, and my heart hurts for him. I don't want to think about the pain he'll likely experience at the hands of my father. I've had to learn how to tune it out, the knowledge of what my father does, because otherwise I'd never survive this place.

One day he won't have a reign of terror here. Until that day comes, I need to make sure I survive.

"Lock him up with the others. I'll have my fun later." My father waves his hand dismissively, and Tenarious drags the boy behind the dais through the door that leads to the cells in the lower basement.

"Father, is that all for today? This really is very tedious." I sigh, feigning a bored indifference. I'd rather fake the indifference than let him see just how fucked up today has left me.

"Fine, begone." He dismisses me with a flick of his hand, and I stand. I'm careful to not stand too quickly to make it look like I'm running away, but it's fast enough that I manage to get out before my hands begin trembling. Kaos stays by my side until we reach the kitchens and I spot Amelia, covered in flour, helping her dad.

I smile at her, and then head back to my room.

No one needs to see the breakdown I'm about to have.

It seems like all my life consists of now are fucking royal summons. I've been sitting through this bullshit for weeks. It's as if my father wants to see how much I can make it through before I break. But the joke's on him because I'll never show him any sign of weakness again. There's too much at stake if I lose control of my emotions, if I lose the tight hold I have on keeping my power suppressed.

The Shadow Fire means one thing. I'm going to be powerful. Even more so than I am now. I might not know exactly what I'm capable of, but I can feel power swirling around inside of me. Dark, wild, and desperate to be free. It's more than I've ever felt from another Demon, and that both terrifies me and excites me. It means that if I can get away from here, I can be free. No one will ever hold me prisoner again.

I didn't think my father could sink much lower than he already had. So when I saw Airon and The Carver enter the throne room, which for some reason is set up like some sort of wedding chapel, it never crossed my mind that it could get worse.

It can always be worse.

My father has the boy he bought from Airon sitting at his feet, the same way Kaos sits at mine, while The Carver and Airon cut up one of the many poor girls sacrificed to my father. I'm not sure what she did to invoke my father's wrath, but no one deserves this.

What's worse is that I'm not sure if this is about the girl or if it's about breaking the boy sitting at my father's feet. The girl looks like she could be his twin. Which makes Airon's part in all of this even more abhorrent. But then again, if I'm going by my father's standards, this is nothing.

Her screams have finally almost died off. We've been here for hours, and at one point, I thought Ares might actually lose his cool. We both know he won't because he wouldn't risk me like that. We discovered early on that Father was well aware of Ares' weaknesses, and the total sum of them is me.

We also know my father takes no issue with breaking me if it suits his purpose. Which is why I've learned just how to shut everything inside of myself down over the past fifty years. Survival is key.

Except I'm not sure how many more of the screams I can take. My gut churns. I want to burn every person in this room alive.

The problem is that I don't have control of my powers, so I wouldn't be able to just take out the people I wanted to. Which is why I'm sitting here like a good little fucking doll, doing absolutely nothing. If everyone knew how truly powerless I was up here, they wouldn't look at me with such reverence, as if they covet my position.

Even the girl looks to me for help. What she doesn't realize is that I'm just as trapped, just as helpless, as she is. The key difference is that my torture happens behind closed doors.

The boy at my father's feet shifts, and the waft of burning skin from the chains around his neck and wrists makes my stomach churn.

I will never understand the depravity of men who enjoy this kind of pain and violence. How broken do you have to be to get off on someone else's screams? We might be Demons, but despite the humans' depiction of us, we're not all monsters. Just like every other race, there are the good and the bad among us. And I'm trapped here with some of the worst for the rest of my existence—unless I find a way to escape it all… or until Ares takes my father's seat of power.

I will never forget the words Ares whispered to me on the day we discovered my newest power emergence.

You are not a monster; we were born of monsters. That

doesn't make you one.

That one line has turned into a daily mantra for me.

"Should we carve up her pretty face?" The Carver's words pull me from the train of thought and bring me back to this stark and horrific reality. His black and yellow teeth gleam as he smiles while the girl sobs in the chair she's chained to. He looks over to my father for instruction.

I'm powerless to do anything other than sit here and clench my fists under the skirts of my dress where no one can see. I wonder how much he'd like it if I carved up his face.

That might be an upgrade, though. Slimy asshole.

Airon's grin makes me shudder as he looks at the boy he sold. I have no idea how a parent could do that to their child. I swore after the hundredth or so beating from my parents that I would never have kids. The only decent parent I know is Amelia's dad, Seth. And even he can be pretty absent thanks to his job. But when he is around, he does at least dote on her.

"Bring me her eyes." My father's menacing laugh booms around the throne room, and the shouts of glee and encouragement from his sycophants make me want to vomit. I can't help but look at him with sheer disgust, though I hide the look quickly when Ares raises his eyebrows at me. It's the only real show of emotion from my brother today. Sometimes I wonder if he just makes one of his dreamscapes and escapes into them while we're in here. I have no idea how he stays the person he is after everything he's witnessed, but I truly hope my father never manages to extinguish the light that's inside of him.

I want to look away as Airon rubs his hands together and moves behind the girl, but I know I can't. He clasps her cheeks in his palms, holding her still for The Carver. Her screams tear through the room, and I swear to fuck my heart shatters as she begs for them to stop.

I jump when my father shouts, "You will watch, boy, otherwise we'll make her pay for your disobedience too!" He pulls on the boy's chains until he's watching the poor girl's torture, and I want to cry for him. For us all.

She passes out when the first eye is cut from her, but that doesn't stop the joy and hunger building in the room. The entire group of them are monsters, black pits of evil all the way to their core.

"Is all of this really necessary, Father?" I sigh, hoping he sees my question as boredom rather than horror.

"You should be watching, learning how to keep this lot in line. All of this could be yours one day, Morganna," he says proudly.

"Yes, Father. I know, though I'd rather not, since that would mean the demise of Ares, but still. She's not even conscious anymore." I glance down at the boy, and it feels like he can see the truth of who I am, so I look away quickly. The anger building inside of me is too much, too close to the surface. If I lose my shit in here, we're going to have a lot of fucking issues, and I really don't want to kill my brother.

"Fine, begone. Take that fucking hound with you," he says, waving at Kaos with a sneer on his face.

"That's fine, he needs a run anyway," I say as I stand. Kaos follows suit, pressing himself closely to my side as I sashay from the room. If I'm still here when Ares comes into power, I'm going to have him tear down that room stone by fucking stone. Maybe even the entire fucking palace.

Knock it down all the way to rubble and rebuild.

Not even the strongest of potions or spells could remove the horrors from this place or the blood that seeps from the stones.

One day… once my father is dead.

After riding my Dàgaan for hours, I feel some of the rage release from within me. I've spent the entire ride lost in my own mind, wondering how the supposed Gods could have forsaken us and left this place as part of their legacy. The mythology states that the Seven Realms were created by the Seven Gods. The Shadow Realm was the domain of the

God of War, which is why he created demons. He thrived on chaos and made us in his image. Bloodthirsty, power hungry, and more than a little crazy.

Except I find it hard to believe that the other Gods would have allowed such madness. I might have never left this Realm, but I've read so much about the Realm's supposed history that I feel like if the Gods had truly existed, surely they wouldn't have left this place as it is. Surely even the God of War would have been reined in. Why would six other Gods just allow this place of horror to exist?

Sometimes an existential crisis is just what a girl needs to calm the rage.

I find the entire pack of Hellhounds waiting for me when we finally get back to the stables, with Kaos pacing until we come to a stop in front of him.

I dismount Smokey and brush him down before leading him to his stall. I make sure he has enough water and raw meat to get him through until the morning when the stable hands will look after him and then head back out to where Kaos waits for me. He offers me his nose, and I close my eyes, putting my hand on his head to let him show me what I missed while I was gone.

Images flicker through my mind, my father meeting with The Carver, my name being mentioned, more of the usual… and then Ares, looking for me.

I open my eyes and find my brother standing before

me, a look of concern flashing in his eyes before he strides forward and hugs me.

"Father has called a family dinner." I go still at his words, and he looks about as happy as I feel when he pulls away.

"Why?" I ask. We haven't had a family dinner since he came to the conclusion that my mother ran away to another Realm. I'm pretty sure that's why so many Demons have been given a free pass to wreak havoc on Earth—they're under the guise of searching for her. I can't help but feel responsible for the terror, but I have no way to stop it either.

"I don't know, but you should go and dress quickly. I'll come and grab you in an hour, and we'll go down together. We need to present a united front against whatever comes." He holds out his pinky to me, and I grasp his with my own.

"United always."

It's something we started doing after the first time Father beat me because of something Ares fucked up. I didn't hold it against him, much to Father's dismay. If anything, it brought us closer. But we've always gone up against things together. We truly are united always.

"Okay, go quickly. The last thing we want to do is be late." His eyes dart around behind me, knowing that we can't be overheard. While we have some people around the palace that are loyal to us, most here are loyal to my father. If they think telling him that we're 'disrespecting' him will gain them points, they will absolutely do it.

I nod without saying another word, and Kaos and Havoc flank me on either side while the rest of the pack go with Ares. I'm not the only one who can use some badass backup in this place. Especially since even with as powerful as Ares is, he really doesn't like to hurt people. We all deal with our trauma in our own way, I guess.

I hurry back to my room and wash quickly. The waterfall of hot water scalds my pale skin, but I enjoy the sting of it. It makes me feel like a real person rather than the ice bitch I walk around here pretending to be, like nothing can hurt me or get to me.

I don't take as long as I'd like to. The fear of being late takes some of the joy from my usual sanctuary under the running water. I hurry and dry my long dark hair into waves until it sits just below my waist then pull a black, floor-length dress from my never-ending closet. I slip it on and check myself in the reflecting glass. Demure enough, but then... also not at the same time. The high neck, with the floor length skirt keeps it subtle, but the thigh-high splits in the skirt and the fact that it has no back makes it exactly what I like. Classy, but then again, not quite.

My own mini rebellion against the image my mother expected from me.

I line my eyes with black kohl and use ink to enhance my eyelashes to enhance the green color of my eyes, before painting my lips a soft pink. This might be a family dinner, but even so, I know the consequences of not presenting myself properly. It was one of my mother's first lessons, and some things scar you for life. That first attack from my mother definitely opened my eyes to a lot of things.

I shake away the memories as a knock sounds at the door. Kaos grumbles low in the back of his throat as he moves toward the door while Havoc moves to my side. "It's probably just Ares," I mutter, but Havoc moves in front of me to ensure I stay where I am. I let them do their thing because situations like these are the whole reason I have them, and I honestly would never be without them. I've never slept as well as I do when the pack surrounds my bed.

The door opens and Kaos sits, looking like a puppy in an instant as Ares enters the room. He's the only male in my world I can truly say isn't a threat to me. "You ready?"

"I am now," I tell him as I slip on my heels. "Let's go face the music, shall we?"

He offers me his arm, so I thread mine through the crook of his elbow, and we head to the dining hall in a comfortable silence. I take a deep breath and enjoy it, knowing that this is probably the last comfort I'll feel all evening.

We reach the dining hall, and unsurprisingly, Father isn't here yet. Hells forbid we be late, but he'll probably keep us waiting an hour on principle alone. The table is laid out in full, as if there will be twenty or so people joining us. I glance at Ares, who frowns when he sees what I do.

"Either this is overkill or our family has grown," he snarks, and I laugh.

"With Father it could be either."

He walks me to my seat, pulling out the chair so I can sit before taking his own. We wait nearly thirty minutes before Father graces us with his presence. When he finally waltzes in, he struts across the room as if he had a full entourage with him. I smirk up at Ares before shutting down any and all emotion.

"Children, so good of you to join me." He grins, and my heart rate picks up. He's never this happy, and it honestly scares the shit out of me. Once he sits, the waitstaff appears from the staff entrance and trays upon trays of food are brought out for us. I spot Amelia's fiery hair, and she smiles at me quickly before disappearing with the others again.

We eat in near silence, though Father does discuss some issues in the Realm that I have no idea about so I stay quiet, just as he likes. Seen, but not heard.

It's only once the dishes are cleared that Father turns his attention to me. At that moment, I swear if Ares wasn't here too, I'd probably just run away and never look back. The way he looks me over turns my blood to ice.

"Morganna, I think it's about time you learn how

the Realm works. We'll never find you a suitable match if you're nothing better than an airhead." It takes every ounce of strength I have not to roll my eyes at him or just straight up slap him. Ares' eye twitches, but I nudge his foot under the table. I can take Father's words. They're not the worst things he's thrown at me.

"With that in mind, I've decided you'll be joining Ares on his quarter century tour of the Realm. He can show you how things work and introduce you to the people you'll need to know before the ball in a few months. We have many relationships we need to cultivate, so I expect to have your full cooperation. Meeting the High Families—learning how to be diplomatic—are some of the skills you'll require when I introduce you to the other royal families attending from other Realms."

I keep the smile from my face, but it's so fucking hard to maintain. "Of course, Father."

I bite my tongue to keep the other choice words I have for him about it from falling through my lips. Because at least this time, there's an upside—it's going to be at least eight weeks that I'm out of this horror show. I tune out the rest of their discussion, trying not to fantasize *too hard* about life away from here. I've never left the inner ring of the Shadow Realm. Only Ares has been granted that privilege. Despite the reasoning behind the trip, I find myself feeling excited. Time with my brother, where we might even be able to relax a little? The chance to see the world, even as dark as I've heard it is? It all excites me.

I'm not going to let my father shit all over it with his agendas.

"Morganna!" I blink, pulling myself from the thoughts in my mind and glance over at my father. I bite the inside of my cheek to keep from wincing. He looks pissed.

"Sorry, Father, I was just thinking about the trip," I say as demurely as I can, and I see Ares' shoulders shake subtly as he laughs at the act.

"I was saying that you leave in two days, and you'll be taking those fucking hounds with you. I expect you to do everything your brother says."

"I understand," I say, nodding before looking down at the table and grinning.

I'm coming, World.

Ready or not.

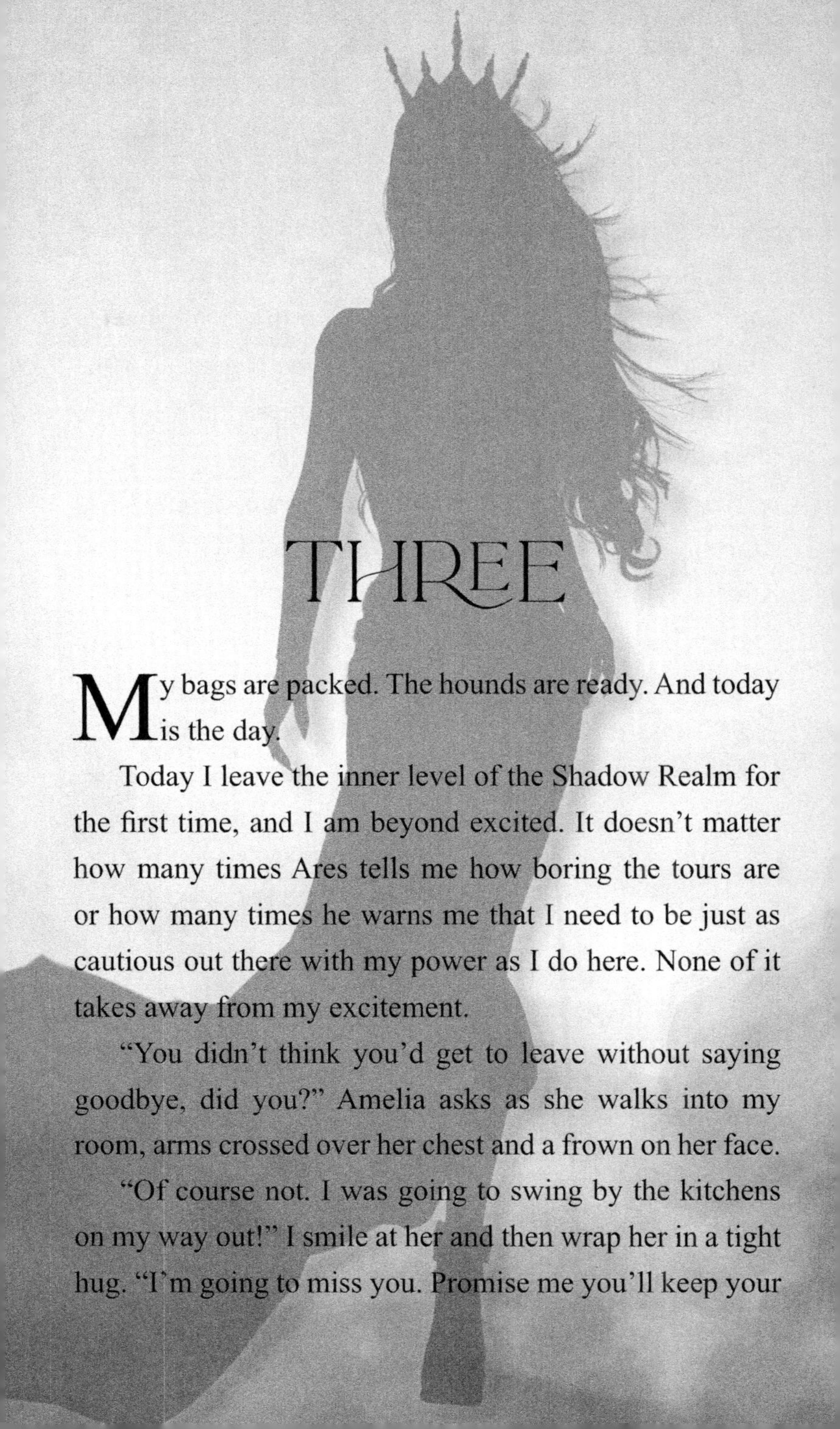

THREE

My bags are packed. The hounds are ready. And today is the day.

Today I leave the inner level of the Shadow Realm for the first time, and I am beyond excited. It doesn't matter how many times Ares tells me how boring the tours are or how many times he warns me that I need to be just as cautious out there with my power as I do here. None of it takes away from my excitement.

"You didn't think you'd get to leave without saying goodbye, did you?" Amelia asks as she walks into my room, arms crossed over her chest and a frown on her face.

"Of course not. I was going to swing by the kitchens on my way out!" I smile at her and then wrap her in a tight hug. "I'm going to miss you. Promise me you'll keep your head down and stay off my father's radar while I'm gone."

"I'm going to miss you too!" she says with a sniff. She's only ten years younger than me, so we've grown up together, living this horror together through thick and thin. "And I promise to not leave our rooms or the kitchen. The last thing I want is to end up in the basement." She shudders before we separate, and a pit opens in the bottom of my stomach. If anything happens to her…

"Are you ready?" Ares asks softly from the door, and while my answer is a resolute yes, I feel awful leaving Amelia behind. I look up at him, and I know he sees the conflict because an aura of sadness radiates from him in that moment too.

"Yeah, I'm ready," I tell him and squeeze Amelia one last time. "I'll see you soon?"

"You're damn straight you will," she says, squeezing my hand before awkwardly waving at Ares and disappearing from the room.

"Could we take her with us?" I ask him, chewing on my bottom lip.

"It's possible, but she wouldn't actually be with you on the trip. If people got wind of you being friends with 'the help' it would get back to Father, and that would be disastrous for you both."

"I know, but at least if she's with the traveling party, she isn't here," I say, hoping he can make it happen.

"I'll see what I can do, but don't think being out there is any safer for her. Especially as 'the help'. People are monsters everywhere, not just inside of these walls," he explains, and I nod.

"Thank you. At least out there, it's not Father."

"Okay, give me a minute. I'm sending Sebastian to get your things. Take the hounds down and get them ready for travel. And I want to be explicit—don't think this trip means we're letting up on your training. I intend to work with you far more than we have, since we'll have more time to ourselves." He turns and leaves, and a small glimmer of hope that he'll bring Amelia with us blooms in my chest.

I whistle for the hounds, and they stand at the ready before following me down to the front courtyard of the palace. They've never travelled by whisper. To be fair, neither have I, so this is a whole new experience for us all. I just hope they handle it okay.

We find Sebastian waiting out the front. He already has one carriage loaded with Ares' trunks, and when he sees me with the hounds, I swear he goes so pale that he's almost translucent.

"Are they coming with us, your highness?" he stammers, and I can't help but smile.

"They are. They won't bite... not unless I tell them to." I wink at him just as Kaos starts to growl, smoke coming from his nostrils. I can't help but giggle quietly.

"Stop terrorizing the poor man, Morgan," Ares says as he approaches us. "It's done, she's just grabbing her things. She'll be traveling with the other staff," he says the words quietly once he's beside me, and I lean into him softly as a thank you.

"Let's get this trip going, shall we?" he says to Sebastian, and I walk the hounds to the metal cage at the back of my carriage. Kaos snorts when I open the door, and I roll my eyes, ushering the pack into the cage. "I think Kaos is going to sit up in the carriage with me," I shout over to Ares, who shakes his head before nodding.

I secure the cage, blowing a kiss at my puppies, and climb into the carriage with Kaos where Ares is already waiting for me. The Dàgaan are strapped to the front of the carriage, and I smile widely.

"Are you ready?"

I nod at my brother, excitement bubbling in my core. "I don't think I've ever been more ready for anything in my life."

"Okay, well close your eyes at least. The first time traveling like this is a bit vomit inducing, but I'm sure you'll be fine. We're starting at the outer ring and working our way back to the inner ring." He bangs on the front of the carriage, and we jolt forward. A giddiness fills me as I watch the Shadow Palace disappear into the distance.

"Here we go," Ares says, grinning widely, and then the

world goes dark. The floor falls from my feet, and I scream into the emptiness as we whisper away from the only place I've ever known.

"So this is Level One," I say, looking out over the city. We're on the outskirts, on a hill that sits high above the main city, and it's unlike anything I've ever seen before. The buildings are smaller on the outskirts and grow taller toward the center where a huge black monstrosity of an estate sits. Two guesses where the High Family of this level live.

"This is Level One. And as you can see, the High Family do take their roles here very seriously," Ares says, rolling his eyes. "The Locklear family are… an interesting bunch. You will have seen Issac Locklear at Father's summonings. He's a beast of a man, and his wife Bethany is meek and lets Issac walk all over her, but don't be fooled. She's a master of potions. They have two children. Noah, who is around your age and a daughter, Riley, who is about sixty years younger than you. She's a spoiled little shit, but Noah seems okay from the very few interactions I've had with him. I don't know much about the children, but I have no doubt we'll see them around this week."

"Okay." I nod, taking in the information as the

carriage leads us through the city. People stop and stare at the procession. Part of me wants to die a little from the attention, but I guess royalty coming to the level is a whole thing. At least that's what I assume from the crowds and the cheers outside.

"Don't worry, you'll be fine. Just follow my lead. I won't hold you hostage, so you at least have a chance to explore, but you have to promise to take Kaos with you."

I smile widely at the thought of being able to go out and explore properly. People here don't really know who I am, so I should be pretty incognito. I've never been able to explore anything or anywhere before, and I hate how sheltered that's made me. I am so freaking excited to finally start living and experiencing my life.

"There is a big dinner tonight, so I do need you there for that. If I need your presence at any other function throughout the week we're here, I'll let you know, but I promise not to be too overbearing."

"Thank you, Ares. You have no idea how much this all means to me."

"I have some idea," he says with a small smile. "I don't think I've seen you smile this much, maybe ever."

"I promise to have my ice bitch facade on when in public," I say, and he chuckles, shaking his head.

"Be whoever you want to be. That's the joy of being second born." He smiles sadly, and my heart breaks for him a little. He's right about that, though. I don't have any of the pressures he has, not really. Even with Father deciding I need to start upholding my royal duties or whatever. Ares is two hundred years older than me, so he's been doing this shit for a long-ass time.

"I'm sorry you already have your life planned out for you." I lean my head against his shoulder, and he pats my leg.

"It's not so bad. At least I know that one day, I can change things. I just need to survive this world first."

We sit in silence for the rest of the journey through Level One, Kaos's occasional snorts break the content quiet, and I just stare out of the small windows taking it all in. It's a very strange place. It's not at all like home, though I haven't been that far out of the palace grounds either, so I can't really say for sure.

When we pull through the gates of the walls surrounding the Locklear's estate, a procession of horns sound out, announcing our arrival. I fucking cringe at the ostentatiousness of it all. As we pull to a stop, Sebastian appears at the door to open it. I move to exit, and Kaos growls at me.

"Fine." I sigh, rolling my eyes at him as I let him climb from the carriage first. I hear the gasps from the Demons outside, and I can't help but laugh. I bite it back when Ares gives me *the look*, but I can't help it. It always makes me laugh how terrified people are of him, especially since he's still growing. I wait for Ares to jump down once Kaos clears the doorway, and fix my ice bitch mask in place before he helps me climb down from the carriage.

By the time I descend, Sebastian has already unlocked the hounds' cage, and the pack surrounds the two of us. Kaos stands at the front, with Havoc and Anarchy flanking him, and the others flare out in a V formation so we're covered fully.

I look up and find the Locklears' watching us warily. There's nothing quite like a pack of Hellhounds for an initial show of power, I guess. Ares steps forward, taking me with him. I whistle low in my throat, telling Kaos to let us pass. He stays at my side as we approach the Demon family who are out in their finery to greet us.

"It is a pleasure to have you with us again, your highness," Isaac says to Ares, not even bothering to look at me.

"It's a pleasure to be here," Ares says with the limitless grace he pulls out of his ass for all of this royal bullshit. "Please allow me to present my sister, Morganna. She will be with me on this tour at the request of my father."

"It is lovely to meet you, Morganna," he says, and Kaos growls at the disrespect. I couldn't give two shits if he uses my title, but apparently Kaos isn't taking any shit on this trip. Good to know.

The man startles at the growl, but I keep my mask of indifference on and don't respond to him. The girl laughs quietly at my snub, but when I turn my gaze to her, she stops laughing quickly.

"Your highnesses, this is my wife, Bethany, and our two children, Noah and Riley. We are honored to have you staying with us this week." Ares thanks them, and I nod, deciding that keeping my mouth shut is probably the best idea right now. I take in the meek Bethany, the cocksure Noah, and the spoiled Riley. I've never been more thankful that my brother is usually the one that has to deal with this shit. The High Families, if they're all like this, are going to drive me to the brink of insanity.

"Let us show you to your rooms," Bethany says quietly. "I'm sure you'll want to rest before the dinner party this evening. Our guests are due to arrive at dusk."

It takes everything I have to not roll my eyes. Who the fuck schedules anything for fucking dusk?

"Please, lead the way." Ares keeps it pleasant and tugs on my arm to keep me at his side. We follow Bethany, the hounds bringing up the rear, through the monstrosity that is their home. It seems as if they built it trying to recreate the horrors of my father's palace but without quite so much blatant grandeur.

Once we've climbed more stairs than I care to count, Bethany leads us down a long hall and opens a door about half way down. "This suite should suit all of your needs."

Havoc enters the room and checks it. Once he signals to Kaos that it's safe, Kaos moves aside and allows us to enter. I stroke between his ears as I pass him, silently thanking him for being so good to me.

The suite is huge. Way too big for what we need, and I can tell that just at first glance. Regardless, Ares smiles at the woman and thanks her before closing the door.

"What a fucking carry on," he sighs before dropping into one of the chairs in the main area of the room. "Take whichever room you want; Sebastian will bring our things up shortly. I'm going to get a bath and soak for a bit before I have to deal with Isaac's bullshit."

"Fine by me." I grin and head toward the room in the farthest corner. The blues and blacks call to me, and I drop onto the giant bed. It's not quite as nice as mine, but it's still soft, and that's what counts. Kaos jumps up beside me, and I smile.

Yes, I think I'm going to be able to get used to this freedom thing.

I walk with Ares to the dining room, my hand in the crook of his arm with Kaos at my side. The rest of the pack stayed in the room because Ares thought that it might seem aggressive, to bring them all with us. I just laughed because Kaos is the real threat out here, but they don't know that.

By the time we reach the top of the staircase, I can already hear the voices. "Just how many people are coming to fucking dinner?"

"More than I'd like." he sighs, running a hand through his floppy dark hair before letting his princely mask fall into place. "Now, let's go deal with Father's allies, shall we?"

We descend the stairs, and as we come into view of the Demons below, the room quiets. I allow my power to seep out just a little more than normal as discussed with Ares, and he lets his come out to play a little too. There's nothing like a power play to start the night.

Literally.

As we approach, I recognize a few faces from my father's summonings. Keeping the sneer from my face is a lot of work, but I manage it, keeping my face as passive and disinterested as I can as Ares moves us around the room, introducing me to people who I have no interest in knowing. Thankfully, most people look over me as if I'm just a doll on his arm.

Got to love being underestimated at all times. That's the problem with being a woman in this Realm. So rarely are we seen as equal to, or more powerful than, our penis-toting counterparts. If the crown were to be mine, I'd have all sorts of plans for some equality, but I know my brother will do what is needed. He's a good guy. I just need him to stay as strong as he has been thus far and not let my father corrupt him.

"I hear we have a potential upcoming wedding…" one of the faceless monsters says, catching my attention. Ares nods stiffly.

"That is Father's hope, yes," he responds, sounding noncommittal. I freaking *knew* my father had shitty intentions with that stupid ball of his. That's likely what this little parade around the Realm is about too. Showing off his prize pony.

Fuck my actual life.

We're ushered toward the dining room, and Ares pulls out my chair for me before he sits to my left at the head of the table. "I also hear that war is brewing."

This comes from Locklear. I perk up, paying more attention than I let on as the rest of the room takes their seats.

"Yes, there are some whispered plans, but Father has a few tricks up his sleeve before then." Ares' gaze bounces toward me first, and my heart sinks. I wonder just how much he's really hiding from me.

I try not to focus on the fact that we might not be truly united in all things despite the stinging in my chest. He nudges me with his knee under the table and discreetly lifts his pinky from where his hands are folded in front of him.

I guess I didn't hide my feelings from him as well as I thought.

It's not long before servers bring out the first course, and like a good little doll, I speak when spoken to and eat my soup demurely. Thankfully, whoever cooks for them does a sublime job, so it's not hard to just shut up and eat. As the meal continues, I can't help but focus on getting the chance to explore the outer ring of the Shadow Realm tomorrow while Ares does his boring princely shit. I intend to go fully incognito and just enjoy life. The city seemed so full, so vibrant, and so far from anything I've ever known. That's what I want to experience, even if I just get to watch from the sidelines.

My curiosity in life has gotten me into trouble more times than I care to count, but Father isn't here now, and I know Ares will allow me more freedom than Father ever has. My heart craves an escape, and I know he won't keep me from that.

"So, Morganna," the meek wife, whose name I've already forgotten, speaks quietly from her seat next to me. "Are you looking forward to seeing more of your kingdom? You'll be meeting all of your potential suitors on this trip, I'm sure. I know for a fact that Noah would like the opportunity to speak with you while you're here."

I glance over at Noah, who is in full dick-wad mode

with the other younger guys at the table. They don't seem to care that there are others here. They're having a party all of their own. Their ale spills over their glasses as they get louder and rowdier.

Oh yes, he seems like a dream husband.

"I'm sure I'd like that," I tell her with my most saccharine smile. It seems to please her, so I obviously sold it. The servers reappear and take the bowl of soup away, replacing it with a steak that is way too pink for my liking, but they at least bring around some amber bubbles and fill my glass. I look over to Ares who just smirks with a small nod. Father would never have allowed it, but he isn't here.

Ares leans over to me and whispers, "You might regret it in the morning. Nectar isn't for the faint of heart."

"I'll take it easy," I murmur back, and he smiles before turning his attention back to the gentlemen opposite me at the table. One of them looks about eight hundred years older than me, and leers at me despite the lack of skin I have on show. Kaos perks up by my side at my unease, his growls causing the room to go silent. He sits up, and he's big enough that he can see over the table at the occupants. He's big enough that it makes more than a few of them shuffle in their seats.

I scratch the fur between his ears, and he goes quiet. "He won't attack unless I'm threatened… or if I tell him to."

My announcement doesn't lift the unease in the room, but people do go back to their meals. I smile down at my Hellhound.

"Who's a good boy," I whisper to him, cutting him off a good half of my steak. He chomps it down before lying down once more, and I turn back to the room. At least the gross guy opposite me isn't staring anymore. He looks a little pale too.

If that's the only entertainment for the night, it's going to be woefully boring, and I can't help but wonder how long this night of sheer boredom will truly last.

FOUR

Last night was about as much fun as watching blood dry. But today I get to escape on my own and explore. To say I'm excited is an understatement.

Ares gave me his plan for the day, and I have more than a few hours to play with. I can slip out unnoticed before my presence will be required for dinner again this evening. He mentioned that I have a formal tea with Bethany tomorrow around lunchtime and a walk with Noah afterward, but if that's what I have to do to get my freedom today, then so be it.

Even though I'd rather pull out my own teeth than walk with Noah, it's totally worth it to have a whole day of doing whatever the fuck I like. I plan on going super incognito. I don't want people to know who I am, so I dress in what I saw most of the people in the city wearing: leather pants, a corset, and a hooded cloak with some badass boots, and a knife tucked in the top of one should I need it. The only other thing I have with me is a small pouch of silver coins from Ares. The chance to go shopping didn't even occur to me, everything has always just appeared for me before, and I can't wait!

"You need to stay here with the others, boy." I crouch before Kaos, who is unsurprisingly unhappy about not coming with me. "I promise I'll bring you back something good. Plus I have my knife, see."

I lift the blade from my boot, and he lets out a humph, laying his head down on his giant paws. Havoc lies beside him, while the others lounge on my bed. I already spoke with Amelia to make sure that someone feeds them while I'm out today. She was more than happy to cover for me.

I pull the black cloak over my shoulders and check my reflection. There's no way for me to really disguise myself further, so I just have to hope that no one recognizes me. It's not like many people know what I actually look like here anyway.

Giddiness builds inside of me along with a shot of fear. I've never done anything like this before. If it all blows up in my face and I get myself kidnapped or something equally as stupid, I am going to be so pissed. I really need to ask Ares how he's going to find a way for him to train me while we're away from the palace. I need to be able to use my powers so that I can defend myself properly. It's ridiculous that I'm one hundred and still as harmless as a child.

I slink out of the room, making sure that the coast is clear before slipping from the estate. No one seems to be paying attention to me. Sometimes being the invisible little doll on Ares' arm has advantages.

Once I pass the gates and get a few streets away from the estate, I let out a deep breath.

I made it.

I pull my hood forward a little more, obscuring my face slightly. I'm glad for the cold cut to the air today so no one questions the hood. I weave my way through the bustling crowds, taking in the wonder of it all. I have no idea where I am or where I'm going, and I don't think I've ever felt as happy as I do right now.

The smells, the sights, the noise… They're not like anything I've ever experienced before, and I feel more alive than I ever have. I work my way through the stores and stalls that line the streets until I reach what I assume is the main square of the district. There are even more stalls here, and the smells of all the food make my mouth water.

I make my way through each stall buying a variety of things I'm sure I don't need, but it makes me happy to see the joy on the vendors' faces when my silver hits their palm. I wonder just how hard the lower families out in the rings of the Realm have it.

After seeing the joy on the first person's face, I spend as much as I can without drawing too much attention to myself, asking for everything to be sent to the Locklear estate under Amelia's name. Thank hells for friends who have your back.

Once I reach the back corner of the square, and having spent more than I thought I would, I take a seat on a bench on a patch of grass. I groan as I get off my feet. These boots might look amazing, but fuck me, they hurt. I guess that's what I get for having never worn them before.

I study the people around me, taking them all in with curious eyes. I eventually spot something so out of the ordinary that I blink and rub my eyes to make sure I'm not imagining it.

Wings.

The girl spots me watching her, and her violet eyes go wide when she realizes I can see her. I get to my feet because she definitely isn't from this Realm. Wings wouldn't be too out of the ordinary, but black-feathered wings, tipped with the same violet as her eyes… yeah, that's definitely not someone from this Realm.

She must be from Avalon.

I've never seen an Angel before, let alone spoken to one. They rarely come here. This Realm is not kind to their power stores, just as mine would be lower if I went to their Realm, Avalon.

I jump to my feet, and she takes off in the opposite direction at a run. Something inside of me tells me to follow her. There's a pull inside of my chest, and the base of my power store calls to hers so strongly that I can't fight the compulsion. I lift the hood of my cape and take off, running as fast as I can on aching feet to try and catch the Angel.

Fuck me, the Angel can move.

Even here with her power supposedly lowered, she's so quick that it's a struggle to even keep her in my sights. I pull on the power within me that calls me to her, and I pick up my pace. I follow her for longer than I should, having no idea where I am or where I'm going as I give chase.

I follow her down an alley, and I see the dead-end at about the same time she does. Her shoulders sink before she turns toward me and frowns. The sparkle in her violet eyes dims a little, and then she disappears with a blast of light.

I lift my arm to cover my eyes, but they water anyway. Once the light recedes, there's nothing to show that she was even here, except for a lone feather on the ground.

Why was she even here? And why would she run from me?

I pick up the feather and put it in the inner pocket of my cloak before heading out of the alley, trying to work out what the hell it is I've stumbled upon.

A loud cheer bursts through the air as two men stumble into the street from a tavern down the way. With nowhere else to go, and no idea how to get back to the estate, I decide to risk it and head to the tavern.

What's the worst that could happen?

I take a deep breath and make sure my power is contained, exactly the way Ares has shown me a million times, and walk inside the wooden door. The change from the quiet outside is startling. The volume in here is deafening, and smoke is cloying in the air. Something about the place feels welcoming, though. It could be the music from the band in the corner or the raucous laughter filling the room, but I feel like I don't need to keep my guard up quite as much as I probably should. I pull my hood down since no one in the Realm knows me by face, or at least, not anyone that I'd find in here. This is definitely not a place of the High Born Demons, and I kind of love it.

I make my way to the bar, a small smile tugging on the edge of my lips as I weave through the happy and loud people. I move to slide onto one of the stools at the bar when I feel a hand grab my ass.

I don't fucking think so.

I grab the motherfucker's wrist who thinks he has the right to touch me, twist his arm, so his back is to my front and smash his face into the bar. I hold him there as I take in who this motherfucker is. I notice his dark hair and somewhat large build and roll my eyes.

"You going to let up on my face, princess?" The asshole groans as his face is mashed up against the bar, and I gasp. I freeze for a second, thinking he's recognized me, but I realize that he has no idea. He's just being condescending. I roll my eyes before lifting his head and smashing it against the bar again.

"Maybe next time you'll think before you touch someone without permission," I say, releasing him. It's only then I realize that pretty much all of the noise in this place has stopped and that everyone is watching us.

Fuck my fucking life.

"Maybe I will, but also, considering where you are, maybe you should've realized that touching is a thing here." I feel the blush creep up my neck at his words, and then I notice the half-dressed women dotted around the room.

Of course I stumbled into a brothel.

The noise in the room cranks back up when they realize there isn't going to be a show or a fight for them to ogle. I've never been more glad to not have all eyes on me. This isn't exactly staying under the radar like I planned.

"Do I look like I'm selling myself?" I cross my arms and jut out my chin, trying not to fall into the depths of his violet eyes as his gaze rakes over my entire body. A roguish smile creeps onto his face. That, mixed with the confidence with which he holds himself and a jaw that could cut fucking glass, makes the heat on my skin go up a few notches. I've never really found myself attracted to people at the palace, but none of them have looked like him either. Dammit all to Hell.

"I mean, it's rare for a girl to stumble in here that isn't looking for a good time, but you're right. You don't look like the other girls around here." As he looks into my green eyes, I feel something inside of me click into place, and I lose all of my breath. He almost staggers on the spot, so I know he feels it too.

"What are you?" he asks, breathless. I shake my head, helpless and not knowing how to answer. All I know is that whatever power lives inside of me wants to claim him as ours, and I'm not all that opposed to it. Even considering how we just met.

"I'm…" I start, not really having the words or wanting to reveal myself to him here.

"How about we go somewhere a little more quiet?" he asks lowly, and I nod. He waves at the woman behind the bar and says, "Tarnie, I'll see you in a few days."

He takes my hand, not waiting for a response, and leads me out of the brothel. I have no idea where we are or where he's taking me, but somehow I know I'm safe with him. It's the weirdest fucking thing, but I've learned to judge people really fucking well over the years. Despite his earlier actions, he doesn't give off the 'I'm a creep' or the 'I'm going to skin you alive' vibes.

I follow without any real struggle, and I eventually start to recognize the streets we pass. We head further toward the square where I spent almost all of my coin earlier. Though as we reach the square now, it's a completely different vision than it was earlier. Now, with the sun set, it's completely deserted. It almost feels barren.

"Where are you taking me?"

"Well, you don't seem like a Low Born, and considering where you stumbled to, I'm going to guess you're not from around here. So, I figured I'd bring you back to the good side of town." I bite my lower lip wondering just how much I should tell him about me considering I don't really know him, even if my power does want to claim him.

"I'm Caleb," he tells me, looking down at the ground. "One of the lowest born in this place, but I swear I have no intention of hurting you."

"I believe you."

He looks up at me, shock clear in his violet eyes. "You really aren't from around here, are you?"

"You could say that." I smile up at him, realizing once again just how much taller he is than me, even in these boots. "I'm Morgan."

"Morgan… it suits you. I have to say, I've never come across a chick that could throw down as hard as you did back there. So yeah... badass Morgan. I like it." He smiles again, and I swear my heart skips a fucking beat. Surely this isn't right. I can't be feeling like this after half an hour with the guy. Especially considering I smashed his face into a bar not that long ago.

"So, where are we going?"

"Where do you want to go?" I consider his words. I don't think anyone has ever really asked me what I want before, and it has me stumbling. Because I have no fucking idea.

"I don't know this place, so why don't you take me to your favourite spot?"

"I'm not sure a High Born like yourself would like my favorite spot." I wince. If only he knew just how High Born I was... but I'm not about to ruin my night here.

"Well, maybe I'm not like the other High Born you know."

He looks me over again, but I feel like he's seeing straight through to my soul. The way his eyes widen when the power inside of me pings again steals my breath away, and I feel such a pull to him that it almost sends me to my knees. If his narrowed eyes and quick intake of breath are anything to go by, I'd say he felt it again too. "That might be the truest thing anyone has ever said."

I lose track of time as I walk alongside Caleb in the most comfortable silence I've felt in my life. Just the sound of his breathing is soothing to me. I feel like I've fallen down some rabbit hole and I'm living in an alternate reality or Realm. This shit has never happened to me, and I've definitely never heard of it either.

I mean, I know that some Demons bond with each other—a heart bond—but I've never heard of someone's power reacting to another's in such a way, like you feel as though you've known them for your entire existence. That's exactly how this feels, and I am beyond thrown. Yet I can't find it in myself to walk away from him.

Ares is going to fucking kill me if I turn up with a stray, and that's exactly how he'll see this. It's the same way he views my relationship with Amelia. Just another person I want to save. But that isn't what this is. At least, I don't think so.

It doesn't feel that way.

He doesn't let go of my hand as we hike up the hill, through the trees, and further away from everything I've come to know of this ring of the Shadow Realm. Further from what should feel like safety, but I don't think I've ever felt as safe with anyone as I do at Caleb's side.

It's so fucked up, but I'm beyond questioning it. I've never examined my power beyond learning with Ares how to keep it shut down and tucked away. That's the limit of my control over my power, but this pull feels too strong to ignore. It's as if the Fates themselves pushed me to follow the Angel and led me to him. I've never been one to believe in a higher power before, but maybe I was too inexperienced, too naive to see the truth of it all. Maybe I just didn't see how a higher power could let my father get away with what he does… but just maybe I was wrong.

We finally clear the tree line, and I gasp as I take in the view. The city glows below us. I can see all of it, even the far outer reaches. From the High Born sector, where the Locklear mansion sits like the monstrosity that it is, to the Low Born shacks, the part of the ring I stumbled into earlier. The divide is indisputable, and I hate how big the difference is.

If I were queen, it wouldn't be like this. But I'll never be queen, so I have to just hope that one day Ares will let me make changes once the power is his to wield.

"This is… I've never seen anything like this." I look over at him and find him watching me, a small smile tugging on his lips.

"This is my spot. It's where I come to escape everything when I need to think… or just get away from the shitty existence of my life. I've never brought anyone else here before, but I thought you might like it."

He brought me to his place. The place he comes to escape. Goddamn my traitorous heart for beating just a little bit faster at this confession. I don't understand what's happening to me at all.

"It's magical," I say, moving to the cliff edge and taking a seat, letting my feet hang over the precipice. He sits beside me, so closely that while we're not actually touching, I am still oh-so-aware of every fucking inch of him.

"It does look beautiful from up here. It's a shame that it's just an illusion." He sighs, and I take his hand. I don't know why, but he doesn't seem opposed to it, so I lock my fingers with his and wait for him to continue. When he doesn't, I can't help but prod just a little. I don't know why, but I want to know him. Every part of him.

"Tell me." It's all I say, but the sigh that comes from him makes me regret my words almost instantly.

"There isn't much to tell. I was a poor little orphan boy who grew up in a group home. I learned how to survive, and I learned how to not be seen, which came in real handy when the brothels came looking for kids to buy and when the King's guard came to round up slaves for the palace.

I learned how to steal to feed myself and the others at the home who managed to evade the buyers and vultures. I learned how to fight to keep us safe. I learned how to earn just enough that we didn't have to be afraid every day. Then I taught them how to survive without me. It's not a great life, but it's honest." He shrugs when he finishes speaking, and I swear my heart hurts for him.

"What about you?" I blink at his question because I'm not sure how he's going to take my answer, especially knowing what I know about him now.

"I…" I hesitate, and he squeezes my fingers, so I take a deep breath. "I am Morganna Voux."

I hold my breath knowing I don't need to say any more. My surname is known all through the Realm. He sucks in a breath as my heart races before releasing it in a shudder. "Well fuck, I didn't expect that."

I smile at him and move to pull my hand from his, but his fingers tighten around mine. "It doesn't matter to me who you are or who your family is, princess. This thing between us isn't something that I've ever felt or heard of. I'm not going anywhere and neither are you."

I smile at his words. I don't think anyone in my life has ever not judged me because of who my father is. Then again, I've never left the Shadow Palace before either. Maybe my views about the world are more than a little skewed.

"I think I'm going to keep you," I say, squeezing his hand, and my power sings again from inside my chest.

"I'm pretty sure I'm okay with that." He grins and tucks me in under his shoulder. As I relax beside him, I feel my power growing restless despite my attempts to keep it contained. I try to steady my breaths, but a shadow rips from me and settles over Caleb's skin. He doesn't even seem panicked by it. Once it coats his entire body, the shadow sinks into him, and he gasps.

"Ouch," he huffs. He flips his wrist over, and a symbol I've only seen in textbooks is there, as if inked into his skin from my shadow. "What the fuck is that?"

I panic but try not to let it show. This can't be happening. I just hope he doesn't hate me for it. I take a deep breath before responding as calmly as I can. "That… that is one of the symbols of the chosen. And I'm pretty sure I just claimed you."

FIVE

We walk slowly back toward the estate, and I try not to worry too much about what's going to happen when I come face to face with Ares. I look over to Caleb again, who keeps ahold of my hand, and I bite my lip before asking, "Are you sure you're good to just drop your entire life?"

"It's not much of a life." He shrugs before looking up to the sky. "I don't have anything or anyone here of importance. The people I had in my life moved on, so yes, I'm sure. There is just something about you, Morganna Voux, and I'm not about to ignore every instinct I have screaming at me that this is the path I was meant to end up on."

He sounds confident, and I try to stop my heart from

hurting at the sadness of his words. I still can't help but worry. I didn't ask his permission for any of this. My stupid power just did its thing, and now I've claimed him.

"Stop worrying so much." He smirks down at me, pulling me to a stop. "If I didn't want to be here, I wouldn't. And it's not just the claiming that's keeping me here, so stop worrying about that too. I've lived long enough to know when to trust my instincts, and I've also lived long enough to know never to pass up a chance at being happy. So let's just see where this takes us, shall we?"

"You're way too easy going. The palace is going to chew you up and spit you out," I sigh, unable to stop my worrying despite his request. It's like telling water not to be wet.

"Oh, sweetheart, you don't have to worry about me." He grins, and I gasp as I feel a pulse of his power radiate toward me. My eyes go wide, and I'm practically speechless.

"How is that possible?"

"I'm not entirely sure. Low borns usually don't have much power, right?" I nod absentmindedly because he's not actually asking me the question, and I stay quiet while he continues. "My working theory is that my dad was a frequent visitor of a brothel, and my mom must have given me up the second I was born. I have no idea where I come from, but I learned early on how to mask my power. I'm really fucking comfortable using it too. So like I said, you don't need to worry about me."

He squeezes my hand and begins walking again, leading me back toward the Locklear estate. My mind whirrs a million miles a minute as I try to process the depth of power I just felt from him. I've only ever felt that sort of depth from my own family.

Oh hells, please don't let us be related.

I wipe the thought from my mind. There is no way my father wouldn't have known if he had another child, especially one this powerful. He would have had him killed, most likely. Being bastard-born isn't exactly a great title back home. Though I can't imagine it's great anywhere in the Realm.

"Stop thinking so hard. It'll all work out. You'll see." He grins at me, and I try to smile back, but I know it doesn't quite reach my eyes. The whole consent thing is really getting to me.

I stop again, not wanting to have this conversation too close to the estate. You never know who is listening. "I'm sorry my power just claimed you without me even asking."

"Morganna, you have nothing to be sorry about. Even if you had asked, I'd have said yes. I promise you, this isn't something I'm going to resent you for further down the line." He pulls me into his arms, and I relax instantly. Placing my hands on his chest, I can feel his steady heartbeat, and I know he isn't lying to me.

"Okay, well if you're sure… then you should probably just call me Morgan. All of my friends do. Only my father calls me Morganna." His face scrunches when I mention my father, and his arms tighten around me a little more.

"Maybe I'll just call you Mor, because I'm telling you right now, princess, I'm not just going to be your friend." He leans down and brushes his lips across mine.

I still for a minute because holy shit, I've never been kissed before, and his lips are so fucking soft. I lean into his embrace, kissing him back with heated fervor, and that seems to be all the encouragement he needs. He deepens the kiss, and I can't help the sigh that escapes me. He takes advantage of my open lips and strokes my tongue with his. My fingers clasp at his shirt, and just before I'm utterly breathless, he pulls back and rests his forehead on mine. "Yeah, we're definitely not going to be just friends."

Sneaking Caleb into the Locklear estate was far easier than I could have imagined possible. Sneaking him into my room though… that's a whole different game. I open the door a little and pop my head through the gap to find Ares sitting in the main area of our suite, waiting up for me with Kaos and the pack at his feet.

Well shit.

"Where the fuck have you been? You were supposed to be back hours ago, and I told you to take Kaos out with you." Ares looks more pissed than I've ever seen him. I mean, I guess some of it is worry, but yeah, he's pissed. I wave a hand behind me, hoping to fuck Caleb understands that I mean for him to wait where he is as I step inside the room.

"Well, you see… I kind of got lost." I bite down on my bottom lip trying to think of a way to explain that I fully forgot about tonight's meal. "But then I found a friend, and we lost track of time a bit."

Ares watches me closely, his head tipping sideways as if he's confused. His eyes narrow slightly as he studies me. "Something is different about you."

Kaos begins to growl at his feet, and I swear I want to faceplant when Ares' eyes go wide. I feel Caleb's presence behind me, so I don't need to ask what's wrong with my brother—I already know.

"You're bonded?" Ares' voice comes out strangled as he starts to his feet, and for a second, I fear he might actually hurt me.

"It wasn't exactly something I planned on, and I don't know that bonded is the right word. It's more as if my power claimed him," I tell him, trying not to fidget. Caleb takes my hand in his, standing there so sure of himself despite the fact he looks completely out of place and is facing down my brother at the same time. I hadn't even really considered the way he was dressed; it's never really been something I've noticed when meeting new people. My brother obviously sees things differently to me if the look on his face is anything to go by.

Caleb taps the door closed behind him with his foot but stays at my back. "Claimed would be the right word." He lifts his wrist to show Ares the mark, who responds by cursing under his breath before he starts pacing the room.

I crouch down, and Kaos approaches me, eyeing Caleb as he does so. Since he hasn't tried to rip his throat out yet, I take it as a sign of his tacit acceptance. "You know he won't hurt me don't you, boy?" I coo at the hellhound, who huffs back. Smoke tendrils curl from his nostrils as I stroke between his ears, and he settles down at my feet.

"And what exactly do you expect to do with him? How are we going to explain this?" Ares finally asks once he looks a little calmer. I mean, he still looks like he wants to wring my neck, but calmer nonetheless.

"I hadn't really thought that far. This isn't something I planned for or intended to do," I tell him, placing my hands on my hips. I get that he wasn't expecting this, and it's likely a complication for my father's plans, but so fucking what.

"I swear to all that binds us, Morgan…" He starts

pacing again, so I stand and wait him out with Caleb at my side.

"He is mine, Ares. He's coming with us. I don't care how you make it work, but it's happening." I can almost feel Caleb's smirk, but I mean what I say. I'm standing my ground. Something about him called to me, and I'm not just going to ignore that.

"Tell me exactly what happened," Ares commands, so we sit, and I tell him everything. The call of my power to Caleb, the weird shadow coating thing, and then the mark appearing. I leave out the details of the Angel, because it's not essential to this part of the story—at least I don't think so. He sits, quietly pondering over my words.

"I don't know what this means, but for now he can stay. I'll arrange some clothes for him, and we'll call him a friend of the royals," Ares states, sounding more tired than I think I've ever heard him. A pang of guilt wrenches my heart. He turns to Caleb and looks him over again. "You need to bathe. I've already made excuses for Morgan not attending dinner this evening, so it won't be any shock when we ask for food to be brought up. Just keep yourself out of sight for now. I'll wrap up our business on this level tomorrow morning, and we shall leave in the afternoon. At least if we arrive with him in the next level, there will be less questions about how you picked up another stray."

He stands and walks toward his bedroom before

turning back to us. “And I’m sure I don’t have to say it, but just in case… not a word about the claiming, or the bond, or the fucking mark. Not to another soul.” He rubs his eyes before looking over Caleb once more. “And if you so much as harm a hair on her head, you will know pain like you have never witnessed before. Am I understood?”

“Completely. But know, I mean her no harm. My power called to hers too. I don’t think I could hurt her even if I tried,” Caleb tells him, and I chew the inside of my cheek as he speaks so that I don’t smile.

Ares just nods before moving into his room and closing the door.

“Well, that could have gone worse,” Caleb says cheerily, leaning back on the couch.

“It could have gone better.” I sigh, and he chuckles.

He grabs me by the waist and pulls me onto his lap. “No one is dead or mutilated. I’ll mark that down as a good night. Plus, I’m in a room with the prettiest, most badass girl I’ve ever met. Today is definitely going in the win column.”

I roll my eyes at him, but he holds me tighter, pulling me closer to him. We’re so close I can feel the warmth of his breath on my cheek. A wave of heat rolls over me, but before I give myself a chance to fall any further to his charms, I push back from him and stand.

“Let’s get you a bath and then get some food. We can

talk more after."

"As m'lady commands." He bounces to his feet and bows at me. I roll my eyes so hard, I swear I see my brain.

"A joker too, what joy." My sarcasm only makes his grin widen.

He stands and moves closer to me, leaving my chest a hair's width from his. "You're going to learn to love it, princess. Of that much I'm sure."

A cough sounds, and I turn to see Ares watching us, the frown on his face obvious. "I suggest you get that bath, the food won't be long."

Caleb nods at him, and I point to my bedroom door. Caleb heads toward it, while Ares just stares at me. "Please, no more surprises," my brother says, his eyes hard.

I give him a sad smile and shrug. "I'm not going to make promises I can't keep."

When Caleb emerges from my bathroom, I'm just lounging on my bed with Kaos. To say I hadn't really paid attention to what he was wearing earlier was an understatement because when he emerges from the door in a black long-sleeved t-shirt that clings to his arms and a pair of jeans, I have to bite down on my lip to stop a groan from escaping.

I'm not sure what it is about him that makes me react

so viscerally, but I'm just going to go with it for now.

His smirk tells me I haven't hidden my reaction all that well, and Kaos just snorts next to me on the bed. "Like what you see?"

"I mean, who would've thought you could fill out a shirt like that so well?" I shrug, feigning nonchalance but grinning because I know it isn't going to work.

"What can I say? I might be Low Born, but I know how to eat." He rubs his belly and grins before dropping down on the other side of me. "So how's this all going to work?"

"Honestly, I have no idea. We're leaving here tomorrow, but we're still visiting each of the other rings in the Realm before heading home. My father has a coming out ball planned once we return. Gag me. This trip was meant to be about me introducing myself to the High Born families officially before the ball, but I'd rather gouge my eyes out than go to a ball with the sole intention of selling me off to the highest bidder."

His eyes narrow, and the room darkens a little. "Yeah, I don't exactly like the sound of that either." He pulls me closer to his side with an air of possessiveness. Even Kaos eyes him, trying to work out if he's going to be a threat. I rub his belly, and he settles back down as Caleb relaxes more with me in his arms. "But what I really meant is how is this thing between us going to work?"

"Oh, erm, yeah I hadn't really thought about it. I figure I'll be able to miss most of the royal bullshit that Ares has going on, so we can just hang out and get to know each other some more. Like we probably should have before I did the whole 'claiming you' thing." He chuckles at my words and kisses the top of my head. I'm not sure if I should feel this comfortable with someone I barely know, but I do. Whether it's because I claimed him, because my power called to him, or because Kaos has deemed him as okay, I don't know. But since this quite literally is my first rodeo with anything like this, I'm going to just go with it.

The door to my room flings open, and Kaos is on his feet in an instant as Caleb maneuvers me behind him before I can so much as blink. "Food is here."

I look over Caleb's shoulder and see Ares taking in the sight before him, more than a little amused. I roll my eyes at just how funny he seems to find the fact that Caleb instantly moved to protect me. On one hand, I mean, swoon. Obviously. On the other hand, I'm a badass bitch. Kinda. At least I will be when I learn how to use my powers fully. I can kick someone's ass all over the Realm if we fight like the humans, but then Demons always tend to play dirty.

"We're coming," I say as I climb off the bed and walk in front of Caleb. Kaos follows me out, and I just hear Ares grumbling, "You better not be."

I can't help the blush that stains my cheeks at my

fucking asshole brother's filthy comment. Caleb snickers behind me, so I guess he heard too.

I pull to a stop when I see the spread Ares had brought up. "Did they think they were feeding an army?"

Ares laughs at me and shrugs. "I told them you were hungry but didn't know what you wanted. Mainly because I don't know what your new pet likes to eat."

"Oh, I'll eat anything." Caleb grins and swoops past me to the table. "I am not a picky eater."

Ares rolls his eyes at me. I guess he didn't get the reaction he wanted from his 'pet' comment. Though it pisses me off. I get that this whole thing wasn't planned and might cause issues for him, but he doesn't know Caleb.

I glare at my brother who holds his hands up in apology before sitting at the table. "Well, since you're going to be around with us for a while, I suppose you should tell me a bit about you. Is there anyone who will object to us running away with you? I try to leave the kidnapping mess at my father's feet. It's not exactly the image I want to give off."

Caleb shrugs. His lack of concern about being in the room with royalty is really fucking refreshing. He isn't fazed by my brother at all, and I have to admit that totally makes him hotter to me. "There's no one that is going to miss me or cause a stink that I'm gone. No."

"Hmmm," is all my brother says before starting to eat. The testosterone in here is off the charts. I really don't want to deal with a dick measuring contest, so I sit down beside Caleb and start to eat as well. We make general conversation while we eat, and it's just when we're almost finished that the door bursts open and a red-headed hurricane storms into the room. The door slams closed behind her, and she gawks at Caleb sitting beside me, one arm around the back of my chair.

"Well, hello, hottie. Who are you, and can I eat you?" Her words make me choke on my water, and Ares just shakes his head. She catches sight of Ares and blushes, looking like she wants the floor to open up and swallow her whole.

"Caleb, this is my friend Amelia. As you can see she has no filter. Amelia, this is Caleb, and he is mine."

"Woah, your eyes did the creepy amber thing," she says, eyes widening at the ease of my statement. "Don't worry, I'll keep my hands to myself."

"As you should," Ares mutters before standing and coming to my side. "I'm going to turn in for the night. Please don't blow anything up before morning."

"You really should stop asking me to make promises I can't keep." I grin at him, but I stand and kiss his cheek regardless. "Good night."

He grumbles as he walks away, and once the door to his room closes, Amelia drops into the open chair and puts her face in her hands. "I really need to think before I speak."

"Nah, I like it," Caleb says, grinning widely.

"Of course you do." I roll my eyes at him and turn back to my friend. "But honestly, it's fine. What brings you up here anyway?"

"The other servants are all in a tizzy that we're leaving so much earlier than planned, so I wanted to come and see what was going on. Now, of course, I see exactly what caused the change of plans." She eyes Caleb again, and when she glances at me, her eyes go wide. "Sorry, I'll stop."

I guess my eyes did the 'creepy amber thing' as she calls it. They change color when my power surges. I have very little control over it. "It's fine. My power is a little all over the place."

"I'm going to head to bed," Caleb says, standing. "I'll give you guys some time to catch up."

He leans down and kisses me again with so much heat that my toes curl in my boots. Hot damn that boy can kiss. I think. Not like I have anything to compare it to, but my body says *yes, fucking please* every time he touches me. He smirks when he pulls back, like he knows just how much he affects me, then salutes Amelia before walking to my bedroom.

I might hate that he's going, but hells how I love to watch him leave. That ass in those pants. Yes, please.

"Morgan, you need to start talking. Because holy

fucking sex on a stick, who the fuck is that?" I grin at Amelia's outburst once Caleb shuts the door.

"I honestly have no idea."

SIX

I'm going to kill someone.

Ares wrapped up everything pretty quickly with the Locklears', and no one really questioned us cutting the trip short until Noah arrived at the door to our suite asking for some time with me despite the fact we were due to leave.

Which is how I find myself mentally restraining from stabbing this prick in the throat with the blade I have in my corset boning.

"As you can see, a partnership between our families would be beneficial for us all. I would bring the brains, and you would bring the beauty. We would be unstoppable."

Someone fucking gag me at his sexist bullshit spiel. I hear Ares snort a laugh and smother it while I try to not roll my eyes so hard that I tear a ligament or something.

Instead, I just smile and laugh as I'm expected to and pat his arm like a submissive little doll. I'd rather claw my own fucking eyes out than extend this any longer, and thankfully, Ares comes to my rescue at long fucking last. "Noah, we really do need to be going. I'll be sure to let my father know that you and Morganna spoke at length."

Noah drops my arm the minute Ares begins speaking, which just confirms every suspicion I have about him. He's a power-grabbing asshole. And I swear, if his hand brushes against my thigh, ass, or tit once more, I'm going to drop the act and just lay the motherfucker out.

I leave Ares to deal with Noah and his pompous ass, heading back to my room where Caleb is tucked away in bed until we can leave. That's two hours of my life I'm never getting back, and I swear I need a good wash because that guy is slimy as fuck.

I reach the room to find Caleb sitting on the floor, the pack circling around him while he reads a book. So much for my fierce protectors. He has them wrapped around his little finger, and it's been little more than twelve hours. Kaos lifts his head when I get close and tilts his head at me as if just realizing I was gone, but then he drops his head back in Caleb's lap.

"You seem to have a way with the hounds."

"I've always been good with animals. Their intentions are far easier to work out than Demons. They won't kill for sport, just to survive or to protect. That's a way of life I can get behind." Shadows dance behind his eyes, and I know there's more meaning behind what he's saying, but considering I've barely known him a whole day yet, I don't think I have the right to pry. Even if I have claimed him. "How was your walk?"

"It was disgusting. That man-child really needs to learn some respect. He has wandering fucking hands and its gross." I pause as Caleb's face morphs. His eyes turn black, and his teeth elongate. Kaos and the pack jump to attention as if we're under attack.

"I'll teach him some fucking respect. He doesn't get to touch what is mine." My eyes go wide as I take in just how pissed off he is right now. The power comes from him in waves, but I'm not afraid. Somehow I know he won't hurt me. I move toward him and place my hands on his chest.

"It's okay, I handled it." My words are soft, and after a minute or so, he goes back to his usual form. His violet eyes look down at me, and he shudders as he wraps his arms around me.

"Sorry, I'm not really sure where that came from." He presses his nose into my hair and takes a deep breath before pulling me more tightly into his embrace.

"We're good," I say softly as I hug him back.

"Are you two about ready to leave?" Ares' voice breaks through the moment, and Caleb pulls back from me.

"Yeah, we're good," he says, and I see the shutters come down as he tucks away the emotion. I'm still a little shocked at Caleb's outburst, but I smile at my brother like nothing ever happened.

Ares eyes us both closely, but I whistle to the hounds, and he gives up searching for whatever he's looking for. "Okay, well, we're going now. Get the hounds downstairs. Caleb, if anyone asks from here on out, you're a friend of the crown, and you're on protection detail for my sister."

"Got it," Caleb says with a nod. I'm not sure anyone will believe it, especially since I'm with my brother, and I have the hounds, but I'm not going to question Ares either. If he thinks this will work, then I'll follow his lead.

"I'll meet you both downstairs. All of your things have already been taken down." Ares leaves, closing the door behind him, and Caleb all but deflates.

"Are you sure you're ready for all of this?" I ask him, trying not to dig my nails into my palms. It's a lot, and despite him saying he's okay with it all, I'm not sure he really knows what he's getting himself into, and I can't help but feel guilty for taking him from everything he's ever known.

He strides back toward me and captures my chin in his thumb and finger, pulling my gaze to his. "I am in this—whatever this is and wherever it leads me. I have never belonged anywhere, and two hundred years is a long time to not belong. This thing between us, no matter how new it is, is the first time I've felt anything close to home, and that's because of you. You feel like home to me, you understand? So you don't need to worry about me. I'm not going anywhere unless you tell me to leave."

He captures my lips with his, and I run my hands through his hair, wishing we could be closer, but time is not on our side. He releases my lips and kisses my forehead softly. "We should get going. Your brother will come looking for us, and I really don't want to piss him off since he's been so good about me being here."

"I guess you're right." I sigh softly. "Let's get this show on the road, shall we?"

We've been in Level Two for four days, and I've never seen so many dull and dreary Demons in my life. I would've thought a place run by Sirens would be more entertaining, but apparently not. Ares has made me tag along to more royal meetings than I care to count, and Caleb has been at my side for every single one. I'm not sure if I feel worse for him or for me for having to live through them.

By the end of day five, I've had enough.

"Ares, please don't make me go to another meeting. I beg of you. If I get dismissed or groped one more time, I'm going to go postal." I drop into the chair in the main room of the suite we're staying in. The High Borns really are a pretentious fucking bunch. I swear this level is more stuck up than the last, and if this is a pattern, I am not looking forward to the next few levels. I didn't think anywhere could ever be as bad as home.

Caleb grunts as he pulls me to my feet then takes my seat and pulls me down onto his lap. "She's not wrong. A few people have nearly lost limbs because they couldn't keep wandering appendages to themselves."

Ares chuckles as he pours himself a glass of nectar and shoots it back. I guess I'm not the only one who's sick of this place. "Just two more days, and then we can get out of here. At least the Trevalans aren't as big ass-kissers as this lot."

I groan and curl up in Caleb's lap. I can survive two more days, right?

I'm not sure I can, but I suck it up the way I've been taught to. "Fine, but can we please start my training soon?"

Ares' gaze bounces between Caleb and I, and I roll my eyes. "Ares, he's fine. He's not going to use my power against me. Trust me, he has plenty of his own."

My brother looks at me skeptically but shoots back another drink before answering my original question. "We can start training once we're in the next level. I trust a few people in Level Three. We can train in a safe space there."

He looks to Caleb as if weighing up his words. "Do you train?"

"I've never trained officially, but I'm in control of my power. I'm not too bad with an axe either." Ares smiles at Caleb's response.

"Not a sword man then? I can appreciate that." Ares finishes another drink before putting the bottle away. "You can train with us. It makes sense for Morgan to train with more than just me. She knows all my moves at this point. And if you're happy to let me see your power, I can help you hone yours too."

"Thanks, that would be great," Caleb says, and I swear I can almost feel him squirm at the affability of my brother's offer.

"Awesome, well, I'll leave you to have a nice night without me. I have another fucking night out with these slimy assholes. Don't wait up." He looks fucking miserable as he walks toward the door, but by the time he waves goodbye, his princely mask of indifference is back in place. I hate how much he hates having to do all of this. That I can't rescue him for once. But I won't lie, I'm so fucking thankful I don't have to spend any more time with the High Born of this level.

The only thing I like about them is that they're so far up their own asses they didn't question Caleb's presence with us. That's literally the only good thing about this entire level of the Realm. I haven't met one being who is even half decent. It's disgusting.

The rumors of what happens for the evening entertainment is enough for me to be thankful that I'm not invited.

"So, what do you want to do with our evening alone?" Caleb asks, and my heart starts to race as he kisses my neck. I swear I can't formulate words with his lips on my neck. My skin feels like it's on fire in the best kind of way. His hands move from my waist and skim my ribs, and I gasp at the contact. "Is this okay?"

"Yes," I say breathlessly as his hands move lower again.

"What about this?" he asks and I nod, my whole body alight.

"I haven't ever…" I try to speak but the words won't form.

"Ever?"

"Never," I confirm, and his hands stop. I try not to pout at the sudden change in his actions, but I get it.

"You've never been with a man before? Or a woman? Just so we're clear."

I shake my head at him. "No, when you kissed me for the first time… That was my first kiss." I feel heat creep up my neck and cast my gaze down. I hate how sheltered I've been from stuff like this, and now I just feel stupid and naive.

He puts a finger under my chin and brings my gaze back to him. “Hey, you have nothing to be embarrassed about. I just wish I’d known before I was so reckless. A first kiss is important. But I won’t lie, the fact that you’re untouched is hot as fuck.”

I squirm on his lap, but smile, trying to trust that he has no reason to lie to me. “Are you sure you want to keep going?”

“Yes,” I tell him honestly. He grips my waist and lifts me from his lap while standing. Not letting my feet touch the ground as he carries me to the bedroom.

“Tell me to stop if you want me to stop, okay?” he says as he closes the door behind us, and I nod.

“Words, Mor. I need words.”

“Yes,” I gasp as he lays me down on the giant bed.

“Better.”

I lean up on my elbows, my dark hair fanned out behind me, and I watch him as he strips off his black t-shirt. Damn, he’s just too freaking beautiful, even with the scars that mar his skin. I’m not sure what I did to deserve him, but I’m past the point of questioning it too much.

Naked from the waist up, he flashes me a rogue grin that makes my nerve endings tingle with anticipation. With a spark in his eyes, he hovers over me and places a kiss on my forehead, then the tip of my nose. He drops a kiss on each of my eyelids before warming my cheeks with his full lips. He doesn't touch me anywhere else, and the thought that he's so close, yet so far, drives me wild. His body warms me from above, and yet our only points of contact are the slowly peppered kisses he's trailing over my skin.

"I want to make it count, princess. Every touch and every kiss."

Tracing my lips with the tip of his tongue, he sighs into my mouth before resuming his tender kisses on my chin. As he continues his gentle path down the column of my throat, my mind is able to forget all the crap I have had to deal with on the first levels of our visit. The only sound I can truly hear is my own breathing. The rhythm perfectly matches the rise and fall of my chest, increasing as he moves closer to my breasts. Every cell in my body tenses at the thought of his mouth on my untouched skin, with nothing between me and his lips. Nothing but his intimate touch.

"I love that I can hear everything you're feeling." His words bring me out of my own head, prompting me to rise on my elbows and look down at where his lips worship the valley between my breasts.

"What do you mean?" I can feel the crease between my brows. There's no doubt my confusion is clearly written all over my face. Can he hear my emotions? Can he tell how nervous I am?

"The lower I go, the louder your breaths grow. It tells me how excited you are, princess. It tells me you want me in the same way that I want you. Your body is speaking to me, and I hear it loud and clear."

The smile I give him feels goofy, like I'm drunk on his nectar. He says the sweetest things.

"May I?" It takes a second to work out what he's asking, and heat spills over my cheeks. I have nothing to be ashamed of. In fact, I'm fully aware that I've been blessed by the hells, but no one has ever seen me undressed.

If I bare myself to him, I'll be exposing more than just my body. I already know that my heart is at risk, and if I do this, I'll be giving it to him more fully.

Even with all of that running through my mind, I don't hesitate.

"Yes."

Putting his weight on one forearm, Caleb slides the pad of his index finger over the spaghetti strap of my dress, running it half over the wispy fabric, half over my skin. That slight touch is like lava running through my veins. I have to bite my bottom lip to keep myself from panting, to keep from throwing myself at him unabashedly.

The uptick at the corner of his mouth tells me he feels it too. That he knows exactly what he's doing to me, and he's enjoying every second of it.

It's when he slides the strap over my shoulder and

exposes me that I realize everything he's been doing is nothing compared to the feeling of his soft lips on my nipple. He licks and bites gently, and on instinct, I clench my thighs and revel in the feel of warm liquid pooling at my center. It's a foreign feeling, something I hadn't expected, yet it feels right. So fucking right.

"I can smell your arousal, Mor, it's fucking delicious."

As his mouth closes over my nipple, he does this thing with his tongue, and I swear it's like there's a direct line connected to my clit. My hips shoot off the bed, and my breath catches in my throat.

Stunned, I lift up and look down to where his eyes are staring back at me, a mixture of lust and utter male satisfaction shining bright.

"What was that?" My voice sounds like I've just run a marathon. I barely recognize it.

"That, princess, was desire. I'll let you in on a secret," he pauses to circle his tongue around my pert nipple before finishing his thought. "That was only a fraction of what I'm going to make you feel."

It seems impossible. I can't imagine anything feeling more potent than what he just did to me. The way he made me feel, but I'm not going to question him. I'm not an authority on any of this. Instead, I swallow any form of protest as he resumes his travels down the length of my body, peppering soft kisses along the way. My sternum, my stomach, a lick around my belly button, all the while pulling my dress down as he exposes more of me to his hungry eyes.

When he reaches his final destination, he lifts his gaze back up to mine and asks without words if he can continue.

I love this about him. He knows how I feel about consent and his willingness to respect that makes my heart swell with respect.

"Yes." It's barely a whisper, but it may as well be a cry over the mountains.

Uncovering my black lace panties, he curses on an exhale before placing one final kiss on my burning center. I know I'm wet, I can feel the slick liquid pooling between my legs, and the thought of his mouth going anywhere near there makes me squirm and pant at the same time.

"Caleb—" he cuts me off with a lick over my panties and a groan of utter male pleasure.

"Fuck, Mor, I can't wait to feast on you."

As if on their own accord, my hips rise up to meet his mouth, seeking relief from a mouth that seems as if it were made for my pussy.

"Yes, please."

I have no idea what it feels like to be touched there, let alone have someone's mouth there. I feel as if I should be embarrassed, but I can't bring myself to be. Everything Caleb says and does makes my confidence rise and my heart beat inside my chest like a battle drum.

"I hope these weren't important to you." Confused by his words, I lift up on my elbows again. By the time my gaze lands on Caleb, nestling between my thighs, I realize he's talking about my undies. My now shredded undies.

"Hey!"

"Shh, we both know you have more than you can count." His smirk makes me roll my eyes, but my protest dies in an instant as his tongue slides through my wetness. The heat, the thickness, the softness—all of it lapping at me and circling my aching clit.

I gasp at the foreign sensation. It's everything I never knew I wanted. Everything I didn't realize I needed.

Falling back onto the bed, I clench my fists over the bedspread and shut down my mind, letting my instincts take over. My chest heaves, my breaths labored as a heat travels through my body. It feels as if a series of electric shocks is hitting every last one of my nerve endings and lighting them up in a way I've never felt before.

Caleb grips my thighs, his fingers digging into my flesh as he devours me like he won't survive if he doesn't get his fill. His groans reverberate on my pussy as his tongue fucks me, his breath warming my skin.

"Caleb, oh hells, I can't..." When his mouth closes over my clit and his tongue flicks the swollen nub over and over again, I lose all semblances of control I was tenuously holding onto.

My entire body freezes as my core begins to pulse. Caleb resumes his tongue fucking as his thumb replaces his mouth on my clit, assaulting it with unprecedented pleasure, before swapping back again.

It's when he bites down and sucks on my clit that my body arches, and a wave of pleasure like I've never known rips through me, starting in my core and building outward until I writhe. I scream out incoherencies and feel as though my entire body is levitating above the bed.

When I fall back down, I don't know how much time passes. I'm eventually pulled back to consciousness by the soft circling of Caleb's thumb on my thigh. I'm basically lying on his chest, and he smiles at me. "Welcome back, princess."

With a dopey smile on my face, I look up at him and acknowledge his promise from before.

"You weren't kidding about that fraction."

Today we're finally heading to Level Three, and I don't think I've ever been so relieved. The hounds are already in their cage, including Kaos, much to his dissatisfaction, while I sit in the carriage with Caleb and Ares.

"Is all this carriage shit really necessary? Could we

not just whisper from one place to the next without such fanfare?" Caleb asks once again.

Ares sighs and pinches the bridge of his nose. "Yes we could, I'd rather it honestly, but this is what's expected. Welcome to the Royal fucking bullshit parade."

Caleb sniggers beside me while Ares looks like he wants to drown himself in a pool of nectar. It's only a minute or so until the Dàgaan take off, and the carriage jerks forward before the ground disappears beneath my feet and we whisper away to the next level of the Realm.

It only takes a few seconds before we rematerialize, and I feel Caleb's hand on mine. My stomach churns again, and I can't help but wonder if I'll ever get any better at traveling this way.

The carriage takes us through the level, but it's much louder than any of the others we've been to so far. I pull back the curtain and see hundreds of people outside, cheering my brother's name.

So fucking strange.

I look over to Ares who just grins. "I told you I had friends here."

"You did, but I didn't expect this." I look over to Caleb who is just chuckling at it all. The carriage weaves through the city until we reach what I assume is the Trevalans' estate.

Ares jumps from the carriage first with a huge grin on

his face. Caleb climbs out next and offers me a hand down.

"Ares, you crazy bastard. It's about time you got here!" I see a woman with blood-red hair embrace my brother. I can't help but smile when I see her, because she looks like a fucking badass. She's a Wraith. I don't know how I know this, but I do. There is no doubt that this woman is a warrior. I look out at the people around the estate and outside its walls, and realize they're all warriors. At least they look and dress like it.

"Brandy, I've missed you!" Ares says with a laugh before waving me over. "This is my sister, Morgan, and her friend Caleb."

"Nice to meet you," I tell her sincerely, and she grins at me before launching at me and wrapping me in a hug. She squeezes so tightly I feel like I can barely breathe, but she laughs and lets me go again before doing the same to Caleb. I laugh quietly as his eyes bulge out a little at the intensity of her hug.

"I've been waiting to meet you for a long time, girly," Brandy says to me once she releases Caleb. "Get your hounds before they tear my people apart, and let's head inside, shall we?"

I turn to see a guy who looks as big as a fucking house trying to open the door to the cage holding my pack, but Kaos is giving him hell. I whistle, and the hounds all turn to look at me. I give them a pointed look, and Kaos howls before the others join him. Little assholes, the bunch of them.

I head over to the cage, with Caleb a step behind me as my brother heads inside the house, and open it myself. "You guys are meant to protect me, not disobey me," I mutter as I open the door and they all pile out. Some might say traveling with eight Hellhounds is a bit much, and I might tell those people to fuck right off.

Once the cage is shut again, the porter takes the carriage along with the Dàgaan around the back of the building, and the other carriages follow him. I see a shock of red hair before seeing Amelia's smile as they disappear around the corner. At least I know she's still here with me and happy. It's much better than the alternative even if I haven't had much chance to see her.

"We should head in," Caleb says, touching my waist. I look up at him, and the intensity of his stare is enough to make me overheat. A blush stains my chest when I think about the way he made me come completely undone the other day, and he grins. "Not what I meant, but I won't say no." He winks at me, and I hide my face in my hands.

"Oh no, you have no reason to hide from me, not ever. Now come on, I can see your brother twitching the curtains looking for you." He places a hand on the small of my back and leads me inside of the estate.

I'm shocked by the interior. It looks like some sort

of home crossed with an armory. There are weapons everywhere. Literally mounted on the walls, hanging from the ceilings, in cabinets, and on dressers.

"This is nothing," Brandy says, waving us through to the sitting room Ares is already in. "You should see the armory."

"I'd like to see that." Caleb grins, and Ares shakes his head.

"You might regret that."

"Ares, stop. We'll let the boy decide for himself." Brandy grins before we all take a seat.

"Now then, why don't you fill me in on whatever little errand your father has sent you on that brings you to my door."

After leaving Brandy and Ares to catch up, Caleb and I decided to explore this level with Kaos in tow. I'd say as per my brother's request, but it was more like a demand that we bring the hound. While he might be loved here, you never truly know a person's motives until it's too late to change the position you find yourself in.

This city is far more basic than Level One, which shocks me, but considering it's full of warriors, they don't seem to have much need for the finer things, beyond armor and weapons.

But what really takes my breath away is what we find outside the city. The mountains and the snow. I've never seen snow before. We walk for what feels like miles to explore the rocky cliffs before heading back to the city.

We're not expected back at the estate, so I drag Caleb into one of the few restaurants on the main street through the center of the city.

"I can think of better things to eat," Caleb smirks as we sit down, and I feel my cheeks heat before I level him with a stare.

"I'm sure you can, but I want to actually eat first."

"Oh, princess. I'm all about sustenance first." I shake my head at him and his outrageousness, because I mean, really?

"I'm sure you are." I smile before picking up the menu that's standing up on the table. I don't recognize half of the stuff on here, but I'm pretty sure that steak is steak. Right? I'm not the sort of girl who's going to pick at a salad, even in front of a guy. The server drops by and puts two glasses of water on the table before rushing away.

"Maybe tone down the scowl, Mor." Caleb laughs. "You're scaring the staff."

"But I didn't do anything," I object, looking over at the server who is still scurrying away from our table.

"Mor, everyone on this level has worked out who you

are. And while I know you won't flay them alive for your fork not being clean, the Voux name comes with a certain reputation. Even if your brother is friends with Brandy. It's rare that there's more than one exception to a rule—they likely assume your brother is the exception." Caleb squeezes my hand, trying to soften his words, but my smile drops. I hate my father a little more with every breath I take, and I didn't think that was even possible. "Don't worry, one day they'll see you. Just like I saw you."

My heart skips a beat when he looks at me like he can see my soul, and I squeeze his hand back before softening the frown on my face. I can do this, I can show them that I'm not a monster.

My mind flicks back to the worst moment of my life, the moment I killed my mother, and I frown again.

We were born of monsters. That doesn't make you one.

Ares' voice flickers through my mind, and I can take a breath again.

Movement outside the door catches my eye, and I jump to my feet.

Wings.

Why on earth is she back here?

"What's wrong?" Caleb asks, going on full alert, and the audible gasps ring out around the restaurant.

"We need to go." I scramble out of the restaurant, just in time to see her ducking down an alley. I can't lose her again. I need to know why she's here. Something inside of me tells me that she's important, and I'm learning to trust my instincts beyond all else.

I chase after the Angel with Caleb hot on my heels. I can hear Caleb cursing behind me, but I pick up my pace as I watch the Angel get further into the distance. Fuck my life, she can move.

"Is that a fucking Angel?" I hear Caleb's surprise as he catches up with me. At the sound of his voice, she stops running and turns to face us. I miss a step thanks to my shock at her sudden stop but catch myself and keep running. As we get closer, I see her eyes grow wide as she watches Caleb.

We fully catch up to her but keep our distance. She doesn't even bother looking at me. She can't take her eyes off of him. I feel my power instantly start to react, and Caleb places a hand on my shoulder. "Mor, your power."

I take a deep breath and rein in the anger and jealousy that's ripping through me. It takes a moment, but I get myself under control. I look down and notice the scorch marks under my feet. My eyes go wide, but I tamper down the shock again before glancing back up at the Angel.

"Why are you here?" I ask her, and she brings her gaze back to me.

"I'm looking for answers." She doesn't say anything else before she disappears before us in a flash of light, and

I let out a scream of rage.

"Cryptic fucking Angel bitch," I growl before Caleb wraps his arms around my waist and pulls me against his chest.

"Why the fuck did you go chasing an Angel in the first place?"

"This isn't the first time I've seen her here. The last time was just before I found you, but she disappeared without a word that time. It doesn't make any sense for her to be here. The Angels have no business with us. They deal with Kavaraí and the mortal Realm. So I want to know why she's here. If she wants fucking answers, why does she keep disappearing?"

"I can't answer that. I don't know as much as you do about the Seven Realms apparently, but if an Angel is here, something must be going on."

"Probably, and I'm going to find out what."

SEVEN

A cheer erupts from the other end of the table followed by rowdy laughter. Brandy Trevalan might not have a traditional family, but the family she's made for herself is definitely a sight to behold. The table in this dining room seats at least fifty people, and it's full to the brim.

The bench seats have me squished between Ares and Caleb, while opposite us are Brandy's closest confidants, Tomas, Han, and Carter. I'm pretty sure she's fucking Tomas considering the possessive hold he's had on her hand all night, but I'm pretty sure he isn't a Demon. I'm not sure exactly *what* he is, but he's definitely not from this Realm—his silver eyes tell me that much. There's something else about him that I can't put my finger on. He notices me watching him and simply stares back at me. At least these three are distinctly less rowdy than the others at the table, yet they easily seem the most menacing.

"Stop staring," Caleb whispers in my ear.

Tomas, who is directly opposite me, smirks. "It's okay. The little princess hasn't seen life outside the palace walls before. I'm pretty sure everything out here is pretty different. She might know horrors that we can't dream of, but she's sheltered in the most obscure ways." I still, feeling more seen and called out than ever, but I don't respond until Ares chuckles beside me.

"Things are definitely… different out in the Realm," I say as diplomatically as I can. Carter stands and moves to Brandy's side, kissing her and shocking the fuck out of me, before he disappears from the room. Did not see that coming. Not even a little bit.

Ares leans over to me while Brandy laughs at something Tomas says. "They're all together, stop looking so shocked."

"All of them?" I ask, never having heard of anything like it before. But then, the only relationships I've ever seen are my parents' and my father's sycophants. I mean, I have nothing against it, I just hadn't realized it was a thing. Though, I guess when I think back to some of the books I've read, it makes a lot of sense.

"Yes, all of them," Brandy answers my question while Ares just grins and Caleb's shoulders shake from his laughter at me. “Trust me, it’s better this way.”

She winks at me before Tomas takes her hand, and they walk away from us. As most of the table starts to stand and move out of the room, Han walks with my brother, whispering about something I’m sure I’d like to know about, but my brother is too protective for his own good sometimes.

I stand from the bench, but moving off of it in my long black dress is not the easiest. Caleb notices me struggling and lifts me over before placing me back on my feet, grinning at me the entire time. “I had it, you know. You didn’t need to lift me.”

“Mor, having my hands on you really isn’t a burden.” I roll my eyes at him and swat his chest before moving toward the door, following the others. He catches my hand and walks beside me until we find ourselves in some sort of party. A deep bass thumps through the dark room, lights flash, and there are so many people jammed in here. Some are dancing, well, grinding up against each other, while others are dotted in groups around the room, sitting at small tables or standing at the small bar to the left of the room. “Do you want to dance?”

I look up at him, his cocky grin is in place, and I smile. “I’m not sure I’m dressed for this.” I wave to the writhing mass of bodies.

“Oh, princess, trust me, the way that dress hugs your

curves? You're more than dressed for this."

He tugs on my hand and leads me toward the group. I've never thought of myself as a prude, despite my virgin status. But I can honestly say I've never danced like this before. Caleb pulls me into his embrace and kisses me before spinning me around. He grips my waist and pulls me back against him. His hands lead my hips in a rhythm with his until I let the music take me away.

Music has always been a great escape for me, dancing too. I guess this is just how the people of the Realm dance.

I raise my arms, wrapping them behind his neck and letting my fingers tangle in his hair as his hands explore my body. I'm sure I should feel more embarrassed than I do about letting him touch me so publicly, but with the crowd we're in, I doubt anyone is even looking. And even if they are, I very much doubt they give a fuck.

So I decide not to give a fuck either. My body is my own, and I'll do what I like with it.

Caleb leans down and bites my earlobe before lowering his mouth to kiss my neck, and I swear my knees go weak. "I don't know what it is about you, Mor, but I don't think I'll ever have enough of you."

I turn in his arms and capture his lips with my own, taking charge of the kiss. I skim my fingers under his black t-shirt, groaning at the feel of his rock hard body. Very soon I'm going to explore more of him. Once I manage to pep talk myself into having enough confidence to go after what I want. I already know he won't push. He's made that very obvious, and it makes me feel safe, but it also means I'm going to have to Demon up and make the first move.

One step at a time.

I deepen the kiss and tangle my hands in his hair once more, feeling the rumble of his chest as he grips me tighter. The music continues to thump, and I sway my hips while I kiss him, losing myself to the night.

After a night full of dancing until the early hours of the morning, I'm sore and tired. I groan as Ares bursts into my room at ass o'clock in the morning with an enthusiastic, "We start training today!"

He leaves without another word, and despite my excitement about finally getting the chance to train—to see what I'm truly capable of—I groan into my pillow. Of course he would pick today to start. He was up later than I was. At least we don't have a suite here, just a room each. I was told before we came to bed that breakfast is a family affair every morning, and I groan again at the thought of seeing all those people again.

Apparently, the Morgan that didn't give a fuck in the dark isn't so chill in the light of day. Not that I'll let any of them see that. I'm a Voux, which means I'm more than a little skilled at not letting anyone see what's going on beneath the surface.

Caleb groans beside me as he rolls onto his back. "Why are we awake so early?"

"Ares said I get to start training today," I tell him as I throw the covers back, shivering a little in my silk cami and shorts. I throw a log on the fire, which is basically down to embers now, before moving to my trunks that are arranged opposite the bed. "What do I even wear to train?"

I'm not really expecting him to answer, so when I feel his heat at my back, I jump a little before settling into his arms as he rests his chin on top of my head. "You wear something comfortable. Something you can move in. And depending on your power, something water and fireproof."

"I don't really know what my powers are," I tell him, shrugging a little. He pulls away from me and turns me to face him.

"What do you mean, you don't know what your powers are? You're at least one hundred, how can you not know?" His face is incredulous, but I guess it does sound more than a little absurd.

"My father," I tell him bluntly. "I discovered some of my powers when I was younger, but then one manifested… there was an incident…" I trail off, and he sits on the edge of the bed, giving me the space to talk.

"Ares helped me cover it up, but if my father knew what I was capable of with that one power alone, he'd have sent me into the mist without a second thought. It's why I've never trained with my power. It's why I have no idea what I'm actually capable of."

"But you kicked my ass so easily when we met." He still looks confused, even if a little concerned.

I take a deep breath and try to explain. "Yeah, Ares tried to make sure that I could still look after myself. He also taught me how to meditate, to contain my power and make it undetectable. Beyond that, I'm pretty useless."

"Mor, I don't think you could be useless at anything even if you tried. You're probably the most capable person I've ever met." He turns me around and looks into my eyes, cupping my cheek. "You can handle anything that's thrown at you, and you know I'll be standing right beside you to help in any way that I can."

I close my eyes and let myself absorb his words. He's right. I can do this. I take a deep breath and let go of the negative energy. "Thank you."

"Any time. Now then, let's get dressed, get fed, and go show your brother just how much of a badass you are, shall we?"

"Morgan, concentrate!" Ares shouts from across the rocky plain that we've been working in all fucking day. I'm exhausted, and he can shove his concentration up his ass. We started the day with some physical training, and I learned that Caleb is a dirty little asshole when he fights. But I did learn a few new tricks.

Since lunch we've been working on exploring my powers. The problem is that I've suppressed everything for so long that the minute I try to coax any kind of energy from the well inside of me, it blasts out, longing to be free. It's a good thing this space is as barren as it is and that Caleb is on our side because my Shadow Fire secret is officially blown too.

That was a fun revelation. I thought Ares was going to have a fucking cat.

But once I figured out how to make sure to keep that one particular power in check, we've been experimenting with other stuff.

"You can do this, Mor," Caleb encourages from where he's crouched behind me.

I close my eyes and try to whisper again. It turns out this shit is hard. Most Demons can do it, so Ares decided to start with that simple trick, but I fucking suck. All I've managed to do so far is make some things disappear and other things appear from nothing. While both of those powers will come in handy, and I'm very happy I have them, being able to escape whenever I want to by whispering away would be fucking awesome.

I picture moving across the plain in my mind, just how Ares told me to. Clearing my mind of all other things, I focus as hard as I can.

My stomach drops, and I feel the ground fall out from under my feet. I don't let excitement grip me. Being trapped in the in-between is something I do not relish the idea of, so I grit my teeth until I feel the ground beneath my feet once more. I open my eyes and realize I'm now behind Caleb and Ares, who are both grinning at me.

"You did it, Morgan!" Ares lets out a whoop, and I smile briefly as my stomach flips. I turn and vomit, trying to keep Caleb from being able to see. He and Ares both rush to my side, and I can't help but groan. This is so not cool.

"Don't worry, everyone vomits their first time." Caleb tries to make me feel better, but I really don't believe him. I need to Demon up, stupid weak-ass stomach. Next time, I won't eat before we train. Maybe then I won't be sick. We move away from the area, which I'm grateful for. Almost as if to prove Caleb's point, Ares hands me a bottle of minty alcohol. I swill the burning liquid through my mouth to rid myself of the taste.

"So gross," I complain with a deep frown. "So we go again, yeah?"

Caleb grins at me, and the proud look on Ares' face tells me he's happy with my question. He nods once, and I give him a grim smile. "Okay, let's do this."

After spending yesterday exhausting myself, trying to get a decent handle on how to whisper, I've spent the morning lounging around with Caleb, doing little more than eating and reading. It's been absolute bliss. I'm not going to lie, the amount he loves to read makes him even hotter to me.

What can I say, a hot nerd is super yummy.

A knock at the door has Kaos' head perking up, but when the door opens and Brandy waltzes in, he puts his head back on his paws and starts snoring again. Little monster.

"There you are," she says with a determined smile once the door is shut. "Your brother told me he's been training you to fight for years. No offense to Ares, he's good, but there are better fighters out there. I wanted to see what you're made of if you're up for it?" Her eyes sparkle with the challenge, and I can't help but jut out my chin. I hate being underestimated.

"Let's do it." Caleb closes his book and grins at the surety of my statement.

"Well, this just got interesting."

Brandy smirks at him and claps her hands. "Oh, don't think you're getting off scot free. Tomas is waiting to see what you've got too."

"Of course he is." Caleb jumps to his feet and offers me a hand to pull me to my feet. Once I'm standing, Brandy frowns.

"That just won't do," she says, motioning to my dress. "I have gear that will fit you. How the fuck does he expect you to fight properly in a corseted fucking dress?"

I can't help but grin at her before pulling two thin blades from the boning of the corset. "There isn't much of a chance of me wearing full armor at the palace, but we make do."

She belts out a laugh and shakes her head. "I knew I liked you. But still, I don't fight like that. Both of you head down to the armory. I'll send word to the tailors to outfit you. Tomas will find you and bring you to the arena. This is going to be so much fun."

She turns on her heel and leaves the room, door slamming shut behind her, and I drop back into my chair with a groan. "I am still so fucking sore from yesterday."

"You got this. You're a badass, remember?" Caleb grins at me. "Plus, you're hot as fuck when you fight. I am so down to watch you."

"Of course you are." I roll my eyes at him and climb back to my feet. "I guess we better head to the armory and see what we can find."

Caleb moves to the door and opens it for me, waving me through. "After you, m'lady."

I laugh again and shake my head.

Another benefit from my power claiming him—life certainly isn't boring anymore.

It doesn't take long for the guys in the armory to get us decked out, but if I thought corsets were uncomfortable, they have nothing on leather armor. Don't get me wrong, the freedom of movement is pretty great, but gods, it's fucking hot. At least my feet are bare, because the cold stone floors help keep me cool.

Tomas finds us once we're dressed and leads us wordlessly to the arena, which is actually a huge basement with a floor of sand. There are three rope rings on the ground, marking out fighting areas, and not much else in here. Well, other than Brandy, her guys, Ares, and a dozen other Demons.

"Welcome to my playground," Brandy says, stretching her arms wide. I smile at her, ready to test myself against a true warrior. Everything about her screams lethality. Caleb peels off to one of the rings with Tomas after squeezing my hand, and I continue toward Brandy. "Are you ready to see what you're made of?"

"Hells yes I am."

"Daggers or sword?"

"Daggers," I answer, and her grin widens.

"Girl after my own heart." She leads me to the back of the room, and laid out on a table is an array of daggers. I pick up a matching pair, about the length of my forearm. "Sai. Good choice."

She reaches forward and picks up wider, flatter daggers that are curved a little with an intricate design through the middle. She doesn't name them, but I can tell she's used to handling them. I move with her to the center ring.

"No holding back or pulling punches. The blades won't kill us, and there isn't poison coating them, so no maiming either. Just good old-fashioned steel. No salted iron here—that shit burns like a fucker, and I don't fancy a slow body death. I like this body." She grins, and I find myself loving how morbid she is. But I am glad there's no salted iron. It's basically lethal to Demons if it breaks the skin. It won't kill our souls, only the mist or Shadow Fire can do that, but it takes a lot of power to regenerate a body, so for most Demons, salted iron is a death sentence anyway. It's slow and absolute fucking agony. Or so I've heard anyway.

It's why my father uses it for the shackles he keeps on his pets. It burns and weakens them, but since he coats them in a healing salve, it doesn't break the flesh and it won't kill them. It's simply another form of torture for him.

I take a deep breath but cling to the anger the thought of my father invokes. A healthy dose of rage is good before a fight. I follow behind Brandy to the center ring and watch as she grins. She barely gives me a chance to orient myself before she attacks.

I raise the blades in an X formation to stop her sweeping blow. She bares her teeth when the steel crashes together, and I just manage to hold her off before she pulls back. "I won't pull any more punches. That's your only warning."

I shake out my arms as she retreats, and I curse myself for not having trained with blades more. I'm going to get my fucking ass kicked. She puts her arm forward and beckons me toward her with her hand, and I grin. She doesn't know what I'm capable of, and while I'm not stupid enough to think I can best her, I'm going to give all I've got.

So I adjust my grip on the Sai and charge. I feel eyes on me as the room goes quiet, but I block it all out, the way I've done time and again. I focus my attention on studying Brandy's movements instead. We parry back and forth until she knocks me on my ass and I find the edge of her blade at my throat. She holds the position for just a moment before grinning and pulling back. I take her hand and stand, noticing Tomas and Carter holding Caleb in place at the edge of the ring.

Brandy nods at me so I move over to him, and the two

Demons give us some space. "I'm okay."

He growls lowly, as his gaze rakes over my entire body. Once he seems satisfied, the black in his eyes recedes, as do his black claws, and he becomes the man I know once more.

"We're not going to be able to keep this thing a secret if you keep beasting out on me," I say, chuckling softly. I know we're safe in this level of the Realm, especially with the people in this room, but if I'm threatened outside of this ring, then we need to be more careful. I know Ares has made it seem that he's my protection, but that side of him coming out if I'm injured or threatened is going to give us away.

"I'll work on it," he says, his voice scratchy. "I just hate seeing you hurt."

"I'm not hurt, and you're the one that keeps telling me I'm a badass."

I poke his abs, and he grins at me. "You are. My Demon just hasn't quite caught up. Don't worry, I'll get him under control."

I hug him quickly to hide the shock on my face. I've never heard of someone referring to their power as a different entity like that. I guess I really am too sheltered for my own good. I know there are many different types of Demons. I just hadn't considered they'd be that much different from me. I make sure to smile again before I pull back. "Go work out your frustration on Tomas. I'm going to go try and kick Brandy's ass again."

He barks out a laugh before kissing the top of my head. "Sure thing, princess. Go kick the warrior's ass."

EIGHT

After that first day of training with Brandy, we've spent pretty much every minute with her and her guys training in the arena. Ares has been with us too, working on his skills. I managed to best one of Brandy's men, which has had me smiling for the last three days. I haven't had the upper hand with the woman herself yet, but I'm not foolish enough to believe I'm anywhere close to good enough to do that.

Yet.

Maybe one day.

We've been working on my whispering and using that in battle too. That shit is exhausting, but I'm finally getting the hang of it. I also made a deal with Brandy that I can come back here and train whenever I like, and now that I can whisper effectively, my world is opening up.

I make my way down to breakfast alone; Caleb came down with Ares a little while ago because I needed a shower to wake myself up. All this training has me completely exhausted.

"She's never going to go for it." Ares sighs as I enter the room. The conversation dies, and I raise an eyebrow.

"Never going to go for what?"

Ares winces as I drop into the seat between him and Caleb while no one but Brandy looks at me. "A party. A big-ass, fancy pants party. For the entire level, plus guests. A way to get your daddy off the trail that Ares and I are as good friends as we are. We found some of your dad's spies lurking around the level yesterday."

"A way to piss off my father? Why would I not be down with that? But also, you guys don't exactly seem like the types to throw a big-ass fancy party."

Brandy's grin widens as she takes in my words. "That's because you see through the glamour."

My brow furrows as I try to work out what she means. "What glamour?"

"Brandy has one of, if not the strongest, glamour in the Realm," Ares explains.

"Even your daddy can't see through my glamour. Usually the only people who can see through it are those who have had a drop of my blood. Which a good percentage of my people, the ones I trust, do have. There are some High Born families who see what I want them to see because despite living in my level, they're still loyal to your father. Outsiders don't see the truth of this place either. We look just like any other level, with their snobby ways."

"Wait, but I didn't see a glamour… neither did Caleb." I look around the room, and everyone smiles at me.

"We know," Tomas answers. "You're the first person ever to see through the glamour without blood. We think Caleb saw through it because of his connection to you."

Holy fucking shit.

I lean back in my chair trying to process what they're telling me, but it doesn't make any sense.

"This means you're powerful, girlie. More powerful than even your brother thought. Which is why we've been training you so hard," Brandy explains. "So, keeping your father dancing along to what we want him to know isn't a problem. But you need to figure out more of your power quickly. The safest way to do that is to keep your father thinking that you're doing what you're supposed to be doing."

I look over to Ares to see that he looks conflicted. "What do you think?"

"She's right. No one sees through Brandy's glamours without her blood, but you did. We've been trying to figure it out since we got here, but the only explanation is your power. The fact that Father's spies showed up here has me worried. I think the party is a good idea, but it means parading you around, and you have enough of that coming."

I groan at the thought of my father's upcoming ball, and then shake it off. "If this needs to happen so I can keep training, let's do it."

Big parties might be my version of a waking nightmare, but if this is for the greater good, then I'm here for it. Bring it the fuck on.

"I told you she'd be fine!" Brandy exclaims before clapping her hands. "Okay, so let's do it tomorrow, since that's your last night here. We'll get everything sorted out, just remember to bring your glad rags."

Caleb squeezes my thigh under the table, and I can't help but smile. Seeing him in a full fancy pants getup is going to be a whole ass thing. I'm excited just thinking about it. "She doesn't mean me too, right?"

"If you think I'm going to this thing and letting you skip it, you don't know me that well. Besides, I'll need my guard to keep all the assholes' paws off of me." I flutter my lashes up at him in the most ridiculous way, and he groans before dropping his head onto my shoulder. Maybe this will be more fun than I thought.

While everyone else is sorting things out for the party tonight, Caleb and I spend the morning lounging around and reading. I absolutely adore that he seems to enjoy it as much as I do. There is nothing better than expanding your mind or getting lost in a whole other world. My life has shown me the benefits of a good escape, and as for the little that I know about Caleb's life to this point, I'd say the same for him.

Everyone needs a good escape.

It's also nice to not be pushing my mind and body to its absolute limit today. After breakfast yesterday, I spent the entire day working with Ares on my powers. I focused on learning how to conjure things from nothing but a picture in my mind, and then making them disappear again.

That was fucking exhausting.

My biggest problem right now though is that my usual escape just isn't cutting it. I half want to jump on Caleb and see just how much I've been missing out on, but considering that he's been adamant on taking things slow whenever I've tried to push for more, I'm pretty sure that won't go over well. I try to not pout about it. I get he's trying to be a gentleman or whatever, but still—a girl has needs. Needs I didn't know I had until he opened my eyes. And now… well now I'm pissed I waited so long to discover just how awesome this orgasm shit is. I'm ready to own my shit and spend more time dedicated to exploring it all.

I look over at him again and find him watching me, a smile playing on his lips. "What's on that mind of yours, Mor?"

"Me?" I squeak out, and I feel my cheeks heat. Just because I know what I want and I want to explore it doesn't mean I'm chill about just blurting it out apparently. "Oh, nothing."

His smirk grows, and he closes his book before giving me his full attention. "Nothing, huh?"

I feel my heart race as he teases me. "Are you sure about that?" I swallow at his words, trying to find a way to speak, but my throat is about as dry as the deserts of Avaenór. He moves toward me and places his hands on either side of my head before leaning down, leveraging the weight of his body against mine. "I think you had a lot more than nothing on your mind."

Licking my lips, I nod, confirming his assumptions.

"Words, baby."

"Yes." That breathy voice doesn't sound like me, it's so sultry and husky, but it makes his eyes flash.

"Does it have to do with this?" He gently pushes his rock-hard erection against my center, rubbing up and down for a beat before lifting his hips and depriving me of his sinful weight.

"Yes."

The heat creeping up my chest and neck tells me I'm giving him the full view of a grade-A blush. Judging from his smirk, he's enjoying this way too much.

"You're not ready for…" he pushes his cock against my core once more, rubbing against me, teasing me mercilessly, "this."

I narrow my eyes at his comment, because I'm capable of knowing exactly what I want and need. He chuckles at my indignation.

"Relax, baby." He traps my lip between his teeth and pulls slightly, all the while grinding his cock between my legs before licking away the sting that his bite left in its wake.

My hips arch toward him, seeking out the heat of his body so when he lowers his mouth to my ear, his breath causes shivers of anticipation throughout my body. "Show me your pretty little pussy, Mor."

In an instant, his body is gone. By the time I open my eyes to act on his command, he's sitting on the armchair at the foot of my bed.

He's way too fucking far away for what I had in mind. The look in his eyes tells me he has a plan, and I'm too curious to ignore whatever game he's playing. I'll show him just how ready I am.

Making quick work of my shorts, I shed all of my clothing below the waist and sit up against the headboard, thighs closed.

"Open up, Mor, show me how beautiful you are."

My swallow is audible, my nerves making me hyper-aware of everything around me.

"Show me, baby." His voice is raw with lust as he encourages me. It's the slight part to his mouth and the outline of his dick in his pants, the evidence of his own desire, that gives me the final push.

I take a deep breath and steady myself. It's not like he hasn't seen me already, but this feels somehow different than before. Exposing myself more than I ever have, I pull my knees toward my chest and then slowly spread my thighs, revealing the most intimate part of me to the man I want most in this world.

His groan as he watches me both embarrasses me and makes me feel bolder. "Fuck, Mor. You make perfection seem average."

My cheeks heat with another fucking blush, and I hate that I'm still so innocent. I want to be able to make the first move, to sit on his lap and fuck him into next week. The thought alone makes me wet.

There's no doubt Caleb notices just how turned on I am. His gaze snaps to mine, lust making his eyes burn until they're black.

"What are you thinking about, Mor?" That gravel in his voice… That's for me. The realization makes me relax. It urges me to give him more.

"You. I'm thinking about how it would feel to have you inside me." The blush returns, but I ignore it. I'm too consumed by this primal need inside of me. It's unlike anything I've ever known.

"Fuck," is all he says before he pushes his pants just below his ass and pulls out his beautiful, thick cock.

I'm frozen in place, watching him as he leisurely strokes his cock like an afterthought. His gaze darts from my lips to my pussy.

"Put two fingers in your mouth, suck, and lick them as if they were my cock."

I don't hesitate. In an instant, my fingers are in my mouth, my lips sucking and my tongue wetting them as much as I can.

"Hmm, so fucking hot."

His strokes seem harder, a little faster. His thumb runs along the head of his cock, spreading the cum that seeps out of his slit.

"Touch yourself for me, princess."

Something about his commands make all of this that much hotter. So I start by placing my fingers at the base of my pussy and slowly run up between my lower lips. As he watches with rapt attention, I notice he's stopped stroking and is just squeezing the life out of his shaft.

He reads my confusion and chuckles. "I'm trying so fucking hard not to come right now. The sight of you pleasuring yourself is enough to turn me into a prepubescent little punk."

Waiting for his next instructions, I slowly rub myself. I've never even done this before, so I'm unsure what to do next. He made me feel so good before, and I know he will again.

"Push your middle finger inside of yourself while pressing your palm into your clit." I barely recognize his voice; it's like sand has transformed it into the opposite of the smooth tone I'm used to.

I gasp as my finger breaches my opening, pushing in as far as it will go, and my palm adds friction to my clit, making my legs fall to the side. I'm so fucking wet I'm dripping onto the comforter. It's dirty and filthy, and I love it. I love knowing that his commands have this effect on my body.

"Fuck, Mor. You're so fucking wet. I want to bury my face in your pussy and eat every fucking inch of you, devour you, consume you completely. And when I'm done, I want to slam my cock inside you and mark you as mine, forever. Keep going, baby, I want to watch you come undone."

My head hits the headboard, my finger pumping in and

out of my pussy as his filthy words ignite a fire inside me I didn't know I possessed.

"Yes," is all I can muster, and still it comes out a mere whisper.

By the time I lift my head to look at him, I can see the vein at the side of his neck bulging with his effort to stay in control.

"Add another finger, baby."

So I do, without hesitation. I'm fucking myself with two fingers, my palm rubbing my clit with added fervor as Caleb fucks his own palm with abandon.

"I can see your wetness, baby. It's dripping all over your hand, your thighs, the fucking comforter. It's fucking beautiful. You're beautiful."

His hips thrust into his fist, and his cock looks angry with need. I'm so close to an orgasm I can practically taste it.

It's when he bites his bottom lip, his teeth indenting the pink flesh, that I know I won't be able to hold off much longer. His eyes spark with acknowledgement, and his teeth release his lip as he gives me a sultry, sexy smile.

My new favorite words drip from his mouth. "Come for me, beautiful."

His command is like a key that releases me from my own prison, unleashing a dam of emotions as my orgasm rips through me, so intense that it shakes my entire being.

My scream is silent, my mouth open, my eyes closed as I freeze all movements. I feel the bed dip and then the heat of Caleb's body washes over me. When I open my eyes, he's there, watching me and fucking his fist like a man crazed.

When I whisper his name, I feel the first spurt of his orgasm hit my pussy.

"Fuck, you're so goddamn beautiful."

Another jet of cum hits my thigh, then another, and another. On a long, heavy sigh, he lowers his head, his lips meeting mine in the softest, most loving kiss he's ever given me.

I've never seen a man orgasm, and I love that Caleb is the first.

"That was…" I trail off, unable to find the words. He climbs from the bed and disappears into the bathroom. He reappears quickly with a washcloth and cleans me up with a smile on his face.

"It absolutely fucking was." His eyes sparkle with his words. He puts the washcloth back in the bathroom before climbing back onto the bed with me and pulling me into his arms. "I'm going to show you everything you've been missing."

I sigh as I snuggle into his chest, his heat is the perfect comfort, and his arms around me make me feel safer than I ever have. "I can't wait for forever."

I stare back at my reflection in the mirror. My crown of sparkling gray stones nestled in between an intricate pattern of precious black metal sits on top of my long, dark hair. I wear a dress in the same colors as my crown, and I feel more like an imposter than I ever have. Kohl lines my green eyes, and my lips are a dark red, the only color on my body.

Amelia came and helped me get ready, curling my hair to perfection while I painted on my face. It was nice to just hang out with her for a few hours. I really need to try and find some more time to do that around all of the other shit we have going on so I don't lose myself. I feel more grounded than I have in a while. If nothing else, being around her is humbling.

"Are you sure we need to go to this thing? Because damn, Mor, you look good enough to fucking eat." I turn and find Caleb leaning on the door jamb, and I don't even feel guilty about perving on him in his black guard's tunic. The tunic is embroidered with silver, with matching silver clasps. I guess Ares had it tailored, because it hugs every damn inch of him. And now I know what he looks like underneath it too… maybe he's right, maybe we should ditch tonight.

If only.

"You have no idea how tempting that sounds." I turn away from him and look back to the mirror.

He strides to where I'm standing and places his hands on my bare lower back, just above where my skirt rests at the top of my ass. His touch is like fire, and I take a deep breath as the warmth from him wraps around me. I look back at our reflection, and I can't help but think that we fit together. Maybe my power did know what it was doing by claiming him. "I have a pretty good idea."

"Are you two nearly ready?" I startle at the sound of Ares' voice and find him in the main doorway. I was so distracted by Caleb's touch that I didn't even notice him enter the room. He eyes how close we're standing together, but I stare back at him. I know my brother is no saint, so he doesn't get to judge me.

"Yeah, we're good," Caleb says, clearing his throat. I guess my brother's stare got to him a little more than it did me. I get it, but at the same time, fuck no. I'm not going to be shamed for finally exploring.

Ares pauses for another beat before turning on his heel and walking away without a word. I love my brother, but sometimes he's such a fuckhead. "I guess we should go."

Caleb takes my hand and kisses it, grinning at me as he does. "We got this. Let's go show them who the baddest bitch in the Realm is."

I laugh at his ridiculousness, but I don't resist when he pulls me from the room. We walk through the estate, and once we reach the entrance hall, we merely follow the noise. We have to climb another set of stairs, but once we reach the top, I just stop and gawk. Brandy really went all fucking out, and I know none of it is a glamour since I can see it.

"Holy shit, you guys party on a whole other level," Caleb says as he takes in the sight before us. The ceiling is clearly a spell, but it's a beautiful illusion of the night sky with a blanket of stars. Black, sheer fabric is draped across the walls with twinkle lights beneath it, making the walls blend seamlessly with the night sky on the ceiling. The stairs before us are carpeted in a dark red, and why there are stairs up and then down is beyond me, but then I reason that all of these High Born types love a good entrance.

"Are you ready?" I ask him, hoping this peek into my world isn't too much, because he truly hasn't seen anything yet.

"With you at my side, I could conquer worlds. Let's do this."

I pull my arm from his and wipe the smile from my face. The mask of indifference that any of my father's spies and the High Born not loyal to Brandy will expect to see slips into place, and we walk through the doorway.

I swear all conversation stops as we reach the top of

the staircase. I lift my head a little higher and jut out my chin, letting Caleb walk just a step behind me to keep up appearances as we descend the staircase.

Once we reach the bottom, I scan the faces in the room. Once I've made eye contact with everyone who deems themselves to be of importance, the conversations start back up over the soft music.

I spot Brandy and Ares toward the back of the room. Motioning to Caleb, he nods, and I make my way over to where they're waiting for me.

"That was some entrance," Brandy says once we reach her. Her usual smile is absent from her face, but I know that's more for appearances rather than from anything I've done.

"Entrances are a speciality of mine," I joke, and her eyes sparkle with the laughter missing from her face.

"Well keep the act up, girlie, and the vultures will never know any different. Now, I suggest the three of us split up and mingle with those loyal to your father. I have no doubt he'll get word about tonight before the night is even over."

I roll my eyes at her words, but I know there isn't a lie in them. My father's reach is wide. Too wide. I'm pretty sure it's the only reason no one has assassinated him at this point. The fear of repercussion from those loyal to him and the crown is too great.

I nod, and turn to face Caleb, who I know won't leave

my side all night. "Let the torture begin."

NINE

I feel so dirty.

Sucking up to the High Born who are loyal to my father has left me feeling gross. I showered when we got back last night, and bathed again this morning, but I still feel gross. I know Caleb feels the same because he's been scrubbing himself under the waterfall of scalding water for at least thirty minutes.

The sycophants, those most loyal to my father, are just disgusting. They fawned over us all, starving for a morsel to take back to my father. I'm sure news of my new guard will reach him. I just hope he doesn't think too much of it. I'm almost proud of the way Caleb managed to rein himself in, considering all the giant assholes at the party who didn't know how to keep their hands to themselves.

No one died or was mutilated, at least not because of me, so I'm calling it a good night.

I finish packing up my trunks with a flick of my hand. This whole learning-to-control-my-power thing really is coming in handy. The more I practice, the better I get with it. Especially the smaller stuff like this. We still haven't tried using any major offensive or defensive powers, but I know it's coming. I'm just hoping that Ares has more friends as we move throughout the levels so we can train with the same sort of ease that we have here.

Caleb appears from the bathroom in nothing more than a towel, and I can't help but stare at how beautiful he is. Scars and all. His smirk tells me just how much he doesn't give a fuck about the scars that mar his torso. We haven't spoken about how he got them, but I'm not the kind of girl to pry. If he wants to tell me, he will. Hell knows we all have our own monsters to deal with.

"You get your fill?" His smirk grows as I blush.

"I don't know that I'll ever get my fill," I admit, and he strides toward me and wraps me in a hug. I don't give a fuck that he's still a little wet; I hug him right back.

"We're in this together now," he murmurs into my hair. "You don't need to face this shit alone anymore."

I'm not sure where that came from, but if I were to hazard a guess, I'd say a very real look into the type of life I've experienced to this point has him rattled. Everyone thinks the life of a royal is like living in a gilded cage. Both the High Born and Low Born always think that my life must be so blessed, never having to worry over anything. How wrong they are.

Don't get me wrong, I know there are things I've never had to worry about. Food, water, a warm bed, and I don't take any of that for granted. But just because I've had things doesn't mean my life has been nothing but roses.

Last night, Caleb witnessed that.

"You're not in this alone either, not ever again," I tell him, and he squeezes me tighter before releasing me and stepping back.

He moves to the trunk allocated to him and pulls a t-shirt and jeans from it. A far stretch from what he wore last night, but honestly, he looks good in everything. "Do you need to talk about last night?"

I look back over at him as he pulls his jeans on and buttons them up. "No, that was nothing new for me. Do you need to talk about it?"

"That's nothing new for you?" He looks at me like I've lost my mind. "Mor, that shit was… it was fucking soul destroying. Do you know how many heads nearly rolled? Seeing those assholes parading around their fucking pets? What they did to them with everyone watching, it was absolutely disgusting."

"My father's sycophants are a hateful crowd. They get

off on the fear, on the blood, on the power. I've seen this shit at the palace my entire life. There's a reason I brought Amelia with us." His eyes go wide, and I realize that it's all really clicking into place for him.

"Did they ever…?" He trails off, but I shake my head to answer his question anyway.

"No, I have always been off limits to my father's sycophants. He taught me his lessons in other ways." I look toward the ground, not able to take the pity I know I would see in his eyes. "But I survived it, and I'm here, stronger than ever."

He wraps me up in his arms, and I feel the pulse of power that comes from him. I know without looking that his eyes are black.

"Mine," he growls, and the rumble in his chest soothes me.

"Yours."

I'm not sure how long we stay like that, but when Kaos perks his head up from the puppy pile the pack is in, I know that someone is coming and we need to get ready. "You should finish getting dressed. I'll get the hounds downstairs."

"Okay," he murmurs before kissing me softly, as if I might break if he does anything else. One day I'll show him that I'm far from breakable, but today isn't that day. He went through a lot last night.

I whistle, and the hounds all perk up and climb to their feet. Anyone else might think they had a late night last night, but Ares wouldn't let me take Kaos with me. It was ridiculous if you ask me, but then maybe there wouldn't have been an excuse for Caleb not leaving my side, so I get it.

I open the door, and Kaos leads the pack outside while Havoc hangs back waiting for me to exit. I look back at Caleb one last time as he pulls on his t-shirt, and I can't help but wonder if what he saw last night changed how he thinks of me. I guess we'll find out soon enough. Heading out the door, Havoc follows me, and I pull the door closed, giving Caleb some privacy.

"Let's go," I murmur to the pack, and Havoc rubs the underside of my hand with his head. I get a flash of his memory, and I see how sad I look, so I scratch him between the ears. "I'm okay, boy, I just need something more."

He grunts in response but presses against my side as if he doesn't believe me. I probably wouldn't either.

We arrive at Level Four, and I swear the levels are starting to blur. Brandy wasn't wrong; a lot of them are very similar. The inhabitants and landscape might be different, but the general way of life is pretty much the same.

It's starting to feel like I'm on a tour of different bedroom suites. Ares has kept me as far from the royal bullshit as possible at my request, and I'm beyond thankful for that, but there are some things even he can't save me from.

Like these fucking dinner parties every higher Demon seems to want to throw in our honor. I know it's just to try to curry favor with my father. Which family looked after us best and all that, but honestly, I'd rather just not deal with any of it. Not that I can say that to these people.

I really just wish the sons of the higher Demons would stop throwing themselves at me. I'm not sure how much more I can take before I start smashing heads. And that's only if Caleb doesn't beat me to it.

What has me most pissed off about the assholes on this level is their blatant refusal to let my hounds in with me. Something about not having animals in the house. I've seen the higher Demon from this household in my father's royal summoning's, so I already know that animals live in this house.

I'm currently sitting at the formal dining table of the Embers'. The ruling family of this level. Emane and Yana have three sons, who on the surface are reasonable to look at, but the minute they open their mouths… let's just say shit rolls downhill. The three of them are sitting opposite Caleb and I, with their father at the head of the table and their mother opposite Ares. She's been giving him 'fuck me' eyes since we arrived, and it's enough to skeeve me out. I have no idea how he's coping. Especially when she's so blatant about it even though her husband sits between them. It's cringey as fuck.

"So, Morganna, how are you enjoying your first tour of the Realm?" the eldest of the sons, Torrin, asks.

"It's been eye opening," I tell him with a demure smile. "But I've met a lot of new people so far that I haven't seen at the palace before."

He grins at me before taking a giant bite of steak. Even the way he chews makes me want to vomit. Caleb keeps his eyes on his plate, but I can almost feel the vibrations of his laughter. Do these High Born really have that little experience with women, or do other women just fall at their feet for the chance of gaining a name and title?

So freaking gross.

Ares manages to steer the conversation away from me to the upcoming ball of my father's, and I swear, their greed fills the entire room like its own entity. The idea of being tied to the royal family makes these people hot. It's repulsive.

But at least Ares has stopped trying to hide the fact that the ball is a way for my father to sell me to the highest bidder. I'm not sure how I'm going to get out of it just yet, but I'm positive that Ares will help me find a solution.

Marrying someone to further my father's power just isn't how I want to live my life. This existence is far too long to bow to my father's whims at every turn.

"We'll be training tomorrow. You should all join us. I'd like to see what the man who protects the princess is capable of," the youngest brother, Edwin, chimes, and I finally tune back into their conversation.

I swing my head from my brother to Caleb, wondering how the fuck the conversation ended here. I don't want Caleb in that position, but if we tell them no, they'll know something is off. Caleb hasn't trained formally like these guys have.

Shit.

My stomach churns at the prospect of it, but Caleb just fixes that classic fucking smirk of his on his face and meets the brothers' gazes head on. "I'm down. It's been a while since I kicked some High Born ass."

Ares chuckles beside me, while the brothers all look shocked. I guess most people don't accept their challenges.

"I think it will be good for my boys to fight against some new blood," Emane, their father, states before chugging down another glass of nectar. How he's not passed out on the floor is beyond me.

"That should be interesting indeed," Ares adds before glancing at me. I see the same fear inside of me flash in his eyes. We are so fucked.

I know I should have more faith in Caleb. He fights dirty—I've learned that much in my own training with him. But up against three swordsmen who will no doubt have trained formally with the guard, because all of the High Born tend to… that's a whole different story.

Shit.

"We should make it more interesting," Caleb adds, and his cocksure grin makes my heart pound.

The middle brother, Zafar, watches him closely, his beady little eyes seeing everything. He's been the quieter one of the three, but I know more than most to never underestimate the quiet ones. They see everything. "How so?"

"I'm sure we can all think of something."

"Enough talk of this," their mother screeches, and I actually wince at her shrill voice. "This is meant to be a nice dinner, not the start of a sword fight. I've had enough."

"Yana, boys will be boys. They simply want to make sure our princess is adequately protected, though I'm sure they don't mean to question Ares' judgement on a guard for his sister," Emane states, and the boys' eyes go wide before they shake their heads. Apparently they hadn't thought about how it might offend the crown to question its decisions. I bite my lip to stop myself from laughing out loud. "But you're right, this is a nice dinner. However, I am done, so let's wrap this up, shall we?"

That might be the first thing the man has said since we arrived that I agree with. I sag a little in relief. I am more than ready to be done here.

Now I just have tomorrow to worry about.

This is going to end badly.

I can feel it in my fucking bones. Nothing about this is going to be okay. Because if they hurt him, beyond whatever he's signed up for by being a dick, I'm going to rage out. And the problem with that is that we don't know exactly how my rage will show itself, and we're trying to keep my power levels under control. And we *do not* want more people to know about my Shadow Fire.

This house has way too much testosterone, and I am all for not being here any longer. This is just a stupid fucking bullshit competition. I can think of so many more ways I'd like to spend our second day in this level, and none of those ideas include sword fighting.

By the time I reach the green at the back of the estate, all five of them are already there. My presence was requested because what fun is dueling without a princess to oversee it? I mean, kill me.

Please.

I'd love to join in and show these idiot Ember boys

just who they should really be afraid of, but that doesn't exactly go with the plan of keeping my strengths under wraps. Though I guarantee that they won't like me when I'm mean. The training I've had since we left home, on top of the years of fighting training I've done with Ares, has given me a whole new sense of confidence in my abilities.

Caleb is warming up with Ares, while the three brothers are on the opposite side of the green doing the same thing. There are four chairs set up, and I'm assuming that's my vantage point. I smile, baring my teeth at the Ember brothers, before turning and softening my smile at Caleb and Ares.

"Are you okay?" Ares asks as he moves to my side.

"I think all of this is stupid and an unnecessary risk, but yes, I'm fine." He grimaces at my words, and I know he agrees. I know as well as he does that this isn't a challenge Caleb could've turned down. He isn't a well-known knight of the guard. People are going to test him, and until he has a reputation for not being a pushover, he can't afford to have those rumors spreading around. Especially when he's been named as my personal guard.

I don't speak to Caleb. He's busy preparing himself, and the last thing I want to do is distract him and be the reason he gets hurt. I'm sure I'm underestimating him, but I can't help the knot of fear in my stomach.

The youngest brother steps up first, and Ares takes a

seat beside me, separating me from the other two brothers.

Ares leans backward and clears his throat before shouting, "begin!"

At his word, Edwin rushes toward Caleb, who parries each blow thrown at him. I cover my mouth with my hand and feign shock to cover the smile I can't control. What's more amusing is how frustrated Edwin becomes when he doesn't instantly best Caleb. Apparently I'm not the only one who underestimated my claimed one.

I watch them fight back and forth, until Caleb manages to take Edwin's sword and lands a kick square in his chest, putting him on his ass. It's over when the point of his sword tickles Edwin's throat, and I press my lips together to keep me from cheering. I've never been a fan of fighting, but watching Caleb dominate has me feeling all kinds of hot and tingly things.

He withdraws the blade and offers the youngest Ember his hand, but like any true butt-hurt youngest sibling, Edwin hits Caleb's hand, climbs to his feet, and stomps off. "How very unsportsmanlike of him," Ares mutters, and Torrin groans.

"My youngest brother has been fawned over by my mother one time too many."

"Who's next?" Caleb asks, flourishing his sword, and I can't help but grin at how cocky and arrogant he seems right now. It's way more attractive than I thought it would be. My guy looks hot in a leather guard with a sword in his hand.

Zafar stands, eyeing Caleb's sword, and lifts a staff from the ground. "That would be me."

Caleb grins and drops the sword, moving to the weapons rack to the right of where they've been fighting and grabbing a battle axe. Gripping it with both hands, he grins and heads back to the space before us. I eye Zafar's staff, usually I wouldn't think much of it, but the green gem held in the tip feels off. Caleb hasn't been using his power to fight, and though I know he told me he was more than comfortable using his power, I don't want this to go horrifically wrong.

Zafar is the quiet one, and he's also the smallest, despite being the middle brother, which just leads me to think he fights dirtier than the other two. There's a darkness in his eyes that the others don't have. Every instinct I have is screaming at me to stop this.

"Ares, something feels wrong." No sooner are the words out of my mouth than Zafar lifts the staff and a green lightning bolt shoots from it, hitting Caleb directly in the chest. He flies back, and Ares pins me in my chair. It's only Caleb's groan letting me know he's still alive that keeps me from throwing my brother the fuck off of me. Zafar stands there smiling, like he's just fucking won something when I see the change in Caleb. His eyes go black, his fingers turn to claws, and his teeth elongate.

Shit. This isn't going to go well.

It's when he stands with shadows streaming from him that Ares utters, "Fuck."

But he and Torrin stay seated. I guess Zafar provoked it, so it's on him. I know that Caleb wouldn't want to truly hurt anyone, though, so I'm torn—because I'd also really like to see what it is he's capable of.

Caleb watches Zafar, who seems planted to the spot. The ground begins to shake, prompting Zafar to move toward Caleb, his staff raised. Before he gets a chance to do anything, a sliver of black shoots through his chest and lifts him off his feet. More tendrils begin to wrap around his extremities before one wraps around his neck.

"Stop this," Torrin hisses, but Ares stays in his seat, hands crossed in his lap.

"That's against the rules of combat. You know it as well as I do. Zafar needs to tap out."

I look at my brother wide-eyed. I thought for sure he'd stop this. Especially since Torrin seems to be growing even angrier, which means he's going to use that against Caleb.

"I do not care about the rules of engagement, call your fucking dog off of my brother," Torrin shouts, but my brother is still unaffected. I, however, am nearly ready to unleash hell on this asshole. Who the fuck does he think he is?

Ares pats my hand, and it's so condescending I want to throat punch him, but I know it's more for appearances' sake than anything, which is the only reason he's still breathing. "You should mind your words and remember who the fuck it is you're talking to."

Torrin pales at Ares' words, and I bite back my grin. I look back at Caleb who has closed in on Zafar. Zafar is trying to clasp the tendrils that hold him, but he's too weak. Nothing he does seems to have any effect on Caleb at all. "Beg me to release you."

The growl of Caleb's voice shouldn't make my pussy tingle, especially right now, but it does. I'm not sure what that says about me, but fuck it.

Zafar opens and closes his mouth like a fucking water dweller.

"Sorry, I couldn't hear you," Caleb growls, taunting the weaker Demon. The tendril around Zafar's neck disappears, and blood gushes from the flesh where the tendril held him. He sucks in air, choking as he does so.

"You're fucking insane," he screeches. "Put me down!"

Caleb roars a laugh before bringing Zafar closer to him, still hovering off of the ground, so their noses practically touch. "Maybe you should have thought about what sort of fucking monster you were playing with before you fought dirty. I've felt your type of power before, and what you hit me with would have been enough to kill a weaker man."

He finishes speaking and steps back before releasing Zafar, who drops to the ground face first, bleeding at every point where he was held by the shadows. Ares lets out a quiet chuckle, but I'm pretty sure it's loud enough for Torrin to hear. Zafar pushes up from the ground, and I notice the bloom of red on his chest too. Those shadows really are a force to be reckoned with.

Zafar storms off the same way his younger brother did, and all that seems to do is feed Torrin's rage.

Caleb manages to rein in the darkness, and looks at me, shame filling his eyes. But I smile at him and hope he can see that I have absolutely zero issues with what he did.

"You!" Torrin shouts, pointing at Caleb. Caleb holds his hands up, showing he isn't a threat, but Torrin throws the sword toward him. Caleb catches it with one hand, and Torrin storms toward him. "I'll show you what a real fucking fight is."

Torrin darts forward, so quickly he becomes little more than a blur, and the only reason I realize he's reached Caleb is the sound of metal on metal as they trade blows. I turn to Ares, who is watching them closely. "This is going to end badly."

"Have faith, little sister. Caleb is far more competent than I realized. Naming him as your personal guard was a good idea. I never would have imagined he'd be as resourceful as he is, even after the training we've done together. It seems as if he's been holding out on us." Ares' interest in Caleb makes me worry too. He is mine, and I'll be damned if I'm letting him become my brother's new toy. Secrets be damned. As if my thoughts are written all over my face, my brother laughs. "Don't worry, Morgan. I won't try to take him from you, but I am going to look into this bond between you some more. I've never seen someone manipulate the shadows the way he did with Zafar. I can't help but wonder if he was capable of it before or if this is something that happened after the claiming."

Having no idea, I don't answer him, turning back to focus on the fight instead. Caleb gives as good as he gets with Torrin. I'm not sure there will be a victor in this particular fight, and I don't want anyone to be maimed any more than they have been already today.

"Enough!" The word booms around us, and I turn to see Emane standing just behind us. Torrin and Caleb separate, both of them bleeding, chests heaving with more than a little venom in their gazes. "We'll call this fight a tie, shall we?"

Emane looks to Ares who nods. "Let's. I think there's been enough blustering for one day."

They face off, so many things unsaid, but I don't claim to know the inner workings of the politics here. I stand, and Caleb comes to my side. I want to ask him if he's okay, but now isn't the time. We all wait until Emane and Torrin have left, and then Ares turns to Caleb. "You fought well, and with more honor than any of them showed. Take pride in that. Do not dwell on your darkness. Have you always been able to manipulate the shadows like that?"

"Yes," Caleb answers bluntly. "Though they've never made anyone bleed like that before."

Ares' brow furrows. "I see."

He turns and leaves, giving us no answers, and I kind of want to slap my brother upside the head. Instead, I turn back to face Caleb and take his hand, squeezing it quickly before releasing it. "Let's go get you cleaned up, shall we?"

"Mor…" he starts, and I shake my head.

"My brother was right about one thing—do not dwell on the darkness. We may be born of monsters, but that doesn't make us monsters. You were provoked, and you fought back. I don't think any differently of you because of it." His shoulders sag, and some of the tension drains from his face.

"I think I might just be a little in love with you, princess."

TEN

Today, we've been left alone. Ares dropped a note under my door last night to let me know that our presence wasn't needed with the meetings, and I haven't stopped smiling since.

Breakfast was brought up to our room first thing. After eating and preparing for the day, we've spent the morning exploring this level of the Realm.

This level has a lot more natural spaces than the previous levels. We've been trekking through a forest for longer than I care to think about, but it's been pure joy.

"Can you hear that?" Caleb asks with a slow smile, so I stop, hold my breath, and tune in to the noises around us.

Water.

I smile widely and pick up the pace as I follow him

through the trees. It doesn't take long before we find the source of the noise. A waterfall and pool.

It's beautiful. The water runs clear, and the pool looks so freaking inviting. More than anything, it's peaceful. It's as if we've found a hiding spot that no one else knows about. We amble down the cliff until we're in the clearing with the pool, and I pull off my boots, dipping my toes into the water. I'm so glad I wore shorts today, because watching Caleb struggle to roll up his pants amuses me to no end. He drops down beside me, nudging me with his shoulder as I laugh at him, before dipping his feet in the cool water too.

"There's something about being around the water that just brings me an immeasurable amount of peace," I say, tipping my head back and enjoying the sun as it beams down on me. I might enjoy how pale I am, but that doesn't mean that I can't enjoy the sun as much as the next person.

"I don't think I ever knew that kind of peace until I met you. My life has been one long fight, and then there was you… like a beacon of peace among the chaos. It's why I couldn't resist touching you. Even if I was a jackass in the way I did it. Something about you called to me in the most visceral of ways."

I glance over at him and find him with his head tipped back and his eyes closed, enjoying the sun as much as I am. But the tightness in his shoulders tells me he's still feeling weird about yesterday with the Embers'. We spoke about it briefly earlier, but I let it go because he still seemed rattled. "You don't talk much about your life before you met me."

"There isn't much to tell that doesn't sound like a tragedy in motion," he shrugs, and I stay quiet, hoping he'll expand. "I told you about my non-existent parents, the group home, and the small pseudo-family I made for myself. There isn't much to tell beyond that."

"What about the scars?" I ask, knowing I'm prying, but I want to know more about him.

I'm tired of waiting for him to open up to me since it's just not happening. This man told me he thought he might love me. I've never been in love before, but I do know that I've never felt this way about anyone else in my entire life. If this is love, I want to experience it all. I want to know everything there is to know about him. We might have forever since I claimed him, but what I've learned in this life is that forever doesn't always mean a long time. There are too many things in this world able to kill us and too many people willing to do the killing.

"My scars are from too many fights, moments when I saved my own life, and some where others did," he says, all without looking at me.

"I'm sorry," I murmur, because I can feel his sadness. It's like a dark cloud that suffocates me.

"You don't need to be sorry, Mor. I get it. You don't

know much about me, but honestly, there isn't much to know. I'll tell you the little that there is." He reaches down and pulls off his t-shirt, his body tight in all the best ways. He turns, showing me his back. "These ones are from the whip of the woman who ran the group home. I was the oldest, and I took the punishment rather than letting the younger ones experience the ma'am's brand of pain."

He moves again, showing me a jagged wound in his ribs. "This is from the day I lost some of my brothers to the King's guard. They weren't as good at hiding their powers as I was. I tried to save them, but I failed."

He shifts, showing me a round scar on his shoulder. "This is from a spear during a bar fight gone wrong." Lastly, he brings my hand to the burn mark on his chest. "And this is from where someone tried to make me a prisoner. They branded me with their family symbol. Once I escaped their clutches, I burned their mark from my skin."

I cover my mouth with my hand, struggling to understand the horrors he's been through. Not all wounds leave scars, so I can't imagine how many more injuries there have been. Then my gaze flicks to his wrist, and the mark I placed on him with my claiming stares up at me. The accusation burns in my gut, and I can't help but frown. I branded him in my own way too without his permission. He cups my cheek and brings my gaze back to his. "Hey, don't even go there. I'd have taken your mark willingly had we been able to control it."

"I'm still really conflicted about it. I can't help but wonder if you're only okay with it because you're claimed," I admit, wringing out my hands. "I've seen a lot of bad shit in my short life. Horrors no person should have to witness, but my father is a special kind of sadist. It's made me very touchy about consent, and because I couldn't control my power, it claimed you. While I wouldn't change anything about what's between us, I do wish I could've at least asked you before it happened."

"Trust me, Mor. I was yours before the claiming. I can't explain it fully, but I knew it the minute you walked into that tavern. I was dumbstruck before I even saw your face. Then you walked by me, and I knew I would've followed you off of a cliff into oblivion without a second thought. This, what's happening with us, would've happened, claim or not." He kisses me softly, and when I curl my fingers through his hair, he deepens it until I think the kiss might consume every inch of my very soul.

He pulls back and tucks my hair behind my ear. "I meant what I said the other day, Mor. The same as I said the first time I kissed you. We were never going to be just friends, and if you think I'm ever going to let you go or let someone else come between us, you've got another thing coming. I am yours: hook, line, and fucking sinker. I'm fully a goner, and I wouldn't change it for the entire fucking Realm."

I wake up with Caleb wrapped around me, and I think I'm going to die from heat stroke. The guy is a fucking fireball. I try to move when he pulls me back up against him, and I feel his dick press into my ass.

Holy shit.

It can't be as big as it feels.

Right?

"Where do you think you're going?" Caleb's voice is deeper when he's half asleep, and as his breath tickles against my ear, my entire body breaks out in goosebumps. I twist in his arms so I can face him, and he smiles down at me. "Morning, beautiful."

I cover my mouth to shield my morning breath and say, "Hi."

"No need to hide from me." He pulls my hand from my mouth before cupping my cheek and kissing me softly. I can't help but think of just how good he made me feel when his lips were on my pussy, and an idea pops into my head.

I pull back from the kiss, and he tucks my hair behind my ear.

"Are you okay?" I ask, pausing moving forward with

my plans because if he's still not good after the other day, I'm going to wait. Him being okay comes first. I know we had yesterday to recover, but I could still see the tension in him a little then too.

"I'm good," he says, holding me tighter, so I smile before I push on his shoulders so he falls onto his back. With a confidence that is entirely a front, I climb on top of him, and his grin widens. "And what exactly are you going to do now?"

His hands move to my hips, and I lean forward to kiss him. The thin layer of silk from my cami is the only thing separating our skin, but that doesn't stop my nipples pebbling at the feel of him beneath me. I've been missing out on this for way too long, and I'm deciding right now to own this shit. My sexuality is my own, and I'm never going to let anyone shame me for owning it.

I kiss down his chest, sliding down his tight fucking body as I do, and I damn near salivate at the 'V' of his hips. I want to bite it, so I do, gently, and he groans, wrapping his fingers in my hair. I can't help but smile against his skin as I keep moving lower.

His hooded eyes gaze down at me as I reach the band of his shorts. "Are you sure?"

I smile up at him and nod. "Yeah, I'm sure."

He lifts his hips and helps me pull his shorts off. My eyes go wide as I take in the size of him, and I feel my blush spill over my chest. He looks bigger than I remember, but I don't let it distract me from the task at hand. I might never have touched a dick before, but I'm pretty sure it can't be that hard.

Okay, I take that back.

As his cock springs out from the confines of his shorts, I have a very real fear that there's no way this thing is going to fit in my mouth. How am I supposed to open my mouth big enough for him to push inside? Better yet, how is it supposed to get completely inside my mouth?

My face must be showing my every thought, because Caleb cups the back of my head and pulls me up for a deep, soulful kiss.

"You don't have to do this, you know?"

"I know, but I want to." What I don't tell him is that I'm just afraid he's going to choke me with that monster cock of his. That, or I'm going to be shit at whatever it is I'm meant to do. It's not like I've had friends or a sister to talk about this kind of stuff with. I mean, I have Amelia, but she's about as experienced as I am.

"So, why do you look like you're about to face your Demons?" I smile at that because… Demons, you know?

"I just…"

"What?"

How am I supposed to explain this?

"I can't possibly fit that thing in my mouth." Or I could

just blurt it out, apparently.

After a half a second pause, Caleb throws his head back and bursts into laughter. I can't help but feel a little self-conscious, but I also know that's not his intention at all. If anything, it makes me feel lighter.

Fuck it.

Wrapping my hand around the base of his cock, I'm only half surprised that my fingers can't quite touch around his girth. He wraps his hand around mine and guides me a little, which makes me feel a bit better. As his head tips back, he takes his hand away, leaving me to play however I see fit.

Taking a page out of his playbook, I lower my mouth and kiss the head of his cock, and a feeling of overwhelming pride shoots inside my chest as he curses and groans at my actions.

"Fuck, princess, you're going to make me come before I even feel the inside of your beautiful mouth."

I grin and decide to taste him, darting my tongue out and tracing the small slit at the top. I'm rewarded with a tangy drop of his essence. When it hits my tongue, I feel my own arousal dampen between my legs.

Feeling bolder, I open my mouth and suck on the head of his dick, taking the time to lick the top before engulfing him deeper and deeper. His fingers wrap around my hair, his muscles tense with his pleasure.

"Fuck, Mor, my restraint isn't going to hold…" he groans as his hips jolt a little, but he pulls back. His instincts must be telling him to fuck my mouth whereas his sensibilities are telling him to be gentle. Hopefully one day I'll get to experience him with no restraint whatsoever.

I take him deeper, my mouth almost aching at the stretch, but the velvety feel of him gives me more pleasure than pain.

"Easy, beautiful, you don't have to—" I cut him off as I slide my mouth down his entire length, save for the base where my hand pumps in tandem with my mouth. "Fuck yes, just like that."

It's a heady feeling bringing a man like Caleb to his knees. The thought makes me want to give him more.

Humming my satisfaction, I lose all control when the head of his cock pushes against my throat and my gag reflex kicks in.

"Breathe through your nose, baby. Easy, breathe slowly."

I do as he says, tears falling from my eyes but that doesn't bother me. I take him down again, enjoying the sounds that come from him.

I want more, but the fear of choking stops me before I remember his advice.

Pulling him out of my mouth, I lick up and down his shaft, suck on the head, and then in one bold move, dive onto his cock, making him buck his hips and curse the fates.

"Fuck, Mor…"

I love that I'm having this effect on him. It spurs me on, giving me the confidence to go further.

Up and down, sucking hard until my cheeks hollow out, I fuck his dick with my mouth and watch, rapt, as Caleb fights the urge to lose all control.

But that's what I want. I want him to lose himself to me.

It's when our gazes meet and I let his cock hit the back of my throat that I feel his fingers tighten in my hair, his eyes pleading.

"I'm gonna come, princess."

I follow my instinct and squeeze his base as I use my other hand to cup his tight balls. It must be the right thing, because Caleb lets out a primal sounding growl.

His body—a work of art that I am more than happy to explore—freezes, every muscle tensing. Each of his veins bulge for two seconds before I feel the first spurt of his cum hit my throat. I swallow it down until he's done.

"Holy shit, are you sure you haven't done that before?" he asks as he pulls me back up his body and wraps his arms around me. I can't help but smirk at him.

"Yeah, pretty sure." I laugh.

"Well, I mean, no one's going to complain about

waking up like that. Now it's your turn." I squeal as he flips me onto my back and cages me in with his arms. His weight presses against me in the most delicious way.

"That's not why…" I lose my words when he sucks my silk-covered nipple into his mouth.

He pulls back as a gasp slips from my lips and grins down at me. "Oh I know, but that doesn't mean I'm not going to eat. I can eat all damn day."

"Well, isn't this cozy." I look up and find Zafar standing in the doorway to my bedroom. Caleb jumps from the bed, naked, ready to defend us, but it's too late. He knows.

"I didn't realize you were such a prude," I purr, hoping that Zafar doesn't see this as any more than a quick fuck, but the grin playing on his lips tells me otherwise.

This could ruin everything.

"Oh I'm not, but I'm pretty sure that this is exactly what it seems—the little princess fucking the help. I'm sure your father would love to know the virgin daughter he's offering up is far from it."

"I'm sorry, did it look like he was dicking me? Are you that inexperienced?" I counter, jutting out my chin, hoping my bravado wins out.

His grin widens and he turns to leave the room before looking back at us over his shoulder. "Your secret is safe with me… for now."

Fuck.

This can't be happening.

Ares is going to kill me. He's going to literally obliterate me. He had one rule. Keep this thing between Caleb and I under the radar. We haven't left the room since Zafar caught Caleb in my bed, and I'm banking on Zafar actually keeping his mouth shut. At least until I can think of a way to fix this.

Caleb is in the bathroom when Ares comes to find us, and the minute he enters the room, he can tell something is wrong. The smile drops from his face as he sees my expression, and he closes the door behind him. "What happened?"

So I tell him, even though it pains me to confirm to my brother that Caleb and I are fucking around. Despite how close we are, this is definitely not something we've ever spoken about.

"I'll handle it," Ares says, pinching the bridge of his nose. "Has he spoken to anyone else?"

"I don't think so. He said he'd keep the secret for now. We both know that means he'll keep it until it benefits him not to." I sigh just as Caleb enters the room. To say the tension ratchets up a few notches is an understatement. They just stare at each other, not speaking, until Ares looks away sighing.

"Just try not to get fucking caught again, okay?" he says before standing to leave. "Oh, and I came here to let you know that my business here has concluded early. We're leaving tomorrow. You're expected for dinner in an hour. I'm going to go and find Zafar to see if I can fix this mess."

He leaves the room without another word, and Caleb drops down into the seat Ares just left. "Well, that could've gone worse."

"Could've gone better too." I shrug and curl up in the chair. "My biggest worry is for you, not me. My father is…"

"Your dad is a giant raging asshole. I get it. I don't know everything you've been through, though I get the feeling he'd kill me just to spite you, so I get it. But Ares has your back. Our backs. We'll get this sorted out." I wish I had his confidence in all of this.

"We should probably dress for dinner." I sigh and stand. I'd really rather not, but if it's our last dinner here, we need to go. I hope Ares can sort something out, but I have a back-up plan forming in my mind just in case. I won't let anything threaten Caleb.

Anything.

Ares caught me before we sat down to eat and assured me he'd made a deal with Zafar to keep his mouth shut. But every glance he sends in my direction at dinner makes the rage inside of me grow.

How fucking dare Zafar hold this shit over my head?

He's no better than the rest of them. Just another person trying to pull my strings and make me dance to their tune.

I've sat through this entire dinner, white knuckled. It's taken every ounce of control to not put my fork through his eye. We finish eating and I stand to leave. As we're walking from the room, Zafar grabs my elbow and pulls me to the side. "You might as well have your fun now. Soon you'll be mine. I'll kill your little pet the minute it's official."

He grins before walking away, and I look over to Ares who looks at the ground. That's how he thought best to keep this secret?

I guess my back-up plan just became a necessity because I won't have him threaten Caleb, and I sure as shit won't be his. I head back to my room like nothing is wrong.

Waiting for the estate to fall silent is torture, but once Caleb is asleep beside me, and all other noise ceases, I put my plan in action.

I swore I would never be this person, but that was a naive thought. You do whatever it takes to protect the ones you love. Without exception. I leave my feet bare as I walk from the room, only stopping to pull one of the salted iron blades from my corset as I leave.

I creep through the estate to the family's wing, and the big, pretentious 'Z' on the door leads me to my destination. I've always been light on my feet, but the constant training as of late has definitely helped.

Opening the bedroom door, I see him asleep in his bed, a smile on his face. Sleeping at ease he isn't trying to ruin my entire fucking world. Closing the door behind me softly, I creep over to the bed, dagger in hand.

I never wanted to be like my father, but being his daughter has taught me a lot. First and foremost, never let someone have the upper hand when you can take it back. Do not let your enemy have the upper hand if there is an alternative.

As I stand above Zafar, I swear he looks more evil asleep than he does awake. I lower my dagger to his throat and put my hand over his mouth. His eyes shoot open and before he can speak, I press the blade harder against his skin. "You should have made a deal with me, or better yet, been a decent fucking person. You brought this on yourself."

I drag the blade across his skin, the blood spatter hitting my face, but I look him in the eyes as the blood drains from him. I see it, the second he realizes that my blade is salted iron. He tries to buck and flail, but I use my power to hold him still, just the way Brandy showed me.

"You crossed the wrong fucking Voux," I hiss, and pull on the Shadow Fire from within the depths of my power. I use my power to lift his body from his bed and let the flames consume him. Sure, I could've just used the flame from the beginning, but I wanted him to know that he brought his death upon himself. Once the body is gone, with no trace of him here, I strip his bed, and remake it until it looks like no one slept here tonight, before burning his sheets to nothing too.

I check the room to make sure there's no more blood to give anything away, but there's no trace left of him except from the blood spray on my face. I wipe it with the back of my hand and let out a sigh. Who'd have thought I'd kill someone before I lost my virginity?

I guess I'm more my father's daughter than I ever realized.

ELEVEN

I wake the next morning, acting like last night didn't happen. No one seems to have noticed I was gone, and it's not until we're down at breakfast that anyone questions anything.

"Have either of you seen Zafar today? I knocked on his door, but he wasn't in his room, and his bed didn't look slept in," Yana asks once the remaining Ember brothers have joined us. Ares looks over at me, but I keep my gaze on my plate and put another forkful of steak and eggs in my mouth.

"No, but he did seem worked up after dinner," Torrin says to his mother. "Maybe he got a little carried away at the tavern. I'll swing by there after breakfast and see if I can find him."

His words seem to settle his mother, and I continue to eat like I don't know I wiped their son from existence last night. He should've known better than to fuck with what was mine. I'm tired of being underestimated and messed with.

He went too far.

Once we've finished breakfast, the boys get the carriages packed up while I handle my hounds. I've missed them while we've been here. There's no way Zafar would've made it into the room without us knowing if they were with us, but it taught me yet another lesson.

Never agree to let them be kept away from me. It can be lethal.

By the time I have them in their carrier, Caleb and Ares have the carriages ready to go.

"We look forward to seeing you at the ball," Yana calls out with a wave as I climb into the carriage. I smile back at her and let Ares respond. Caleb follows me in, and after a moment, Ares joins us.

"If you thought this stop was hellish, you guys better buckle up."

I look at Ares with a frown. "What the fuck does that mean?"

"That means that our next stop in Level Five was cancelled due to infighting, so our next stop is Level Six, the level run by The Carver. And you and I need to talk."

He watches me closely, but I keep my face blank other than a sneer. I won't keep the secret from him of what I did, but I'm not telling him until we're far from here.

"I fucking hate him."

"The Carver? Yeah that doesn't sound ominous at all," Caleb jokes, trying to lighten the mood.

"You have no fucking idea." I shudder, just thinking of the last time I saw him in my father's throne room.

Ares sighs and pinches the bridge of his nose. "Thankfully, we're only there for one night. Father is aware of my issues with his friend. Plus, he doesn't need to ensure the loyalties there. This is more because of appearances, so we only have to survive one dinner."

"Survive is the best fucking word there," I grumble, and Caleb squeezes my hand.

The carriage starts to move forward, and my stomach sinks. Just when I thought things couldn't get worse.

Well, here we go I guess.

We whisper between the levels, and the darkness that greets us on Level Six isn't a real shock despite the fact that it's mid-morning. Everything about The Carver screams darkness. He might not control the shadows or the mist, but there is an evil inside of him that I've only seen in one other.

My father.

He enjoys the screams of his victim. He feeds on their

fear like a succubus does on sex. I'm not sure what type of Demon he is as he's always been an enigma, but I can't stand to be around him. He practically bleeds darkness.

So I'm looking forward to this about as much as I enjoyed destroying Zafar last night.

I lean into Caleb, taking comfort in his warmth as we head through the pitch black to what I assume is The Carver's home. It's hard to see much of anything out of the windows. I'm not sure exactly what's happening here, but the silence both in and out of the carriage encourages me to stay quiet. The only sounds are the hooves of the Dàgaan. Even my hounds are quiet.

One thing is for sure, I will not be separated from my hounds here. Not even for a minute.

You never know what lurks in the darkness.

We continue to travel for a little while until the carriage draws to a stop.

"We'll talk later, but please, both of you, stay in your fucking room and stay out of trouble. Even the smallest inkling that you two are more than what meets the eye will get back to Father." Ares eyes me, as if he already knows that the Zafar problem is now non-existent, but I don't give anything away. He's right, this place is not a place to be spilling secrets. I'm also not sure I'm comfortable with Caleb knowing what I did. I'm pretty sure he won't judge me for it, but I don't want him to look at me differently.

I'm pretty sure I've fallen in love with him. It might be quick, but this thing between us is undeniable. I don't think anyone has ever seen me as much as he sees me. I don't want to fuck this up, but Zafar was going to ruin everything.

I chew on my lip, contemplating telling him. Then I remember where we are again, and I know I can't tell either of them anything until we leave this place.

At that thought, Ares climbs from the carriage, and I look over at Caleb. "Lets just hope we all survive the night."

It's hard to hold my tongue.

The Carver's pets are everywhere, catering to his every need. Some of them are more cut up than others, but each of them looks at him like he hung the moon.

It blows my fucking mind.

They're like mindless zombies in love with their tormentor, and it makes my stomach churn. Caleb has kept a reasonable distance from me since we arrived and has his own room next to mine. The pack hasn't left my side since I let them out of their carrier. They're currently on full alert and dotted around the room I'll call mine for the night.

Caleb is in here with me but sits across the room in a

chair reading a book rather than sitting with me on the bed like he usually would be. Because in this place, the walls really do have eyes. It creeps me out thinking about the fact that we are literally being watched at all times, but I just have to keep telling myself it's just one night.

We can survive one night.

I hope.

"I'd like to take a walk," I announce as I place my book on the table beside the bed and stand. The pack comes to attention immediately, and Caleb nods.

"Yes, princess." He keeps his face straight, and I hate the distance we have to put between us here. Hopefully, if we can escape the grounds of the house, we can be a little more ourselves.

Caleb moves to open the door, and we find Ares standing there about to knock on the door. "Oh good, you're both still here. We need to talk."

He strides into the room, and Caleb lets the door fall closed behind him, looking at me apologetically. I smile at him because it's not his fault my brother has shitty timing. "What brings you by?"

"Dinner tonight. I need you both to be on your fucking best behavior." Ares shudders in his seat, and I hate to think what he's witnessed in the small amount of time he's spent with The Carver so far today that has him so on edge already.

"What's going on?" Caleb asks, standing just behind me in what anyone could call a security pose. Thet soldier look seems to be one he's nailed, and I can't say I like it. It's so far from the man he really is.

"The Carver has a… surprise for us at dinner tonight. He wouldn't say more than that, but considering who he is, I'm expecting the worst." I feel exhausted just at the thought of surviving tonight already.

"Well, doesn't that just sound like a good time." Caleb grimaces, and I close my eyes, leaning my head back on the chair.

"Can I be ill and just sleep through this entire stay? Please?"

Ares gives me a sad smile but shakes his head. "You know if I could, I would let you. But we both know that more than any other stay we have, this one will be reported back to Father in the most detail. So this is one we just have to grin and bear. At least our next stop will be a longer stay, and a much better one too."

"The next level is a friend I assume?" I smirk at my brother, and he laughs.

"Not in the way you're insinuating, but yes. He's more like a brother than a friend. I think you'll like him and his family a lot. His father has been more of a father to me than ours ever has." He smiles fondly, and it makes my heart happy that Ares had someone who showed him love and kindness. Hells knows we never got it from either of our parents.

"Anyway, back to tonight, I know black is usually your go-to palette anyway, but I definitely recommend it tonight. And I'd cover as much skin as you can get away with." He frowns again. "We both know The Carver has never touched you because of his friendship with Father. But Father isn't here, so just be on alert, okay?"

There's nothing quite like an ominous warning to set my teeth on edge. "You can count on it."

"Okay," Ares says, standing. I can't help but notice the tense set to his shoulders. "Dinner will be in about two hours. I suggest you use the time wisely." With that, he slips from the room as quietly as he appeared. Kaos moves to lie by my feet, and I pet him gently.

I'm not going to be able to bring them to dinner, I don't trust The Carver not to use them against me or to not harm them. I don't really relish the thought of leaving them here alone either. My fingers still when a thought slams into me like a runaway freight train.

Amelia.

She'll look after my pack, and I know they'll look after her right back. At least this way I know that all the beings closest to me will be as safe as I can make them. I look up at Caleb and grin. "I need you to do me a favor."

I step into the dining room, led by one of The Carver's pets, with Caleb and Ares at my back. Ares breaks away to speak to The Carver, possibly in an attempt to distract him from my arrival. Caleb pulls my chair out for me before moving to sit next to me. There's no way for me to get out of sitting next to The Carver tonight. He has no family, so Ares will sit to his left while I sit to his right as is only proper.

Once we're seated, I hear more voices, and more people fill the room. I recognize some of the faces from my father's throne room, but I don't know any of the names. I can do nothing but assume these are some of the High Born of this level. I look over to Ares whose face shows no sign of surprise at the newcomers, but that doesn't mean anything. Not tonight.

Everyone takes their seats, and I'm just grateful that no one tries to speak to me. I really, really don't want to engage with these people. Hell, for the first time in existence, I don't even want to eat. I'd cut off my left tit with salted iron if it got me out of this.

Once all of his guests are seated, The Carver moves to the head of the table and raises a glass. "Welcome, friends, old and new." He smiles down at me, and I suppress a gag. "Let us celebrate the presence of our crown prince, and the soon to be announced princess. May the royal family stay prosperous for many centuries to come. In their honor, I have arranged for some dining entertainment for us."

He sits and claps his hands together once. At the sound, his girls appear around the room and place the first dish in front of us. I look down, and my eyes bug out of my head. Caleb looks at me, and I shake my head subtly. That can't be a heart. Right?

"Wolf's heart. A speciality of this level," The Carver says with a wide grin, and the others at the table coo over such a treat. Me… I try not to vomit on my plate. I look across to Ares who looks about as miserable as I feel as he picks up his knife and fork.

They can't expect me to eat this, right? I will legit vomit all over The Carver's shoes.

The rest of the table tucks in, and I see Caleb just watch the plate like it offends him. I mean, I get it. The Carver leans over to me, blood trickling from his mouth where he's plowing into his raw heart. "Don't you want to at least try it?"

I turn to him and act the part of the doll my father has shaped me to be in public. "I'm sorry, but I'm not sure my delicate stomach could handle such finery."

His grin widens, and I know he sees what he wants to. The breakable little princess everyone thinks I am.

"I'll have yours, then." He jams his fork into the heart

and moves it to his own plate, a little blood squirts from it as he does so and stains the white table cloth. I have a very horrible feeling that won't be the only blood stain on this cloth tonight.

I sit back and try to stay quiet as much as I can, and by the time the fourth dish comes out, it's finally something that is a semblance of normal food.

"Steak tartare!" The Carver announces, and I have to wonder what the fuck his damage is to make him this way. It's not enough that he enjoys torture, but he eats everything fucking raw too. I have a few small bites, much to my stomach's protest, but I know I need to eat something just to keep the peace.

After six courses, the food portion of the night is nearly done. Just when I think I'm free, The Carver stands again. "And now, my honored guests, tonight's entertainment."

The chill of his tone sends a shiver down my spine, and I can't help but sit up straighter. That's when the laughter begins, and Caleb tenses beside me. A girl floats into the room, and then she hovers above the table. She looks at me with sheer desperation as a tear slips down her face.

I look over to Ares whose fists are clenched, but his face is as passive as ever. I guess this was the surprise The Carver alluded to. Fuck my fucking life.

"I thought each of you here would like to break her with me."

I take a deep breath and shut down my power quickly. I cannot let my rage get us into trouble tonight. Gripping Caleb's thigh under the table, I squeeze, hopefully reminding him of the same thing.

"Thank you for the offer, but with so much travel, I think I'd quite like to go to bed," I say to The Carver.

"I must insist, then, that you take the first blow if you wish to leave. Of course you need your rest, as any princess does." Fuck him, fuck everyone here, and fuck my father for putting me in this fucking position.

I look back at Ares, and I know he can't help me. No one can fucking help me. So I sigh indignantly and stand. "If I must."

Caleb stands and takes a step behind me as The Carver lays out his roll of knives, offering them to me. "Use whichever one you'd like. Don't worry, she won't scream. I'll keep her quiet for your first time."

I smile at him like I'm thanking him, and take a small needle-like blade from the roll. The rest of the room watches me with such eager anticipation that my hand shakes. I can feel their fucking excitement for what's about to happen. If only they knew that this isn't the first blood I've drawn in the last twenty-four hours.

The difference here being that this girl doesn't deserve this, but I am absolutely fucking powerless to help her. I look at her face and try to convey just how sorry I am, and I push the blade through her ribs, puncturing a lung. Maybe I've jabbed the salted iron in such a place that it will be enough to make her torture end quickly.

I hand the blade back to The Carver, and he looks at me like he just won a fucking prize. "Nice placement, that one will have hurt like a fucker. Have a good night, princess."

I smile back at him and nod. "You too." Then I move from the room as fast as would be deemed acceptable with Caleb at my back.

I hope I can make it back to my room before I lose the meager contents of my stomach.

TWELVE

I barely slept last night. Caleb checked the room before escorting Amelia back to wherever she's staying and then spent the night in his room. Or so I assume. I didn't see him again after he left my room. Either way, I was uneasy.

I tossed and turned all night. The pack was either on the bed or surrounding it, but I couldn't get the image of that girl out of my head. It doesn't help that it felt like I was being watched all night either.

So to say I'm a grouchy asshole this morning is the understatement of the fucking century, but I'm so glad to be leaving that it almost balances out. It doesn't take me long to wash and dress then get my shit packed away.

I don't want to spend a minute longer here than

necessary. Once I'm done, I sit and wait with the hounds, knowing that someone will come and get me when it's time to leave. It's not long until there's a knock at the door. The hounds don't move, so I know that it's Caleb before the door even opens.

"Are you okay?" he asks once the door is closed behind him. He looks like he's had about as much sleep as I have.

"As okay as I can be," I say with a shrug. I'd really like to find refuge in his arms, but I'm not stupid enough to think that we're not still being watched. "Have you spoken to Ares this morning?"

"Yes, I just saw him. He's having the carriages loaded so we can leave as soon as we've eaten."

"We have to eat again?" I ask, and he grimaces.

"Believe me, I'd also rather not."

"I know, I know. Let's head down. The sooner we eat, the sooner we can be on the road." I stand and the hounds follow suit. This is all practiced movement at this point as Caleb opens the door and the hounds check the hall before Havoc allows me to leave.

They're all good boys, really.

We make our way down to breakfast and find one of The Carver's pets waiting for us. She doesn't even blink at the hounds at my feet.

"The man of the house regrets to inform you that he won't be able to make breakfast, but we have laid out a spread for you so that you can eat before you travel. We've also arranged food for your hounds." She waves us into a smaller dining room than the one we were in last night, and for that I'm grateful. I'm not sure I could go back to the room we were in last night.

The table is laid with toast, preserves, biscuits, sausage, gravy, eggs, and a whole fucking buffet. So these people *do* know what real food is.

The girl leaves, and I stop Caleb before he reaches for the food. "This might look okay, but I don't trust it. We'll eat when we get to the next place, just eat as much as necessary so as not to look rude."

He nods and makes himself a small plate. I play it safe and eat half a slice of dry toast. I'm pretty sure the Carver wouldn't poison us for snubbing his 'delights' last night, but you can never be too careful. The hounds don't even sniff the food laid out for them, and I look at Kaos. He snorts at me, and I know he can feel my unease.

Ares doesn't appear until we've eaten the small amount we picked up. "Good, you've eaten. Let's go."

He doesn't hang around for us. He merely walks out of the door and climbs in the carriage that I can see through the window before we even stand up.

It doesn't take long to get the hounds secured, and we're in the carriage with Ares in minutes. He's silent until we whisper away and are safely in Level Seven. "We can talk freely now."

"Good, because what the actual fuck was that last night?" Caleb roars, startling me. Even Ares looks taken aback. I guess we're almost used to The Carver, even if we're both still appalled by his actions.

"The Carver is everything that is wrong with this Realm," Ares tells him, sighing. "He's one of the things on my list that will be dealt with as soon as I have the power to. Trust me, I'm working on it, but there is only so much that can be done right now. I did what I could to reduce the girl's suffering. I placed her in a dream state, so she wasn't aware of anything that happened once you left, and I manipulated her mind enough to make her scream when expected, but she felt nothing. Her death was as peaceful as I could make it."

Caleb looks at me like Ares just spoke gibberish, and I realize he probably hasn't learned of my brother's various powers. "Ares is a Dreamscaper, a really fucking powerful one. He can manipulate what you see not just while you're asleep, but while you're awake too. He can also talk to you through your dreams. He wouldn't do it to you, but he's used it more than once in the throne room so that my father's slaves do not suffer as much as they would otherwise."

"Oh," is all he says, like he's reeling.

"Are you okay?" I ask Ares who lets out a deep breath.

“No, but I will be. Teddy is a dear friend of mine, and his father, Theodore, is as close to a real father as I’ve ever come. Their entire family are basically my extended family, so we’re safe here, and we’re here for two weeks. Theodore is also an archivist, so I’m going to ask him about your claiming and your mark. He might have some answers where I’ve been unable to discover any.”

“Okay, that sounds like heaven. Even one night at that place was too much,” I tell him and lean into Caleb’s warmth. He’s staring out of the windows, and I smile when I see the flying beasts he’s fixated on. “There are Tulane here!”

“Did I forget to mention that?” Ares smirks and I swat his arm. Tulane were my favorite creature as a girl. They’re giant and scaled with pointed teeth, and they breathe fire, but everyone misunderstands them. They’re gentle beasts really. Just don’t mess with their young, and they won’t harm you.

“I didn’t think they were real,” Caleb says, such wonder in his voice makes me remember that he’d never left his level until this trip with us. I can’t wait to take him up on one. I’ve always had a way with animals, and Tulane have always loved me. I’ve never met one I couldn’t fly.

I clap my hands like an excited child as the herd fly past the carriage, their screeches of happiness filling my heart.

This is exactly what I needed after last night. I squeeze my brother's hand and mouth 'thank you' to him. He squeezes back and smiles at me. I haven't seen him this relaxed ever, not even when we were with Brandy.

I think this place is going to be good for us, and I can't wait to meet my brother's other family.

The carriage draws up at a small cottage, and I wonder if we're at the right place until a dozen people spill from the doorway, calling out Ares' name. He jumps from the carriage before it's even fully stopped and is enveloped by all of the people coming in for hugs and welcoming him so warmly.

"Is it terrible of me that as much as I want to say hello to his chosen family that I'd rather just run away and find the Tulane?" I ask Caleb, and he laughs.

"Not at all, I am so here for finding them, but maybe we should say at least a hello first and get the hounds settled. I'm pretty sure that Kaos and the Tulane wouldn't mix too well." I snort a laugh at his very astute assumption. My hound can be a little jealous.

"Okay, let's do this." I climb from the carriage with Caleb less than a second behind me, and we walk toward the ruling family of this level. While Ares said we're safe with them, I still won't take Caleb's hand until I've assessed them for myself. After The Carver, I'm still a little on edge.

An older gentleman, the oldest person in the crowd, walks toward me with a saunter in his step and a warm smile on his face. "You, little lady, must be Morgan. It is a pleasure to finally meet you, though I must admit, I've heard so much about you, I feel like I already know you."

I look from him to Ares, who just starts to laugh.

"My apologies, my name is Theodore Dutton, and this is my family." He wraps me in a hug, and I freeze for a second before hugging him back. I am so not used to all of this hugging, but he seems very genuine. He pulls back and looks at Caleb. "And who might you be, son?"

"Caleb Sinclair, sir," Caleb tells him, standing straight. I realize that until this moment, I didn't even know his full name. Hells, I'm such a fucking moron. He shakes Theodore's hand, and the older man smiles at him.

"That's a good shake you've got there, son." He goes around and introduces us to his wife, Tammy, his children, the twins Teddy and Lani, and their youngest Neva, before waving us all inside the cottage. I'm not sure that we're all going to fit, but we follow them anyway.

The cottage is bigger on the inside than it looked.

"Now you kids will be staying in one of the guest cottages across the farm, but we sit down for family breakfast and dinner every day, ya hear?" Theodore announces once we're all sitting down, and Tammy hands out iced tea.

I sit quietly, leaning against Caleb as Ares catches everyone up on our journey so far. Tammy eventually interjects, "We should let the kids get settled, it sounds like they've been through a lot. We can finish catching up later."

"That would be amazing, thank you," I say to her. "But really, I'd just love to go find the Tulane."

"Now there is a girl after my own heart," Neva says laughing freely. "You guys get settled in, and I'll sort you out with a map."

It doesn't take long to get the hounds settled, and Neva equips us with a map. It leads us from the back of the farm out to the mountains. Thanks to my new found ability to whisper, it doesn't take long to find the spot she mentioned. I whisper us to about a mile out, so we don't startle the creatures.

"Slow and steady, and we'll be alright," I tell Caleb as we get closer to the nest. I hear their calls before I see them, but when we reach the nest, my mind is officially blown.

This has to be the biggest nest of Tulane that exists. I

can't even count how many of them there are.

"Oh, and stay away from the small ones. The moms don't fuck around with their young."

"Noted." Caleb nods, his eyes wide as he takes in the sight before us.

I close my eyes and reach out to the Tulane in the way that I've always just instinctively known how to do. It doesn't take long before two of them approach us. One is a beautiful fiery red and orange while the other is a blue-green.

Their scales sparkle in the sunlight as they dip their heads to us. "Slowly," I remind Caleb as I reach forward and pat the head of the blue-green one.

Thunder.

The name rolls around in my head and I smile. "Hi, Thunder."

Caleb looks at me, puzzled, until he puts his hand on the Tulane before him. He jumps a little, and I know the Tulane has spoken inside his mind.

"Echo," he says out loud, almost breathless.

"Time to ride," I say with a smile, and Thunder lays down his giant wing to help me climb on. Caleb watches me before doing the same with Echo. I wait until he's mounted and show him where to hold on.

Let's fly, I tell Thunder, and with a few beats of his wings, we're airborne.

Echo and Caleb take flight seconds later, and as we soar through the skies, his carefree whoop brings me so much joy.

Let's show them what real flying is, shall we?

The Tulane doesn't respond with words, but he banks left, cutting before the other creature, and they both let out a screech of excitement.

We tear through the skies, and a freedom that nothing else could ever compare to rushes through my body. There's just something so freeing about flying that little else even comes close to. The Tulane race one another, maneuvering in loops and corkscrews, and I can hear Caleb's laughter ring out around us as the creatures play with one another.

The Tulane zip through the skies, and I spread out my arms as if I were flying myself, the same way I used to as a kid. Thunder seems to feel exactly what I want as he takes us over the lake and nose dives until we skim the water. Echo follows suit, and I let out a cry of joy.

There really is nothing like this.

We fly until the sun starts to dip in the sky, and I tell Thunder to take us back.

Once we dismount, Caleb lifts me in his arms and spins me around. He looks happier than I think I've ever seen him. "Mor, that was… it was fucking incredible. Thank you so much for showing me that, for helping me experience it. I've never felt so alive, so free."

His eyes dance like I've never seen, and my heart nearly explodes with happiness.

"I'm so glad I could give that to you."

"Me too. Me too." He grins before kissing me. "Now let's head back, after all that, I'm fucking ravenous."

I can't help but laugh at him as my stomach growls.

"Yeah, let's do it."

"Really though, Mor. Thank you. This is easily in the top five moments of my life, and so far, you star in all of them."

"You say the sweetest things, Mr. Sinclair." He blushes at my words, and I kiss his cheek. "Now let's go get me fed before I resort to eating you."

He barks out a laugh before taking my hand. "I might just hold you to that."

The bathroom in the cottage is fucking extravagant, and I am so here for it. There's nothing better after a day of riding the Tulane than a long soak in a tub. The smell of the oils as they mix with the steaming water relaxes me before my skin even touches the water.

I sink into the high-sided tub, hissing at the burn against my skin. I'm not sure anything will make me feel clean again after staying with The Carver, but I'm willing to try soaking in this tub for as long as it takes.

I let out a sigh before slipping fully under the water. There's something peaceful about being fully submerged. It could be the absolute quiet, the burn of the oxygen trapped in my lungs, or the thought that even if I did drown, it wouldn't be the end of me. Morbid maybe, but I've heard of some weirder kinks in my time around the palace.

I raise my head out of the water and lie back, enjoying the alone time. As much as I adore being around Ares and Caleb, I'm a creature who is used to being alone. I didn't realize how exhausted I'd become from just being around so many people constantly.

I soak in the water, thinking over everything I've learned about myself since I left home. It's been six weeks, but it could easily have been a lifetime. So much has changed. I've changed, dramatically.

I finally have a better idea of my powers, though we haven't found anything that I *can't* do yet… That should scare me, but it just makes me feel more comfortable in my skin. My entire life I've been afraid of my father's wrath and the despicable actions of his sycophants. But if I can truly defend myself against them, I have no need to fear for myself.

My biggest concern has been Ares. Every time we've discovered something new, it's like another weight is placed on his back, and I hate that he feels so responsible for me.

Once the water starts to cool, I wash myself and climb from the tub. Grabbing the robe hung on the back of the door, I wrap it around myself before heading into the bedroom. I open the door and freeze, finding Caleb standing on the other side, waiting for me. He pauses when he sees me. The only light in the room is from the fire, and it makes him look even more mysterious than he already is. The hunger in his eyes is obvious as they flash black.

Feeling bolder and braver than I have up to this point, I decide, *fuck it.* We've seen all of one another, tasted each other's flesh… Why am I holding back?

I untie the robe and let it fall from my shoulders. We've been dodging around taking the next step, but I'm ready. It's time he figured out just how ready.

"Mor…" he chokes out as I sway my hips, walking toward him. I rake my nails down his torso as he remains still, his eyes never leaving me. "We don't have to do this…"

I cock an eyebrow and meet his stare. "I want to do this."

Running my hands to the edge of his t-shirt, I lift it, and he helps me finish taking it off. He's too fucking tall for me to do it otherwise. I lean forward and press my lips above his racing heart.

"Are you sure?"

I can't help but smile as he clenches and unclenches his fists at his sides, a reminder of the small level of control he has currently. I stretch up on tiptoes and kiss him with every ounce of fiery passion I have inside of me. I might have held out this long, but I don't want to wait a moment longer. I've very much come to enjoy the way he makes my body feel, and I can't think of anyone I'd rather be with for my first time than the man I've come to love. We might have had a weird start, but now I can't picture any part of my existence without him by my side.

Without releasing his lips, I untie his belt and pop the top button of his pants. "I'm more than sure."

It's like my words give him permission to let go of the firm hold he has on himself. His hands encircle my waist, and he lifts me, throwing me onto the bed. "Oh, princess, you have no idea what you're in for."

I lean up on my elbows and smirk at him. "Well, I guess you'd better show me."

Naked and completely unashamed, I watch him with rapt attention as he stands there, half naked, the outline of his massive erection peeking through the vee of his open pants. He's beautiful in the masculine, possessive sort of way he has about him. Although his presence is potent, it's his heart and soul that call out to me. The sincerity with which he shows his emotions despite the mysterious air about him.

"What are you thinking about over there?" He looks like he's trying to solve the mysteries of the universe.

"Well, I'm trying to figure out how I'm going to sink my cock inside the perfection that is your pussy without coming on the first thrust." It takes me a second to absorb what he says before I burst out laughing.

"Seriously?"

"Mor, you don't understand. The way I've wanted you for so long, and the fact that you are the very definition of perfection... At this point, I'm thinking I should rub one out now so I don't embarrass myself." He's not joking. The crease between his brows tells me he's seriously considering taking himself in hand without me.

"Absolutely not!" Fuck that, I'm ready to be a participant, not a bystander.

"Mor—" I cut him off because this has gone on too long.

"If you don't come over here and fuck me like you own me, I'm going to find someone else to do it." I'm bluffing. He knows it. I know it. If his growl is any indication, my words still hit their intended mark.

"The fuck you will!" He kneels between my legs before he even ends his curse. Caleb's right where I want him, but I give nothing away. I want this, and I want it now.

Hovering over me, his forearms cage my head in and hold his weight. He offers me his signature grin, and he's all heat and beauty, blinding me with his boyish charms.

"That was dirty play, Mor. Didn't know you had it in you." His mouth is at my lips, his tongue sliding across my bottom lip before he bites the plump flesh and takes advantage of my gasp to kiss the life out of me. I give as good as I get, and when Caleb puts his weight on one arm to bring his other hand to my breast, my sigh gets lost in his mouth.

Rolling my nipple between his thumb and forefinger, I feel the zing right down to my clit, but it's when he pinches harder than he ever has, I feel the slickness grow between my legs.

Reaching up to take hold of his shoulders, I dig my nails into his skin and rake them down to the middle of his back. My hips surge, searching out the feel of his cock against my burning core.

"Caleb, please." I'm begging, though I have no idea what for, exactly. Is it for more of his kisses? More of his teasing, where he walks the line of pleasure and pain? Is it for more of everything I've never had? I may not know, but Caleb does. It's like he can decode my needs and read my body like a map.

"I've got you, Mor. Do you trust me?"

I don't hesitate. "You know I do."

Of everyone and everything in this world, I trust less than a handful of people. Despite the short amount of time we've known each other, I probably trust him the most of them all.

I whimper as he rises back up. He quickly takes his pants and shorts off before slowly making his way down my body, one hot kiss after the other. Over my chest, my nipples, my stomach, and my belly button. He kisses each of my hips, licking my skin like a lollipop before reverently sliding his tongue from clit to slit and all the way back to the darkest hole of all.

"Caleb." I chant his name over and over as his mouth prepares me for what I truly want. With his hands tucked under my ass, he feasts on my pussy, rewarding himself with a hefty serving of my juices.

"I could do this all night, Mor." I don't have the chance to respond because he does this thing with his tongue just as one finger penetrates me. I'm so turned on, I'm not sure what to do with my hands or the rest of my body for that matter. I want to tear him apart and kiss him back together again. The dueling sensations are going to drive me to insanity.

"I'm going to worship you like you've never known, Mor. It's going to hurt a little but I promise you, I'll make it feel so much better after that."

"I know, I trust you."

His gaze stays on me for a beat before he lowers his mouth again and makes sure I'm ready for him.

One of my hands lands on his head, my fingers digging into his scalp as he pushes in two fingers and stretches my walls as best he can.

Meanwhile, my entire body is on fire. I'm restless, I'm wet, and I'm humming with pent-up energy only he can relieve.

"Please, I need you."

Licking his way up my body, he aligns his hips with mine before sliding his heavy cock through my pussy lips. When the head of his dick rubs against my clit, I can't stop the moan that slips from my lips, and he grins down at me. "Are you ready, baby?"

I nod at him, and he looks at me like I'm a naughty girl. "Words, Mor."

"Yes, I'm so fucking ready for all of this with you."

Cradling my head with both of his palms, he lowers his mouth to mine at the same time the thick head of his cock nestles against my opening. Just as his tongue spears through my lips, his cock pushes inside of me just a little before he pulls out. I gasp, more from anticipation of pain than the real thing, but his kiss is intoxicating. As his torso rubs against my erect nipples, he pushes back in a little bit further than before and holds himself there, letting me adjust to the size of him a bit.

I'm panting into his mouth, my body buzzing with excitement mixed with a little fear as he pushes in a little further still.

"Are you ready, baby?"

I don't answer with words; I latch onto his shoulders from behind, my legs wrapping around his waist, trying to impale myself further onto his cock.

"Shhh, baby, patience." He kisses me again, and just like before, he pushes in, but this time a lot further and a lot harder.

The sting that follows is definitely worse than I thought it would be. It's quick, and the pain isn't as bad as I thought it would be as Caleb pushes all the way to the hilt with not an inch separating us. Stilling, he breaks the kiss and looks into my eyes, searching, assessing, protecting.

"Are you okay?"

I grin up at him, pushing through the lingering pain, and lift my head to initiate another kiss. "I'm perfect."

"You fucking are, Mor. It's like you were made for me."

"I need—"

"I know what you need. I'll always know." His hands palm the sides of my head, and Caleb pulls all the way out before slowly pushing back to the hilt again. Slowly, he takes my virginity like a treasure.

"Caleb… I need more."

He once again understands me, picking up the speed of his movements, pushing in a little bit harder with every single thrust. We're no longer kissing. He's staring into my eyes, watching me, telling me things with his gaze that no words could ever hope to convey.

He's showing me his emotions, and they are vivid, melodic, and unmistakable. I know, at this moment, that even if he hasn't said it outright, he loves me just as much as I love him.

"Fuck, you feel so damn good. So perfect. Your tight fucking pussy is beyond what I imagined."

I'm practically climbing all over him, our movements slick against one another, and the sounds of our skin slapping against skin adds to it all.

He leans back and rubs my clit with his thumb, and it's like every fucking nerve in my body lights up. With every thrust inside me, now relentless and erotic, there's a mounting force of emotions rising. My toes curl, and I cry out as I come all over his dick. He slows his movements but doesn't stop as I ride out my orgasm.

"You're beautiful when you come, Mor."

He starts to fuck me harder, his thumb starting up again on my clit, and faster than I thought possible, I come all over again as I give into the sensations coursing through me. I let it all go.

And when I do, the world explodes behind my lids. Colors and sounds and sensations I'd never felt before gather at the center of my chest as Caleb thrusts two more times and then joins me in his own climax.

By the time we both come down from our high, Caleb's chest is heaving from the pleasurable assault on our senses, and he slowly pulls out. I immediately miss the feel of him inside of me, but watching him make his way to the bathroom, after placing a tender kiss on my nose, is enough to distract from the loss of him.

That tight ass is a woman's wet dream.

Or my reality.

When he comes back with a warm, wet towel, I lift my gaze to see him smirking at me.

"Enjoying the view, princess?"

THIRTEEN

If I said that my time on this level with the Duttons' hasn't been the best two weeks of my life, I'd be straight up lying. Between spending more than a little time getting to know Caleb on a deeper level, to family dinners and games nights, it's been the most mundane yet happiest time of my life.

Ares' little extended family welcomed me with open arms, and I honestly have never felt so at home anywhere before. To say I'm sad to go is an understatement, especially when I know we're so close to going back to the palace. I'd much rather just stay here for the rest of time. Fuck the palace and my responsibilities. Seeing Caleb and Ares so free and at ease has made my heart so happy. I even caught Kaos and Havoc chasing fucking butterflies yesterday.

This place has had the best effect on us, and I don't want it to be over.

Which is exactly why I'm still in bed, keeping my eyes closed despite the fact I've been awake for ages. I'm pretty sure Caleb knows I'm awake too, but I get the feeling he wants to leave here about as much as I do.

I smile when he pulls me tighter against him, his rock hard cock digging into my ass. I might be more than a little fond of his cock, but it's not going near my ass. Not yet anyway. He grinds into me, and I let out a breathy moan. "As much as I'd love to continue with your train of thought, we've slept in. If we're not at breakfast, you know Neva will kick down the door at Tammy's behest. While I'm not sure whether voyeurism is something I'll enjoy, that's not exactly how I'd like to find out."

When he groans at my words and rolls away from me, I can't help but laugh.

"Fine," he says, throwing back the covers. "But I'll need a cold shower."

I continue to laugh as he sulks across the room and closes the door to the bathroom. I stretch out in bed and take a deep breath, trying to steel myself against the sadness I can already feel trying to edge its way into my consciousness. Nothing can ever take away the memories I've made here or the knowledge that this sort of life exists. All I can do is try to work toward carving this kind of life out for myself somewhere down the line.

I get dressed while he showers and head to the main cottage with the Hellhounds at my feet. They've stayed in the cottage with us the entire time, but it hasn't been necessary. I've never not needed protection before, and it's been so freaking strange not having it be a requirement of survival.

The grass tickles the bottoms of my bare feet as I make my way across the large patch of land, and the smile never leaves my face.

"There's my girl," Tammy calls out as I reach the main cottage. She's in the kitchen with the back door open wide, and I can smell the food from here. My mouth starts to water already. When I reach the kitchen, she wraps me up in her arms, dusting me with the flour she's covered in, and kisses my cheek. "I'm really sad to see you guys go today."

"Me too, Tammy. Want to adopt me?" I grin, and she waves me off.

"If I thought I could get away with it, I'd bundle all of you up and run away with you." Theodore walks into the kitchen with Ares and Teddy just behind him.

Theodore embraces me in a big bear hug, the way he has every morning since we arrived here, before pulling back and clasping my arms. "There you are, my girl. Do you have a minute before breakfast? We should talk."

Caleb walks through the back door just as Theodore

finishes speaking. Theodore looks at him and says, "You too."

We follow him through the cottage to a small office he has on the other end of the building. I haven't been in here before, but when he opens the door, I decide I want to live in this room. It's not a big room; it's a small freaking library. Caleb chuckles when he notices just how distracted I am and places his hand on the bottom of my back to lead me to where the others are seated. Once the door is closed and everyone is sitting down around one of the tables, Theodore pulls out a huge, dusty tome of a book and opens it for all to see.

"I've been looking into your mark," he says looking at Caleb. "Ever since Ares explained to me what happened with your power, Morgan, and showed me the mark it placed upon Caleb, I've been poring over the old texts that my grandaddy hoarded like the creature of knowledge he was. The texts talk of one of great power who is coming, who will reshape the world. With the one of great power, there will be four who are gifted greatness, a bond between them and the one of power like the world has never seen." He pauses and looks over to me. I gulp, because he can't be going on about me, right?

"I mean that sounds very ominous, but it doesn't really explain too much," I say with a shrug.

"I know, but it does have a picture with five symbols.

They're all various patterns that I'm sure make up one image, though that isn't in this text. If you look at the patterns, you'll recognize the resemblance to the marking on Caleb's wrist." I look at the pattern he points to, and he's right. It does resemble it. But what's most disturbing to me, is that I recognize the middle pattern. I recognize it because it's on my inner thigh. I always just assumed it was a birthmark.

Shit.

I look at Caleb, and I shake my head subtly, but I know he's recognized it too.

"Do we know anything more about what this is all means?" I ask, looking back up at Theodore, and Ares frowns.

"No, not yet, but I intend to keep looking. The problem with old men who had knowledge is that they were cryptic about it because they didn't want other people knowing what they knew." Theodore sighs before sitting back in his chair.

Teddy stands and clasps my brother's shoulder. "Don't worry, we'll keep searching."

"Oh, I'm not worried about you guys, I'm worried about what this means for Morgan… and what could happen if my father found out about it." The frown on his forehead deepens, and I hate that our amazing stay is ending on such a downward note.

I stand, and Caleb follows suit. "Don't worry so much, big brother. It likely means nothing at all."

"So we're not actually stopping in Level Eight?"

Ares shakes his head, like I'm not just repeating the words he said seconds ago. "No, Level Eight is the smallest of the levels. While it technically has its own leader, it is mainly ruled by the Outliers, which is on the outskirts of the lands of Level Eight. The Outliers have always been separate. It used to be a prison of sorts, but when Airon arrived at the palace—one of the Shadowed just like Father—he was gifted his place here. He had plans of grandeur, and they were to father's liking, and so the Outliers as we know them today were born. It's a very closed community though, so access without permission, or without knowing someone here, is basically impossible."

"Good to know." Caleb nods, while I just try and take in the information. I know the whole point of this trip was to learn about the Realm, and while I have learned so much, some of it just makes absolutely zero sense to me. But then again, I've never claimed to understand my father's methods in anything.

"Morgan…" Ares pauses as if trying to find the right words. "There is another reason we will only be here one night, just as we were at The Carver's."

I shudder merely from the memory of being in The Carver's home but sit quietly waiting for Ares to continue speaking. "You will recognize Airon from Father's throne room. He is as close with Father as The Carver is. If not closer since they are both Shadowed. I've never had to stay here before because his allegiance with Father has always been so tightly wound. We're here purely because this is your first outing, but that means I can't know what to expect. So keep your guard up. Do not let Kaos out of your sight, and keep a decent distance from each other."

His warning is heard loud and clear, and I nod. "Got it."

I stare out of the carriage windows as we trail down the bleak road. There are black mountains in the distance, but before that, dark walls as high as those that surround the palace sit among the black sand that stretches as far as the eye can see.

It's as if nothing grows here, and I can't help but wonder what devastation this land saw to make it so bleak and lifeless, or if it is just a product of being watched over by one of the Shadowed.

Demons are created in many different ways. Like me, a Demon can be born. A Demon can be created from a human soul if it is dark enough. Or a Demon can be born of the shadows that create the Realm. They are called the

Shadowed because they even bleed black.

I've yet to meet one of the Shadowed that has any ounce of kindness in their heart. They're usually cruel, power hungry, and ruthless. Yet even if two Shadowed have never met before, their loyalty will be to each other beyond all else. It's the strangest thing. I don't claim to understand it; I just know a little about it from the tutors I had as a child. Since my father is one of them, my main tutor, Rainanne, thought it best I know as much about them as she could find. Unfortunately that wasn't very much.

But the little I do know makes me more than a little apprehensive about this visit. At least it's just one night again.

The carriage pulls to a stop at the walls, and then after a short pause, we start moving again. It isn't long before we pull to a stop in front of what I assume is Airon's house. It's a black offense to my eyes. I mean, really, what is with these Demons and wanting to create themselves in my father's image? It's so gross.

When we get there, I see the man who sold his son to my father, and my sneer is instant. Ares tuts at me, and I gather myself before following him from the carriage.

"Ares, there you are. I'm sorry to say that you'll be here without me tonight. I've been called away on business, but the staff are prepared to look after you as they would if I were here. I am sorry to miss officially meeting your sister, but I'm sure you both understand."

"Of course, Airon. If it suits you better, we could just head home?"

"No, no, it's fine," he utters, as if the question itself is an inconvenience. "My home is yours, and your sister will want to see this level as she has the others, I'm sure. Take your time. I'm sure I'll see you at the palace soon enough." He nods at Ares and whispers away without even looking at me. I mean I'm not sad about that, but it's still fucking rude.

"Well, that makes life a little easier," Ares says, pinching the bridge of his nose when a meek, dark-haired woman appears.

"If you'll follow me, I'll show you to your rooms." She keeps her gaze down, so I head to the carrier and release my hounds. They howl in a chorus, so loud it makes even Ares jump.

That can't be a good thing.

The woman practically starts to run back inside of the house, and I follow behind Ares and Caleb, with the pack surrounding me. This place is as grim inside as it is outside. Though considering that the man sold his son, I'm not sure why I expected anything different.

The woman scurries toward the staircase to our left and beckons us to follow her. "This way, please."

I didn't want to spend any more time in that house than necessary, and the others agreed, which is why we've been outside of the walls of the Outliers most of the afternoon, exploring the very few offerings Level Eight has. Ares disappeared a few hours ago with a warning not to let our guard down. Since then, Caleb and I have just been wandering in and out of the little stores and stalls this place has to offer.

There's more food than anything, and at this point, if I eat anything else I might be sick. I'm a girl who can eat, but when vendors discover who I am and push their wares in my face, I can't find it in me to turn them down, despite how full I already am. The hope on their faces as I enjoy their offerings has been enough to keep me chewing and smiling, but if anyone else offers me anything, I'm going to burst.

"Maybe we should sit?" Caleb offers as I groan again, rubbing my stomach in the most unprincess-like way imaginable.

"That might be a good idea." I follow him through the streets, as if he knows where he's going, but he, at least, has likely been paying attention to where we've been. I, however, was solely focused on the food.

So much food.

He leads me away from the small city, and we keep walking until we find a small lake with seating around it. How very quaint.

I drop onto the first bench I spot and let out a groan of relief once I do, while Caleb just chuckles and shakes his head at me. He sits beside me, keeping a decent distance because even here, it's not truly safe. We sit quietly, enjoying the silence and each other's presence. A flock of ravens flies over us, screeching as they head to the nesting of trees on the other side of the water. The sounds of life are like a balm, though it does make me wish to be back with the Duttons some more.

I close my eyes and lean back, taking deep breaths until my stomach feels less bloated. I startle at the feeling of Caleb jumping to his feet. "What the fuck?"

I open my eyes to find him standing partially in front of me. Before him stands the Angel I've seen a few too many times for this to be a coincidence.

"You!" I gasp, clambering to my feet. Her gaze bounces between us. "What do you want? Why are you here? Are you following me?"

"I…" she starts but then pauses and tilts her head. "I shouldn't have come. I'm sorry."

She looks torn, but she keeps looking between Caleb and I like we hold all of the answers to her problems. "If you ask your questions, we might be able to help."

"I'm not sure you can," she says, her lips tilting down at the sides. "I was just searching for some answers…"

This Angel is frustrating as hell. What is with the constant trailing off and not finishing her sentences?

"Well then, what are your questions?" I ask, my impatience growing. "And how did you get here? I didn't think Angels came to the Shadow Realm."

She turns to face me and smiles. Something about her feels familiar to me, like I should know her. But beyond the times I've spotted her here, I definitely don't recognize her. "They usually don't. I'm different, which is why I'm here."

Turning back to look at Caleb, she tilts her head, and her smile grows. "Do you know your parents?"

He looks back at me like he's asking me if he should answer her. Except I have no fucking clue. He turns back to her and shakes his head. "No, I'm an orphan. I don't have any family."

"That is where you are wrong." She steps toward him until there's only a few feet between them.

"How could you possibly know that?" I ask, crossing my arms. I don't like how close she stands to him or how familiar she seems with him. Am I a ragey, jealous beast? You bet your ass I am.

She grins at me and shakes her head a little. "You have no need to worry about me, princess. I'm not here to tread on any toes. I'm just here to discover the truth, though I think I've worked it out for myself." She turns back to Caleb, a serenity flowing from her like I've never experienced in my life. "Do you mind if I try something?"

"Er, sure?" Caleb says, rubbing the back of his neck, and I can feel his unease. This feels so weird, so I don't blame him.

She lifts her palm, and a small black ball of flame appears. "Is that Shadow Fire?"

She grins at me and nods. "Hold out your hand," she says to Caleb, and he does. My heart just about stops in my chest when she hands him the ball of flame before I have a chance to stop her.

Except, instead of burning before my eyes, the ball of flame transfers to his hand like it's his own. "I thought so."

"What the actual fuck?" he asks, his eyes wide as he looks back to me.

"I have no idea." I look back at the Angel, who is smiling so wide I can see her teeth. "How did you know that would work?"

She looks a little coy and apologetic before taking the flames back from Caleb and extinguishing them. And just when I thought our lives couldn't get any more complicated, she says, "I told you, I've been here looking for answers. I was pretty certain before I tried this anyway, but the Shadow Fire confirmed it. He is my brother."

FOURTEEN

This whole day has been just a total mindfuck. After her little revelation, the Angel said she had to leave, but that she'd be back, before disappearing in a flash of light.

We didn't even get her fucking name.

No, we got fuck all from that interaction except more secrets to carry. At the very least, I'm pretty sure this means that Caleb can either control my Shadow Fire or create his own. That's something to look at later because tomorrow we head back to the Shadow Palace, and that comes with a whole new set of dangers lurking around every corner.

Caleb hasn't said much since the Angel did her disappearing act, and I want to wring her bloody neck. Sister or not. One thing I do know is that no one can ever find out that he has an Angel for a sister. There are way too many conflicts within the Seven Realms, and the Angels tend to be on the other side of Demons… Being related to one in any way is just going to get him killed.

Though I have to say I didn't think it was possible for the species to mix. And does this make her half Demon, or him half Angel?

It's so fucked up that we didn't get the chance to ask any questions.

Which is exactly why I'm pacing the floor of the room I'm in for the night, waiting to be summoned for dinner. Staying in the house while Airon isn't even here is just weird. As much as I don't want to go home, I'd rather be home than here.

That's how fucking skeeved out I am by this place.

I literally would never rather be home.

Or you know, back with the Duttons'. Either way, I'd rather be anywhere but here. Even the pack is on edge—they haven't stopped pacing since I got back to the room. That could be because I'm a fucking mess, or it could be this place. Either way, something isn't right.

A knock at the door startles me from the never-ending loop of woe is me that I'm trapped in. I open the door and find Ares chewing his bottom lip. I haven't seen him do that since I was a kid. I thought mother beat that nervous habit out of him, the same way she stopped me from playing with my hair. Certain things were simply not done by a prince or princess.

"What's wrong?" I ask him, stepping back and letting him in the room.

"Where's Caleb?" he asks, looking around the room.

I shrug and close the door. "I'm not sure, I think he's in his room. It's been a day. He was going to get some rest before we ate."

He watches me closely, but the words slip from my tongue as if there's nothing else to the story. I'm pretty sure he knows me well enough to know when I'm withholding, but he also knows me well enough to know that I'd only withhold from him if it was needed. Plus, we can't exactly talk freely here. "I was just thinking about heading home tonight. I got a message from one of the levels that needs my attention, so I'd rather get you home so I can deal with it."

I sag in relief at his words. "That's fine by me." Going home comes with its own set of issues, but I'll deal with that once we're back. At least at home I'm not usually watched as much as I have been here.

"I've also spoken to a friend of mine in the King's guard, and he's someone I trust. He's prepared a bunk for Caleb and arranged the necessities so that he can slip into the ranks without any issues. Bryce will take care of him."

"Thank you." I smile sincerely at him. "Is the message anything you need help with?"

"No, I have it handled. I should also warn you, though, Father has been planning that stupid fucking ball in our absence. It's happening in three days." He pinches the bridge of his nose, so I guess he's looking forward to that about as much as I am. "I'll do what I can to help you, but Father…"

"Father is a sadistic asshole who wants to sell me to further his power. I know. I have a few ideas of just how I can dodge that bullet."

"I wouldn't hold your breath for dodging it, but I will do what I can," he tells me, and he looks sadder than I remember ever seeing him. What he seems to underestimate is my desire for freedom.

I haven't survived everything I have just to be Father's puppet.

Ares hugs me, and I startle because I wasn't expecting it. He pulls back as quickly as it started. "Get everything packed. I'll go tell Caleb that we're leaving."

"Is everything okay?" I ask, because I'm starting to suspect there is more going on than I'm aware of.

"Everything will be fine," he says as he leaves, and I frown. That was not the yes I'd been hoping for.

We arrive back at the palace late enough that we don't have

to see Father, and I head with Ares and Caleb to the guards' building, which I'm ashamed enough to say I've never been to. I had no idea that within the wall that surrounds the palace a whole other world exists. I thought it was just a wall.

It turns out this is where the guards and their families fucking live.

Ares sweeps us through, saying hello to some people and brushing past others. I try to catalogue as many faces as I can, but it's a lot busier here than I would've thought. Caleb seems way more at ease in here, and it hits me just how different we really are. The smell alone makes me want to die a little, but as we head further in, everything seems to scale up a little. I guess this is where the higher-ups stay.

"Wait here," Ares says before knocking on a door. When it opens, he grins wide at the tall dark-skinned man in front of him, but the shock on Caleb's face is what hits me.

Caleb blinks a few times before saying, "Bryce?"

"Holy shit! This is the guard you brought me, Ares?" Bryce lets out a quiet laugh before embracing my claimed.

What the fuck is going on here?

"How are you even here?" Caleb asks as the two of them separate. Bryce just laughs, still seemingly in shock and shakes his head.

"Maybe we should take this inside," Ares suggests, and Bryce nods.

"Yeah, you're right. Come on in." It's only then he seems to notice me standing here. He looks me over, seeming confused as to why I'm here, but doesn't say a word. The power inside of me stirs at his presence, but I lock everything down.

My power going haywire out here is so not on the agenda for today.

Once I'm in the space, I realize this is an office, and the bars on the guy's jacket means that he's not just a guard. He's a Captain. Not a bad friend for Ares to have... or Caleb either, it would seem.

"So you guys know each other?" Ares asks as he takes a seat, but I stay standing toward the back of the room. Bryce glances over at me, seeming wary.

"You don't need to worry about Morgan," Caleb tells him as he sits next to Ares while Bryce sits on the other side of the desk.

"I'll assess that for myself," the Captain says, and I roll my eyes.

"Captain, you can assess what you like, but if you think I'm leaving here before I know exactly who the fuck you are, you can think again." I cross my arms and stare at him until he smirks.

"Well, who knew the ice princess was really made of

fire?"

Ares and Caleb both laugh softly, but I don't say a thing. The guy seems like a bit of a jerk, but if Caleb and Ares both trust him, I'll withhold my own judgments for now.

"As for your question, Caleb and I grew up together. If it wasn't for him, I wouldn't have lived long enough to be dragged away to the guard."

"Man, I thought you were dead," Caleb says, scrubbing a hand down his face. "I haven't heard from you in, what, seventy years?"

"It's been about that." Bryce nods. "I never was as good as you at hiding my power when the King's recruiters came knocking. I tried to get word out to you, but by the time I was in a position to, I couldn't find a trace of you."

It hits me that he must be one of the people Caleb told me about. The kids from the group home who were sold or kidnapped. The ones he thought he failed. I look Bryce over again, and I soften toward him a little, but I still don't trust him. My power reacted to him for some reason, and until I find out why, I'm going to play my cards somewhat close to my chest.

Or at least as close as I can considering Ares and Caleb are blurting out our dirty little secrets right now. Nothing like someone I don't know knowing all about my life.

"Maybe before we tell him everything, we can just get

settled in," I say, interrupting them. I'm sure I sound like a spoiled bitch, but also, I don't know this guy.

"Mor…" Caleb starts but I shake my head.

"I get it, you know this guy, or at least you did. Ares seems to trust him for whatever reason, but I don't know him. You don't know what's happened with him in the past, what did you say, seventy years? That's a good amount of time. I'd rather not let him know all of my secrets before I get to know him myself."

"She's right," Bryce says, shocking me to my core, but I'm not going to let it show. "She doesn't know me from fucking Bill down the way. It'd be remiss of someone who's seen as much as she has just to trust me off the bat. I know enough for now, Caleb has a place here that is safe and secure, and as far as the rest of the boys know, he was a private hire as security for the princess, which he'll continue with. Anything else, I can learn as I need to."

"Thank you, Captain." I nod at him, and he returns it. Even if I don't trust him, I respect that he honored my choices. And I'm going to ream Ares and Caleb out for not consulting me with what the fuck they were going to tell him too, but that's for later in private. "If that's all, I'll be getting back to my room. Caleb, I will see you tomorrow."

Ares stands at my words, smiling apologetically to the other two for my bitchiness. He knows better than anyone how I feel about people I don't know knowing my shit. He's the one who's drummed it into me for the last however long that it needs to be that way. Just because he's cozy here doesn't mean shit gets to slip. "I'll walk you back. Captain, Caleb, I'll see you both in a few days. I have a quick trip to make once my sister is settled."

Caleb smiles at me sadly, like he realizes he fucked up in his excitement, so I give him a tight smile back before walking out of the door Ares holds open for me.

I have a feeling the next few days are going to test us all.

With Ares gone until the Ball and Caleb training with Bryce to keep up appearances, I've been a little lonely. Especially since Amelia has been back with her dad, catching up, as she was gone for weeks without him. I know she was with us, but I didn't exactly get to hang out with her much while we were gone either. It might have only been two days since we got home but still… It's lonely.

Which is why I'm having a woe is me moment like a princess locked in a tower.

I already know that my tailor will be coming along soon to do a fitting with me, and to pick out colors for my dress tomorrow—it all seems a little pointless since my sizing hasn't changed in decades, and we all know that black is my go-to color. I am not a bright and shiny colors kind of girl. In that way, I am truly not my mother's daughter. It's probably why I like to stick to black as much as I do. My mother would beat me in all of her finery, and so the bright reds and yellows lost their shine to me.

I flop down on my bed and stare at the ceiling. The hounds are back out in the stables because, at the palace, it's deemed unnecessary to have them in my room at all times, which pisses me off. I'm about as safe in here as I was with The Carver, but my father and I see some things very differently.

A knock pulls me from my misery, and I look up to see Amelia in my doorway rather than the tailor I expected. "You feeling sorry for yourself all locked up in your ebony tower?"

I can't help but grin at the sarcasm dripping from her words and climb from the bed to hug her. She hugs me right back and just like that, I relax. I swear between The Carver, Airon, that fucking Angel, and the Captain, my nerves are fucking fried.

"Something like that. How has time with your dad been?" I ask as we sit in the chairs at the far side of my room.

"It's been nice being home, but I forgot how suffocating he can be. He doesn't even know I'm here."

"He's still not totally cool with us being friends?" I

sigh and slump in my chair. This isn't anything new. Her dad knows just how much danger being my friend puts her in, but she just tends to dismiss it. It's why I was so hesitant about caring for her when we were younger, but she wormed her way into my heart, and the rest is history.

"Something like that. I mean, he likes that you can protect me, like you did by taking me with you. But he still thinks I'll be hurt to get to you or some shit. He's lost a lot, so I get that he's wary, but also, I really wish he'd recognize that I'm a grown-ass woman. My life is my own to make mistakes with as I see fit. Not that our friendship is a mistake, but you know what I mean." She blushes so hard her skin is almost purple, and I can't help but laugh.

"Yeah, I know what you mean." I wave her off, and her blush dies down a little. Another knock at the door sounds, and she scurries to open it, just as she would if she were my lady in waiting. It's usually our cover for her being with me so often just in case anyone should be watching me too closely.

This time, my visitor is the tailor. A stern rail of a woman. Her hair is pulled back into a bun so tight I think she might actually be getting a face lift from it. She has a tape measure around her neck and frowns as she enters the room. I swear, she might be the tailor, but this bitch always looks down her nose at me.

"Please, come in," Amelia says, waving the woman

into the room as I sigh and stand.

The tailor enters with her apprentice who is weighed down with bolts of fabric and the platform that I'll have to stand on to have the materials measured out properly. Amelia moves to help the girl, and I hate that I just have to stand and watch them struggle.

Princesses don't help the help.

Another rule on my mother's list. So fucking stupid.

Decent people should help those struggling around them. It's not that hard. Who actually gives a fuck about someone's station? It won't hurt me to carry a bolt of fabric, but I get the feeling that if I tried to help, the girl would be punished for it. So I stay where I am and feel like shit instead.

I wait as they prepare the room, and once it's finished, Amelia waves before scurrying out the door. I don't blame her. I'd run away if I could too.

"Up you get," the tailor instructs, so I do as expected and just stand, watching them struggle, waiting to be poked and prodded by her. "Are we going with a different color this time?"

"Why would I do that?" Disdain drips from my words, and she rolls her eyes at me, but I pretend not to see it.

"Well then, I guess we had better do something else to make you stand out in the crowd then."

As if I've ever had a problem with that.

FIFTEEN

Kill me.

Please just fucking kill me. I've spent the whole day being poked and prodded and burned while my entire body has been exfoliated, my hair styled, and my mask painted on. I'm fucking sick of all the preparation for the ball, and I'm not even dressed yet.

I'm just sitting on my bed in my fucking underwear waiting for the tailor's assistant to bring it by. I'm not sure what I hate more, that I have to dress up like a fucking doll for my father, or the fact that I've still not fucking seen Caleb since we got back to the palace.

How the fuck are we meant to say he's my personal protection when he's nowhere even near me? Ares hasn't even been around for me to complain to, and I swear, if his ass isn't back in time for this stupid night, I'm throwing my goddamn tiara and saying fuck it all.

I hate how much I'm living up to my spoiled princess persona right now, but my frustration is real. A girl gets used to certain things, and orgasms are something I got used to real quick. So yes, I'm pissy I haven't seen Caleb, and not just because of his magical penis. Being in this place is like a living nightmare and being around him makes everything better.

Our relationship hasn't exactly been conventional, but I know I love him, so being separated from him and having to live in secret… It just fucking sucks.

"You look like you got slapped in the face with a fish," Amelia teases as she slips into my room. "Anyone would think you were prepping to be hung, not to go to a party."

"Being hung might be more fun than this party." I sigh dramatically as she bounces onto the bed.

"Oh, I don't know about that. I've seen the ballroom, and it looks like something out of one of your books. It's beautiful. And as for the people starting to arrive, I have to say, I wouldn't mind falling into some of their arms." She wags her eyebrows at me, and I burst out laughing. Thank all the Gods and the hells for her.

We talk about basic bullshit to pass the time until the tailor's apprentice delivers my dress. "Do you need any assistance dressing?"

"No, you're fine. I have Amelia," I tell her with a smile. "Thank you."

The girl blushes furiously, and after tripping over her goodbyes, she practically runs from the room.

"Let's see what magic they've spun, shall we?" Amelia skips across the room and hangs the dress bag from one of the rails along the top of my bed, and she gasps as she opens it. She pulls the bag off and steps back, and I let out a gasp myself.

"Holy shit. They really outdid themselves." The black material looks like a night sky. There's just enough shimmer to it to catch eyes without making me feel like a fucking spectacle. It has long sleeves and a high neck and what looks like a floor length cape coming from the shoulders. It's utterly stunning. I guess this is why my hair is pinned up rather than cascading down my back like usual. I'd want to show this dress off too. "Help me get it on?"

"Of course," Amelia says, taking it off the hanger. "But you're going to need to ditch the corset. I don't know what it is with this tailor and your back, but there's no back on here. Just the cape."

Of course there isn't, the tailor knows my style, but I keep that little snippet to myself. She might not like me very much, but she also wouldn't purposely piss me off too badly either. I unclip the corset I pried myself into earlier, thankful that I can breathe again, and Amelia helps me maneuver into the dress without fucking up my hair.

The material is so fucking soft, and it fits like a second skin. This might be my favorite dress yet. At least if I'm going to have to parade myself around tonight, I'm going to feel good while doing it.

"Damn, princess." I look up in the mirror to see Caleb standing in the doorway.

"And on that note, I'm going to go. Have fun tonight... well, as much as you can," Amelia says before dashing out of the door, giggling.

"You like?" I ask as he takes a step toward me before halting.

"Oh, I definitely like… I like it so much I'm going to keep my distance, otherwise our secret is going to be fucking blown." His voice is scratchy as he reaches down and readjusts his dick in his pants. He has on the same tunic and pants he wore for the party at Brandy's, and he looks no less delicious now than he did then.

I smile at him before purring, "It might be worth blowing." I wink and he groans, looking up to the ceiling. I chuckle softly. "Okay, I guess we should get going. This night is going to be long enough."

"This night is going to be fucking torture. If any of them touch you, I'm going to be dead because I'll likely lose my shit. But if we survive this night, then tonight I'm going to show you just how good that dress looks on the floor."

Amelia was right, the ballroom is beautiful. It's decorated in silvers and blues. My father's usual taste is beyond gaudy, so it's obvious that someone else must have overseen this because it's almost tasteful. There are standing tables dotted around the edge of the space with the main portion of the room taken up by a dance floor, with a bar on each of the walls that doesn't contain the staircase.

For that much, I'm thankful because nectar is going to be necessary to get through this night.

"Are you ready?" Ares asks, making me jump from where I'm peeking around the door to the entrance of the ball room.

I turn to face him and smile. "You look good, brother."

"You don't clean up too bad yourself." He grins.

"Enjoy your trip?"

"Not exactly, but stop changing the subject. If I don't get you in there soon, Father is going to lose his shit," he says, nodding toward my father at the back of the room, throwing back more nectar than any Demon should drink.

He's going to be a fucking nightmare.

"Let's do this then, shall we?" Ares offers me his arm,

which I loop my hand through before dropping my ice princess mask into place. Caleb follows us at a respectable distance as we enter the room. As we descend the stairs, everyone turns to look at us. The whispers start up as they always do, and I'm thankful to see some familiar faces in the room among the sea of unknowns.

I remember playing in this room as a child. I liked playing hide and seek with Ares behind the heavy drapes that used to hang from the rafters.

What simpler times they were.

Once we reach the floor, Caleb moves to the edges of the room, but I can feel his heated gaze on me as we work through the room toward my father. "Don't leave my side," Ares murmurs as we get closer, and I nod subtly.

"About fucking time," my father huffs quietly once we reach him. "Ares, you know who I want her introduced to. Make sure it fucking happens."

He grabs my arm and pulls me away from Ares, who looks about as happy as I feel. "As for you, girl, you should know better than to think you can keep secrets from me. You best be on your best behavior tonight, or that maid you've befriended will pay the price. Am I clear?"

I swallow down my burning rage and nod once. He squeezes my arm tighter, and I'm glad the sleeves on my dress are full length, because I know I'm going to have bruises. He doesn't say another word before he struts off to stand with The Carver and Airon, who both smile at me in the creepiest way.

A drop of icy dread works its way down my spine, and I shudder at the thought of what price Amelia could pay if I fuck this up. Ares looks at me, studying me closely once I get back to him. “What was that about?”

“Just a not so subtle threat to Amelia’s well being if he isn’t pleased with my performance tonight.” My rage spikes again from just saying the words, and he clenches his jaw. I take a few deep breaths to try and push it all down and place my hand on his extended forearm. “Now come on, brother, let’s go find my suitors, shall we? Where do we start?”

“There are a lot of higher Demons here tonight that want to meet you, but Father wants you to meet with all the Princes of the other Realms we have here tonight. Prince Xavi Allaire is the Crown Prince of the Bronze city in Eteryia from the Fae Realm of Avaenór. With him is his good friend, the Crown Prince of the Glass City—Killian Chastain. He is a hybrid, part Fae, part Demon. Do not stare at him.” He pauses, and I can’t help but wonder why he’s offered forewarning, but I bear it in mind. “We have Prince Malik Favreau of Kavaraí—the Realm of the Dead. Prince Titus Laurier of Einar—the Realm of the Merfolk. Then lastly the Elven Prince of Silvius, Prince Callisto Desai.”

"Please don't expect me to remember their names just from that." I sigh, and he laughs softly.

"I won't, don't worry."

"No one from Avalon or the Mortal Realm?" I ask, more curious considering our Angel visitor.

Ares shakes his head and takes two glasses of nectar from a passing server. "To say things are tense with those Realms currently is an understatement. Michael, the leader of Avalon… let's say there have been issues there, and the Mortal Realm doesn't have just one leader. Father sees them as no better than cattle. He wouldn't lower himself to invite them here."

I shrug, feigning indifference, but I have to say, I am intrigued about the apparent conflicts with Avalon. I had no idea that there were issues. I really have been far too sheltered. "So where do we start?"

"You pick," he says, his eyes sparkling with laughter, and I want to stick my tongue out at him.

"Well then," I say, glancing around the room like I have a fucking clue who anyone is. All I want to do is go and say hello to Brandy and the Duttons', but no. "Let's start with the Fae, shall we?"

"If you insist, but please, if you have any love in your heart for me, do not thank them for a fucking thing."

I blink at him, wondering what the fuck that's about, but nod. "Whatever you say. Lead the way."

We glide across the room, a few people stopping us to say hello, but eventually we make our way over to two men who couldn't look more different if they tried. One is tall, with golden skin and dark hair and eyes, the other is pale, with long white silver hair and piercing blue eyes. That's when I notice the pointed ears, and I figure this must be Killian. Until I notice they both have them, and then Ares' words make zero sense to me.

"Ares, how wonderful to see you again." The dark-haired one smiles at my brother, before glancing over at me quickly. He has kind eyes, and doesn't look at me like a piece of meat, so he's earning points already. "You remember Killian?"

"I do. It's good to see you both. I'd like to introduce my sister, Morganna. Morgan, let me introduce Princes Xavi and Killian."

Xavi takes my hand and kisses it, his charming smile makes me feel at ease, but something about him screams player. "It's a pleasure."

"I'm sure the pleasure is all mine," I respond, my voice sickly sweet as my power reacts, though I'm not sure which one of them it's reacting to. Either way, I stomp it down and lock it up tight.

Not today.

Xavi laughs and glances at Ares. "She's nothing at all like you've described."

"That is because Father is here," Ares tells them both, and Xavi's smile widens.

"Ah, I see." His eyes dance with laughter, and he nudges Killian. "She is beautiful though, no?"

"That she is." Killian's voice is like silk against my skin, and I swear I shudder just at the sound.

"Such a shame that the Fae have fated mates," Xavi adds, but I don't let my smile drop. Dammit, I just know the other guys here aren't going to be as nice as these two. Of course they're not in the race. While I don't intend to sell myself for my father, if I can secure a partnership that gives safe passage to Caleb and I, it might be worth it. Either one of these would've been open to that, I can just sense it.

"Fated mates?" I ask, playing the part that is expected.

"Yes, each Fae is fated to another. We have no real say in it, but when you meet, there's almost no way to deny the bond. Because the pull is so strong, there have only been very rare occasions when a mate has been rejected," Xavi explains. "Though Killian is an anomaly, so who knows what will happen with him."

Killian winces at the comment, but Ares steers the conversation to other things. After a few enjoyable minutes, soft music starts to play.

Killian turns to me while Ares and Xavi talk and asks, "Would you like to dance?"

"Of course." I smile and take his outstretched hand. He's very tall, and very pretty to look at. He has a jaw sharp enough to cut glass and eyes that show just how broken he is underneath the shiny exterior. But he's not Caleb. I place my hands on his shoulders and sway with him to the slow music with his arms around my waist.

"You are very quiet for a princess," he comments, and I shake my head. Ares trusts him, so I let my guard down a little.

"I am not like most other girls, and I am certainly not like people think I am."

He smiles a little, and it changes his entire face. He seems softer somehow. "Of that, I have no doubt."

Taking one of my hands, he spins me out before pulling me back and then twirls me around the dance floor. "But you can certainly dance like a prince."

"Are you kidding? My mother would have my hide if I did not show a lady a good time on the dance floor."

"Is she here?" I ask, looking at the faces around the room as we move. I can't see anyone else who looks like him in attendance.

"No, my parents do not bother themselves with the other Realms so much. I am only here for Xavi."

The song comes to an end and Killian pulls back from me, bowing and placing a soft kiss on my hand. "Thank you for the pleasure."

I nod, remembering Ares' warning and don't thank him back. "The pleasure was all mine."

He turns and leaves, heading back toward Xavi, and I catch Caleb's stare as he goes. I try to convey everything I want to say with a simple look, because I know there's no reason for me to speak to him if I'm not in danger.

"There you are," Ares says, as he tucks my hand in the crook of his arm again. "Let's continue the introductions, shall we?"

The night has been a sea of faces and dancing. The Elven and Mer Princes were not as nice as the Fae ones, but I fully understand why my father would like them. They both seemed to have a cruel streak, a darkness in them that made me want to fully run away.

We have only one Prince left to entertain, the Prince of the Dead. Malik.

He sounds like a bucket of fun.

I don't know much about Kavaraí except that it is the place where Demon souls go once they decide not to regenerate. It is an afterlife Realm of sorts, a little like the Shadow Realm and Avalon are for the mortals.

"Malik is… well he's not to everyone's tastes," Ares warns, giving me a breakdown the way he has with the others.

"Shocker there, Prince of the Dead isn't a charming ball of sunshine and joy." Sarcasm drips from my words as Ares tries not to spit out his drink.

"Well yes, I guess it's not that much of a shock. His people have had some hard times, and he has seen more than his fair share of loss. Just bear that in mind."

I nod and finish my own drink. "Noted. Now let's get this over with, shall we. My feet are fucking dying in these shoes, and I'd really rather be curled up in bed than at this meat market. If it wasn't for Amelia, I'd have left already."

He grimaces but finishes his drink and walks me across the room to who I'm assuming are the royals of Kavaraí.

"Pardon me for interrupting. Your highnesses, please allow me to introduce my sister, Morganna Voux. Morganna, please meet the King and Queen of Kavaraí and their son, Prince Malik."

I smile and shake the king and queen's hands, but the prince looks at me with such disdain and hatred I'd rather cut my hand off than fucking touch him. My power reacts to the visceral emotions, but once again I shut it down. I'm not sure what Shadow Fire would do to a Demon not of this Realm, but I'm still not exactly ready to let that little secret out.

"You can move on now. We're not interested," Malik sneers, his words dripping with contempt.

"Malik, where are your manners," his mother scolds before looking at Ares apologetically. Apparently I don't deserve the apology.

"If you wanted manners, Mother, you should have brought Nasí with you instead of me."

The King drags his son away from us, his rage obvious in the tightness of his grip.

"Please forgive my son, he has had a few trying years," the queen apologizes, again to Ares, who waves her off.

"There is nothing to forgive. But if you'll please excuse us, we have many other introductions to make." The queen smiles at Ares and pats his cheek before turning to find her son and husband while Ares pulls me in the opposite direction.

Once we reach the bar and I have a drink in hand, I lean against the wall. "That could have gone better."

"It could have gone worse. Overall, you did your part, so Father can't hold that over you."

I take a sip of the sweet drink and wince. I don't think I'll ever get used to nectar. "Well let's hope not. The thought of my friend being gifted to The Carver because I fucked up… I'd probably burn us both up with my fire instead and be done with it."

Ares looks at me with sad eyes, because he knows I mean it too. "Let's get you out of here, shall we? You've done as Father asked. I can make excuses for the rest."

"Thank you," I say, slipping under his arm as he signals to Caleb. "For everything. I know you didn't have to stay with me all night."

"I'd never leave you to these monsters alone. Even if it seems like I'm going astray, just know that I'm always on your team."

I smile up at him before composing myself and taking his arm as expected. "Always."

He leads me from the shark tank that is our ballroom to the safety of my room, leaving me with Caleb before heading back down to the party.

"Watching you tonight was torture," Caleb groans as he runs his hands over the bare flesh of my back.

"Everything about tonight was torture," I whisper against his lips before kissing him. "Now make me forget."

SIXTEEN

It's been six weeks since the ball.

Six weeks of fucking bliss. My father has spent a lot of time away, which means I've spent most of my time with Caleb. I've come to know more of the guard, including the Captain, but I'm still not sure how much I can trust him. I'm pretty sure he knows that Caleb and I are together, though I doubt he knows the full truth of it. He probably assumes it's simply a dalliance of the spoiled princess, slumming it with a Low Born.

But if he does, then fuck him.

We know the truth of it, and that's what counts. We've both spent a lot of time training. With all of his extra training and workouts with the guards, the muscles Caleb already had are growing larger and more defined.

It's enough to make a grown woman drool. And drool I do.

It almost felt like our time on the road… a time that I've missed dearly.

Except today my father is home, and according to Ares, he's bringing guests. We're expected at dinner, and the happiness I've felt is slowly slipping through my fingers.

Ever since Ares told me about father returning with guests, dread has wrapped itself around my heart. I don't know where Father has been, but I'm pretty sure he's been working out who best to sell me to. I know Ares has been trying to work things out behind the scenes, but even he hasn't been able to get any straight answers.

Which is why I'm currently dressed up like a fucking doll again, barely able to breathe in this corset, and waiting on Ares to collect me. Because of course it wouldn't be proper for me to arrive without an escort.

This is all so fucked up.

These archaic practices drive me insane. For now, I can do nothing but grin and bear it.

I stand once I hear the knock on my door and find a forlorn Ares waiting for me. "Is it bad?"

"I don't know yet. I've tried to work out a deal with Xavi. I'm fairly certain Father wouldn't have been able to deny that request."

"With the Fae? Ares, what did you do?"

"It doesn't matter. Getting you away from here, somewhere you'll be safe, is all that matters. Finding somewhere *all* of you will be safe is my highest priority. It's only until I come into power, of course. I'm hoping that isn't too far away, but this way, you will all be safe until then."

"Caleb?"

"Yes, he and Amelia will be with you."

"Ares…" I'm speechless. My brother's love really knows no bounds. "Does Caleb know?"

"He does. I briefed him so he doesn't lose his shit at dinner. Now then, look as miserable as you can. We both know Father will prefer it."

He walks me down to the formal dining room in silence, and it takes all of the restraint I have to keep my face straight when we enter the room. Caleb glances at me from his post at the side of the room, but I don't dare pay attention to him with everyone else that is in here.

Each of the princes who were in attendance at the ball are sitting around the table, some with parents, others without, but I don't feel great about any of it. The two Fae smile at me, and I'm grateful that Killian is in the seat beside mine, but a glance at the others gives me nothing but sneers and glares.

The most hateful one coming from the Prince of the Dead himself. How fucking delightful that he's here and sitting opposite me, between his parents no less.

Awesome.

Ares leads me to my seat, pulling it out for me before sitting himself. My father glares at me before turning to Ares. "I'm glad that you could both finally make it."

"Apologies, my business kept me a little later than I intended." Ares' words seem to soothe my father, who is all smiles once he turns back to our guests.

"Thank you all so much for joining us on this delightful occasion. We have much to discuss, but first, let's eat!" He claps his hands, and the servers bring out the first course. I keep my mouth shut and just eat what's put in front of me. The food tastes like ash in my mouth.

Of course my father is dragging this out. I can only hope that Ares' deal won out. At least with the Fae I could be happy. They would have their fated, and I could have Caleb. It's a win-win situation. Kind of. As much of a win as being sold for power can be.

It's a shitty situation, but that would be the best outcome of all on offer.

I lose track of time and the food that's put in front of me. No one bothers to speak to me, so I keep my head down and wait for the axe above my head to fall.

Please let us win... just this once.

Once the food has been cleared and my father has drunk more than his share of nectar, he taps a fork against his glass, quieting the others in the room, and stands.

"Thank you all again for joining us here. I would like to thank each and every one of you for your proposals, offers, and kind wishes. As you each know, I have spent time with each family that wished to compete for my daughter's hand in marriage, to secure a strong tie between your Realm and that of the Shadow Realm."

He pauses, and I think I'm going to be fucking sick. He can't possibly expect me to just go along with this. Even if Ares has arranged a safe place for me, my father couldn't possibly know that. This is fucking ridiculous.

What if he didn't take the Fae's offer?

Oh hells. My stomach rolls again, and I clench my fists in my lap. Caleb is standing behind me, as any personal guard should, but I can feel the heat of his gaze on my back. I'd give anything to go back to Level One and then just run the fuck away with him.

I always suspected this day would come, but I thought I might have even a little say in it. And that say would be absofuckinglutely not. I am not a chess piece to be pawned away to the king's advantage.

Killian squeezes my hand under the table, and I let out a deep breath, hoping beyond all hope that just this once, things go my way.

"As much as I would like to accept all of the offers put forward, unfortunately I only have one daughter, and though I'm sure she wouldn't mind, I'm sure the rest of you wouldn't exactly like to share such a meek morsel."

I feel Ares go rigid beside me, but there's nothing I can do right now. Except to burn my father away to nothing. Though with this many witnesses in attendance, that probably wouldn't go too well for me. I'd likely be thrown in a prison cell even if my brother fought against it.

Long live the king, right?

My fucking ass.

"With all of that said, there obviously can only be one match made. Prince Titus and Prince Callisto. Your offers were found the most lacking, so yours are the first I will refuse. I do appreciate your attendance, and I am sure we will do business again." My father waves his hand before the princes have a chance to air their grievances and they, plus their guests, disappear from the table in a whisper. I'm hoping it's back to their Realms and not to our cells.

War probably isn't on my father's radar right now.

Maybe.

At least those two are gone, and this leaves me with a fifty-fifty chance of things going my way. Ares gives me a small smile and hope starts to bloom in my chest.

This might go our way for once.

Please let this go our way.

"The last two offers on the table were both very tempting, and I must admit, it was hard to pick between them. I almost wish I had another child, except I need one as heir." My father chuckles and sits back in his chair with a thud.

I think I might actually be sick. Nerves and excitement clash inside of me like a fucking hurricane mixing with rain. I'm a mess. If my fists weren't clenched, I'd be shaking like a leaf. I am not cut out for this sort of bullshit.

"But it is with a heavy heart that I must refuse you, Prince Xavi. While tempting, the offer from the Favreaus was too much to decline. Maybe we can work together again soon." Killian squeezes my leg once more before my father waves his hand, and they disappear too. Ares shakes beside me, his rage coming from him in waves, and I dare not look back at Caleb.

"Which means that Prince Malik, you will be marrying my daughter." Malik looks like he'd rather stab me through the heart than accept my father's words, but his parents are fawning over my father like he's the second coming of the Gods.

If they ever truly existed. With the way my life has gone up to this point, I really do question any idea of a higher power.

My heart sinks as my fate sets in, and the Favreaus disappear with their son, leaving me at the table with my brother and father.

"Clear the room," my father booms, and each of the guards slips from the room. I catch sight of Caleb as he leaves, his eyes pure black before he glances away. This couldn't have gone any fucking worse.

My father chuckles in his seat and looks at my brother. "You made their offering too sweet. I knew you were behind the Fae offer, boy. Anything to save your pathetic and weak sister. You're too soft, but once she's gone, I'll change that for good. You almost had me fooled that you were the man I wanted you to be, and then you wasted all those years of servitude with this."

"You cannot do this!" I scream, pushing back my chair to stand. "You cannot make me do this."

"Sit down, you stupid little girl. I can, and I will. You both might have thought you had friends out in the Realm, but my friends are much better hidden. You think I don't know of your little lover?" he says to me before turning to Ares. "Or yours? Pathetic the pair of you. If anything happens to stop this marriage, this deal… Well, there are fates worse than death for the ones you love."

He stands and leaves the room as a tear slips down my cheek.

"I am so sorry, Morgan. I really thought I had bested him." Ares looks defeated, and my heart breaks a little more.

"It is not your fault that he is a monster, Ares."

"I will find a way to save Caleb and Amelia… even if I couldn't save you." His head droops, and I can't help but wonder about the lover my father mentioned him having. Now is not the time, so all I say is a 'thank you' before I leave the room.

They say misery loves company. But not today.

"He can't fucking do this, Mor!" Caleb rages, and I wince as another vase smashes against the wall. I knew this was going to go down about as well as it is. We knew it was coming, Ares warned us, but I guess knowing something and it becoming our reality are two different things.

"It's not like this is something I want," I tell him softly. "But I have no choice."

"You don't even fucking like each other."

"I know. This isn't an arranged marriage for love. It's for power. I hate it, but I can't stop it either."

"We could kill your father," Caleb hisses, and I shake my head.

I move over to him and wrap my arms around his waist. "As much as I wish it were that easy, killing him would just mean our deaths at this point too. I'm not willing to lose you."

"Then just tell him no, Mor. I can't lose you. I won't."

I haven't told him about my father's threats. I won't. I don't want him to feel any kind of responsibility for this. We were foolish to think we could keep this thing between us hidden from him. The palace has too many eyes and ears. But I won't let my father hurt him. No matter what it costs me.

"You will never lose me, never," I tell him vehemently.

He wraps me in his arms and holds me tight. His hands grab my ass, and I gasp as he lifts me, before devouring my lips with his. I clasp on to his hair as he grinds his dick against me, and I can't help the moan that escapes my lips.

"Mine," he growls, and I nod.

"Yours."

"Wrap your legs around me," he instructs, and I do. Once I'm secure, he pulls my dress up and off of me in one go, leaving me in just my purple bra and panties. He groans when he sees them, and I wrap my arms around his neck again.

He moves us around so my back is pressed against the wall. "This first time won't be soft and gentle, but I'll make up for that later."

I suck in a breath at his words and acknowledge them with a nod.

"Words, Mor."

"Yes, okay. More than okay." I'm breathless already,

and then he undoes his pants, his cock springing from the gap, as he has nothing on beneath. I hear the tear as I feel him rip away my panties, but before I have a chance to protest, his lips are on mine and he thrusts into me in one go.

"Fuck!" Caleb throws his head back, releasing a roar colored with anguish and devastation that echoes throughout the room and likely the entire Realm too. I bristle at the sound. Not because I'm afraid, but because his pain is written all over his features and in the strain of his muscles.

I hate this, I hate what it's doing to him, but my life has never been simple.

It's when he lowers his head back and pins me with his Demon's gaze that I measure the extent of his anger. He's never been this way, this raw and feral, and as he rears back his hips and slams into me, I know this fuck will be anything but loving.

He's claiming me. Marking me. Making sure I'm aware of just who I belong to. I might usually complain, but since he is mine, I have zero issues.

Gasping with every rough thrust into my pussy, I hold on for dear life as my back bangs into the wall every few seconds, accompanied by one word: "Mine." Over and over again.

His growls grow in volume until he roars, "You. Are.

Fucking. Mine."

"Yes, Caleb. I'm yours, all yours. Always."

With a grunt, he snakes his hand into my hair at the nape of my neck and pulls back, hard, tilting my head back just enough so he can claim my lips as well.

He's fucking my mouth, fucking my pussy, and making sure I'm going to feel this for more than a few hours.

I bury both my hands into his hair and curl my fingers around his silky locks, digging my nails into his scalp and whispering, "You can fuck me into this wall all you want but, Caleb?" I bite his lip to make sure he hears my next words through the haze of his rage. "There is nothing in the Seven Realms that could take me away from you."

My words get through to him, and I can see the haze lifting, but it doesn't make him slow the claiming.

"Prove it." Confused, I blink up at him as he brings one hand to my clit and flicks it just so. "Come for me."

With one, two, three thrusts that will probably bruise later on, I explode in his arms and practically see stars.

He pulls me from the wall, his cock still inside of me and walks over to the bed. He slips from me, before placing my feet on the ground. "Turn around and bend over."

I do as he asks, and he slaps my ass. I yelp in surprise, but the sting of it just adds to the haze of pleasure I'm already experiencing.

I feel him slide his dick between my ass cheeks, putting

pressure on my asshole before sliding down until he thrusts into my pussy again. He leans forward, and I try to keep my arms locked and take his weight as he ruins me.

"You're not going to forget how my dick feels in your pussy, princess. You're not going to forget one fucking thing about me, and I'm not letting you go." He wraps his hand in my long hair and yanks it backward, arching my back. He grips my hip with his other hand hard enough that I know he's going to leave bruises, but the mix of pain and pleasure does things to me that I never thought I'd feel.

He pounds into me, his hand moving from my hair to tweak my nipples, and I cry out. It feels so fucking good, and he's right, I'm definitely not going to forget this. Wrapping his hand around my throat he pulls me upright, his other arm wrapping around my waist, his cock not missing a fucking beat. He grips my throat harder before whispering, "Come for me again, Mor."

He bites down on my shoulder and my orgasm rips through me harder than ever before. He follows me over the cliff with a roar of his own. We collapse onto the bed, and he stays on top of me. It's only then I feel the trickle of warmth by my neck. I reach up and see red on my fingertips.

"I'm not even sorry." He grunts before pulling out of me and moving to my bathroom. He brings back a washcloth and cleans me up, before licking at the wound on my shoulder. "Now you have a mark of mine too."

He pulls me up into his arms so I'm lying on the bed, draped over his naked body as he runs his fingers through my hair. We're silent, each thinking of what lies ahead for us.

"We'll figure out a way, we'll negotiate."

He doesn't answer, he just keeps running his fingers through my hair methodically.

"I love you, Caleb, that never changes. Ever."

Fisting my hair and pulling my head up so he can look at me, he lifts himself up and crashes his mouth against mine, a kiss full of promises.

I don't know what he's thinking, but it's worrying me. I hear love is capable of so many things. Good and bad.

But I'm not sure that love can conquer all. Especially my father's wrath.

SEVENTEEN

My father has left me alone since his announcement, but I've spent every day wondering what the fuck my future holds and worrying about Ares. He's been spiraling, and I've been able to do nothing but watch.

I've felt so fucking useless.

But today, I'm saying fuck it.

Even if it is just for a little while.

After the ball, I warned Seth that Amelia was at risk, telling him that he should get her as far from here as he could manage. Considering I haven't seen her since, I think he took my warning to heart. I'm going to miss her like fucking crazy, but I'd rather miss her and know she's alive and safe than have her here and end up another one of my father's play toys.

So today, I packed what I could, and I told Caleb and Ares they need to meet me here this morning, and we are getting the fuck away from this madness. Even if just for a moment.

Something broke within Ares at the dinner, and for the first time, he seems even more broken than me. His guilt at not beating Father, coupled with the fear that Father now knows where his loyalty actually lies… it's been hard to watch, so I can't imagine how hard it is to live.

Which is exactly why I'm making us all run away while my father is too busy to notice. Even if it can only be a temporary respite.

I already know he would hurt way too many people if I tried to run away for good, and I can't have that on my conscience.

My door opens, and I find a forlorn Ares held up by Caleb, who pants, "We're ready."

"You guys look like you've been dragged backward through a bush… I'm not even going to ask yet." I move toward them and take each of their hands in one of mine. I touch Kaos' head, and the pack bundles together so everyone is touching. I'm not sure it's necessary but that's how I'm going to do this regardless. "Hold on tight."

I close my eyes and whisper us to the Duttons' cottage.

We land in a heap at their door, and within seconds the porch light is on and the door opens. Tammy stands above us with wide eyes in her night coat, gasping. "Oh my heavens…"

"Sorry to just, er, drop by. It's been a bad few weeks. I needed a safe place," I tell her as I dust myself off and climb to my feet.

"Of course, sweetheart, we heard all about it. Come on in. I'll call for the others." She ushers us in and starts a pot of tea before going and waking Theodore. I hear him grumble lowly before he clomps out the backdoor with a quick, "I'll be right back."

Caleb helps Ares to the sofa, and he just kind of flomps down. "Is he drunk?"

"I have no idea; I just found him like this," Caleb murmurs as we sit on either side of my brother, trying to get him to at least sit up. Tammy brings through the pot of tea and a tray of cookies before sitting opposite us in silence while we wait for Theodore to get back.

I hate that I've brought this mess to their door, but I didn't know where else to go. Ares is spiraling. My world is falling apart. He's always been my rock, but this time... This time I need to be the strong one. So I'm doing the only thing I can think of.

I'm asking for help.

It's not something I'm used to doing, but then again I've never had people like the Duttons' in my life before. Sure we could have gone to Brandy, but I get the feeling that Ares wouldn't want them to see him like this.

"What the fuck happened?" Teddy asks as he rushes into the room. Caleb stands and moves so Teddy can take his seat just as Lani flies in and drops to her knees in front of Ares.

"He's been poisoned." I look at her like she's lost her mind, but she's already examining him. "Look, his fingernails are tinged blue. It's the death rose. Who the fuck would do this to him?"

I don't have an answer, so I stay quiet. My only assumption is my father, but surely he wouldn't kill his heir, especially after selling me off to the highest bidder. I shake off the thought, because this isn't about me right now.

"Shit," Teddy hisses, lifting my brother from the sofa and into his arms.

"What happened?" Neva asks as she and Theodore arrive.

Lani fills them in before she disappears with Teddy and my brother. "I'm sorry I brought this to your door. I didn't even know he was poisoned. I thought he'd just had too much to drink."

"Don't worry, sweetheart. The twins will look after him," Tammy says, patting my knee as she drops down beside me. Caleb sits on my other side.

"Those two love Ares like no other. They won't let

anything happen to him," Neva adds before she slumps into the chair opposite us, next to her father. My eyebrows rise and her eyes go wide. "Oh wait… you didn't know?"

"Didn't know what?" I ask, waiting for her to confirm what I think she just said.

"Neva," Theodore sighs, shaking his head.

"Well, I already put my foot in my mouth, I might as well explain," she murmurs, tucking her dark hair behind her ears. "Ares has been with both of them for what, thirty years? I don't know how it started, or how their dynamic works. I don't ask because I don't need to know. All I know is that they love him, and he loves them."

After being given reassurances that Ares would be okay from Lani, Caleb and I went back to the cottage we stayed in when we were here before. We passed out pretty much as soon as we got there, the stress and adrenaline finally wearing off from everything we've been going through.

Not to mention that the little bombshell about my brother had me all kinds of reeling.

I find myself awake, though, staring at Caleb while he sleeps beside me. I hate how distant we've become since we returned to the Shadow Palace. With everything going on, we haven't found the time and space to just be us.

When I'm with him, I feel so much more capable, more powerful, like I can achieve anything.

It's selfish of me, but I want that feeling always. I don't want to be separated from him. So I need to find a way to break this marriage contract without getting us all fucking killed.

"Stop thinking so hard," Caleb murmurs as his eyes flicker open. He smiles lazily up at me. Getting lost in his violet gaze isn't hard to do, and I find myself smiling for the first time in days. "There's that smile."

"You always know exactly what to say," I sigh, dropping my head back onto the pillow and watching him.

"Only to you, Mor." He kisses me softly, rolling me underneath him. "And if I ever don't have the right words, I'll find something else to make you smile."

His arms cage my head, and I place my hands on his chest—I missed this. So freaking much. I swear, I used to be innocent, and then he opened my eyes to everything I didn't even know I was missing. He kisses me until I'm breathless, and I want nothing more than to lose myself in him, just for a little while.

A knock on the door has him groaning and resting his forehead against mine. "What?"

"Caleb," I hiss, and push him off of me, laughing before heading to the door.

I find Neva on the other side with a wicked grin. "Sorry

to interrupt the festivities, kids, but I thought you'd want to know that Ares is conscious again. The twins got him an antidote in time. He'll need some time to recover, but he's going to be okay."

"Thank you!" I utter, and she gives a weird salute before heading back toward the main cottage. I spin around and find Caleb sitting up in the bed, the sheet pooled in his lap with that smirk of his I find so freaking irresistible on his face. "He's going to be okay."

"He is, but we should probably start worrying about who tried to kill your brother." The smile drops from his face at his words, and I realize he's right. I hadn't even thought about that.

Like we don't have enough to worry about, now someone is trying to fucking kill my brother.

"Yeah, that should probably go to the top of the list. Or at least, top three." I sigh and pad back over to the bed. He cups my cheek in his hand and strokes it with his thumb.

"We'll work this out, Mor. I've got you. I'm not going anywhere. Even if this fucking marriage bullshit has to go ahead for us to come out alive on the other side… I'm not going anywhere. There isn't a force in any of the Seven Realms strong enough to stop me." I lean into his hand and close my eyes, trying to find refuge in his words.

He really does always know the right thing to say.

"We should probably go and talk with Ares to see what

he knows," I say, sighing before I stand. "We also need to come up with a way for him to stay here for as long as possible. It isn't safe for him at the palace."

"We'll think of something. Now you get dressed. I'm going to have the world's coldest shower because you in those short shorts isn't something I can see without needing you on a primal level." I laugh at him until he stands, unabashed as the sheet falls from him.

He swaggers across the room, knowing exactly what he's doing. I bite my lip as he grins over his shoulder at me before closing the door to the bathroom.

The world really needs to stop imploding so we can enjoy each other properly.

It doesn't take long for us to get sorted out and head over to the main cottage. We find everyone else already sitting around the dining table with a breakfast spread that makes my mouth water.

But before I focus too much on the food, I head toward Ares. He still looks fucked up, but at least his eyes are clear today. He tries to get up, but Teddy puts a hand on his shoulder and shakes his head. "Keep your ass in the damn chair."

I can't help but smile at them. How I didn't see it

before is beyond me. I was clearly too wrapped up in my own shit. Lani is on his other side, looking tired as fuck. I guess they both stayed with him all night. I drape myself over his shoulders and give him a hug before kissing his cheek. "Glad to see you up and about."

"I guess we should talk about some things," he murmurs with a coy smile.

"Yes, we probably should. You look half dead, though, so let's eat first, shall we?"

Theodore's laughter booms from the head of the table. "The girl knows what she's talking about. Let's eat!"

I move around to sit next to Caleb and Neva, digging in like my life depends on it.

Once everyone's had their fill, and we've all helped get everything cleaned up, Tammy, Theodore, and Neva leave the cottage with the flimsiest excuse known to Demon, leaving the rest of us to talk.

"Subtle as a hammer to the face, my sister," Lani says, shaking her head.

Ares squeezes her hand before looking over at me. "So, I'm guessing you have questions?"

"I have so, so many questions, but first, who the fuck poisoned you?" Caleb grips my thigh under the table, reminding me to keep my shit in line. My power seems to be linked to my emotions, that much I've learned. While I usually have a pretty decent grasp on things, the more out of control my emotions get, the worse hold on my powers I have.

I should really spend some more time training with my power, or fucking meditating or something, but with the world going to shit around our ears, there hasn't really been much of a chance for any of that.

"Honestly, I wish I knew. I was dining with the guard, and I was with men I trusted. There were some that I didn't know, but I've never had an issue with anyone before."

"Before Father discovered how you're more loyal to me than you are to him you mean?" I ask with a sigh, and Ares winces.

Oops?

Teddy and Lani look toward Ares, and they look more pissed than I've ever seen them. Though, last time I was here, life was sunshine and daisies, so that's not really saying much. Teddy runs a hand through his hair before taking a deep breath. "What the fuck does that mean?"

Yep, I definitely just dropped my brother into a pile of shit. I look at him apologetically, but he shakes his head. "It means I tried to save my sister from my dad's fucking archaic ways, to give her a life where she won't basically be a prisoner, and I failed. He found out somehow. He also knows about one of you. Not both, pretty sure he would've used you both against me otherwise. Though, I'm pretty sure it's only Lani he knows about. It turns out my father's spies are everywhere. Even here."

Lani gasps and covers her mouth with her hand while Teddy curses. "Are we in danger?" she asks, her voice soft and meek. She's definitely not the person I would have ever pictured my brother with, but I guess I never thought he'd be with a guy, or twins, either. So what the fuck do I know?

"Not for now. No one is in danger as long as I marry the Prince of the Dead," I tell them, and Teddy thumps his fist on the table.

"This is so fucking stupid. We had a plan," he grunts at Ares. "Why couldn't you just stick to the plan?"

"What plan?" Caleb asks before I get a chance.

"We had a plan; we've been gathering allies across the Realm. Or at least, we thought we had. If your father is on to you, and he knows about us, it's likely he knows more than that. For fuck's sake," Teddy shouts, and Caleb's eyes turn black as he moves me backward.

"Caleb, it's fine. He would never hurt her," Ares says, trying to soothe my claimed one, but Caleb doesn't move. He just faces Teddy, who grins back at him sardonically.

"He wouldn't hurt her, even if it meant keeping the three of you safe? Not sure I trust that Ares," Caleb growls, and Teddy's grin only grows.

"Boy, you have no idea who or what I am. I suggest you tone your shit down."

"Teddy!" Lani scolds, but the pissing contest seems to only just be starting, so I decide to take control of the situation. I move in front of Caleb, and light a ball of Shadow Fire in my hand.

"I suggest everyone calms the fuck down, shall we? Maybe instead of fighting with each other we can focus our anger where it's deserved, instead," I say, looking at Teddy who just kind of staggers back into his chair before I turn on Caleb. "As for you, I can keep myself safe, you don't have to monster out all the time."

"Morgan, I love you, and I'm going to keep you safe. I'm not going to apologize for it," Caleb growls, and while my heart dances around in my chest, I keep my face straight and stare him down. "Fine, *fine.* I'm sitting. Let's work out a plan."

I smile once he concedes and turn back to find the twins staring at me like I'm a monster they never saw coming. Ares smiles apologetically, but I shrug it off. I trust them because he does. Plus, they saved him when I couldn't.

Now it's my turn to do the saving, except I might just have a different idea of what that means than they do.

EIGHTEEN

Leaving the Duttons' home was possibly one of the hardest things I've ever done. More so because I know how much danger the people I love are in back at the Shadow Palace. But Ares and Caleb refused to stay behind once the Duttons' received the official invite to celebrate my engagement to the Prince of the Dead.

Caleb's burst of rage over the invitation only makes me worry more that he's going to do something stupid, but the plans he made with Ares, Teddy, and Theodore seemed to keep him mostly occupied. His strategic mind shocked us all, and the guys almost gave him the floor to get everything lined up. One day he'll stop surprising me, but I doubt that day is coming anytime soon.

While they've been plotting ways to overthrow my

father and make a safer world for us all, I've been working on my own plans.

I just need to make sure everyone else is safe, but distracted, so I can do what I need to. Which is exactly how I find myself in the guards' quarters, standing outside the Captain's door.

I knock and wait impatiently, fidgeting with my hood to make sure it's up to help disguise myself, though I'm sure that's pointless here. The only upside is that it's the ass crack of dawn, so most people aren't awake yet.

The door swings open, startling me, and the Captain growls, "What?" before he notices that it's me standing there. "Oh, it's you. What the fuck do you want at this time of day?"

It's hard to be offended by the growl of his voice when his very toned and shiny torso is on show. The man literally just wrapped a towel around his hips to answer the door. His dark eyes glare down at me, and I feel smaller than I have in a long while, but I'm here for a reason, and he's going to help me whether he likes it or not.

"I'm here about my brother and Caleb," I say as I sashay under his arm and into the room, invading his space with no regard to his muffled protests. I hear him huff before he closes the door.

"Just wait here a second." He moves across the room to a door on the other side. When he opens it, I spot what must be his living quarters. He slams the door behind him, so I make myself comfortable in his office until he returns. "It's too fucking early for you to be a brat, so this better be good."

He drags a hand down his unshaved face, and I have to say, I quite like seeing the Captain a little ruffled. I brush off the assholeish comments and give him a moment. He stares at me like he can't figure me out, and that only makes me smile on the inside.

"I'm sure you heard that my brother nearly died after being poisoned," I start, and he nods before dropping into the chair on the other side of his desk.

"I did, but what does that have to do with me?" He raises an eyebrow at me. He might be a man of few words, but he might just not be a huge fan of mine.

"Well, considering my brother was poisoned when he was with your men, I'd say it has a fair amount to do with you. If he'd died, do you really think that just the person that did the poisoning would be held accountable?" He swears at my question, and I smirk because I know he knows I'm right. Even if my father ordered the death, he'd make a show of doling out a punishment. That's the special brand of asshole that my father is. "Exactly. So first things first, I'm here to find out if your loyalty is to my father or my brother."

He looks at me, as if seeing me for the first time, and

smiles. "Aren't they one and the same?"

"Only a fool would think that." I sit back in the chair and wait for him to actually provide a satisfactory answer. I'm pretty confident I already know the answer to my query, but I want to hear the words spill from his lips before I do anything else.

"You already know where my loyalties lie. I'd be dead if it wasn't for Ares, but considering Caleb too, my allegiance is to my family. The King is not my King."

"Good." I smile. "Then you'll help us ensure the right King ends up on the throne."

"I'll do what I can, but I don't see how that can be much." He leans back in his chair, running a hand over his crazy short black hair and watching me with slightly narrowed eyes.

"For now, I don't need you to do anything other than help me keep my brother and Caleb safe. The engagement party the King has announced is likely to be a fucking shit show."

He nods before leaning forward and placing his elbows on the desk. "I can do that."

"Thank you. And I need you to know, before we're done, you'll have your freedom back," I promise, and his eyes go wide.

"Those are some big words from a little girl."

"Oh, Captain, you have no idea who I am. You

shouldn't believe everything you've heard." I wink at him before I stand. "I'll be in touch. I have an errand to run this morning, but if you can keep them both distracted, maybe some intense training for the day, I'll be greatly appreciative."

His lewd grins elicits a roll of my eyes at him.

Men.

"I've got you covered, princess. They won't have a chance to think about where you are, let alone ask any questions."

I move to the door and raise the hood of my jacket back up. "Perfect. It's been a pleasure, Captain."

His gaze roams over me, despite the cloak, and his eyes practically sparkle. "I get the feeling the pleasure will be all mine."

Ensuring my brother and Caleb don't notice my absence is just one small part of today's challenge. I got word from a little bird in his court, that my father is with The Carver and Airon today which means he's distracted too.

Now I just have to figure out how to travel between Realms. I might be able to whisper between levels, but I've never even thought about how to travel between the actual, honest-to-hells Realms. It's not ever been something I've had to consider, but of course my father is the person to drive me to explore more of my power capabilities. He's the whole reason I tamped down all possible expressions of power until now. Because of him, here I am, taking risks and using my power in ways I never thought I would.

I whisper to Level Three and search out Brandy. It's early in the day so there's still hardly anyone awake, making it easy enough to move around undetected. I make my way to the estate and slip through the gates. Luckily the guard recognizes me from the time I spent here and doesn't question me.

By the time I reach the dining room, I find Brandy and her trio of lovers already sitting at the table. I'd hoped they'd be here. Thank the Gods that for once luck seems to be on my side.

"What's wrong?" Tomas asks, standing as I enter the room and drop my hood. The others all jump to attention, and the tension in the room skyrockets.

"Right this second, nothing. But I need your help," I tell them, and Brandy waves me to sit down with them.

"I assume you all heard about Ares?" I ask, and they each nod, all frowning deeply at the implications of my brother's poisoning. "Well, that's only a part of it."

I explain the threats to people around us, Ares' murder attempt, the stupid fucking wedding match, and everything else we've had going on. These are Ares' people, and I wouldn't be here if he hadn't reassured Teddy and Caleb the other day that these four were loyal and one hundred percent on our side in everything we do.

When I finish explaining everything that's been going on, Han narrows his eyes at me and asks, "So why do you need our help?"

I take a deep breath and bite down on my lower lip before saying, "I need to get to Avaenór."

Brandy bursts out laughing and throws her napkin on the table. "At least you don't come here with boring requests."

"Can you help me? I've barely had a chance to explore my powers since we left here, and while I'm gaining better control every day with the things I do know I'm capable of, traveling between Realms isn't something I actually have any idea about."

"Why isn't Ares helping?" Carter asks, watching me closely.

"He doesn't know she's going," Brandy says, shaking her head. "She's a clever girl and is used to the men in her life stopping her from doing shit that matters. Of course she's not telling him yet. I assume you need to speak to Xavi?"

I nod in answer but don't dare speak. I don't know how this is all going to go, so I don't want to tell anyone what I'm up to until they need to know.

"I can help you, but just know that we're on board for whatever you have planned. I don't give a fuck if your father knows we don't stand with him. If he knows, it just means we can drop all the pretentious bullshit."

"I'm not positive of exactly what he knows, just that he's privy to *some* things. Someone told him about Caleb... and somehow he knows about the twins, or at least one of them. So it's better to play it safe, at least until we're ready. His destruction is coming one way or another. We just have to bide our time until all of the pieces are on the board," I tell them. I know I sound cryptic as fuck, but there's no way I'm telling them what I have up my sleeve if I haven't even told Ares or Caleb.

"Okay, fine. We'll stick with that for the time being. Now, you eat up. When breakfast is done, I'll help you get to the Fae Realm," Brandy says, silencing her men with no more than a look. That is a super power I need in my arsenal. I want to object to eating as I'd rather just get on my way. There's so much that could go wrong at any point, but I also need her help, so I'm not going to push my luck.

I shrug off my cloak, and my stomach rumbles, which just makes Brandy smile wider. I prepare myself a small plate because the first time I whispered, I really wished I hadn't eaten a lot. I'm pretty sure traveling between Realms isn't going to be any better, so I'm not going to risk it.

It doesn't take long to finish eating, and despite their skepticism, Tomas, Han, and Carter leave me alone with Brandy. I'm not a fool, I know they don't trust me. At least, not like they trust my brother. They know some of what I'm capable of, and I'm guessing leaving the woman they love with me, when my powers can still be somewhat unpredictable, is a risk. I'm just glad Brandy doesn't seem to have the same hesitations they do.

She looks at me before standing and smiling. "Well then, let's go see the Fae, shall we?"

Brandy gives me a stone to help me open a portal through to the Fae Realm, and once I am in the Bronze city, with the palace in view, she leaves me alone. I'm mostly grateful for that, because she is not the inconspicuous type. I also want to speak to Xavi alone if I can.

My only problem now is figuring out how the fuck to get into the palace.

I take a deep breath and continue the walk through the city, which despite the still rising sun is already very much alive. It's easy to understand how this place got its name. The whole place is beautiful, each detail an intricacy built from burnished metals. Even things as simple as the windows are works of art.

The city is alive with the sounds of children playing, the bartering of vendors and shopkeepers, and there's something about this entire place that just feels happy and wholesome. I'm sure there's an underbelly to the beauty. There always is, but I know already that I could've been happy here if my father hadn't fucked with everything Ares tried to make a reality.

By the time I reach the palace gates, I've stripped off my cloak, and I'm pared down to the floor length black leather and lace dress I put on this morning. It's fucking warm here with the sun beating down on the city. It's such a strange heat, so much drier than at home. I'd never even thought about things like that being different.

I really have been far too sheltered. Once Ares is King, and life is safe, I'm going to travel the Seven Realms and really explore what else there is in this universe of ours. I want to experience it all.

"Halt!" a guard yells, and I find a spear tip at my neck. I glance up to see three archers staring down at me, their arrows nocked and bows drawn. "Who goes there?"

"I am a friend of Prince Xavi. I wish to see him," I announce, and the archers laugh at the apparent absurdity of the statement.

"Sure thing, the crown prince has *friends* showing up here all day. I'm sure they'd all like to see him, but I also like my head on my shoulders," the guy holding the spear says, and I roll my eyes.

My frustration ratchets up a level. I've never been refused entry to anywhere in my freaking life. I get that I've not exactly been to many places, but still… I don't know why I hadn't considered that this would be a problem. Sometimes I hate how shut away I've been. "This is insane. If you could just please get Xavi, or Killian, they will vouch for me."

At Killian's name, they start to murmur, and one of the archers disappears. I guess Killian's name isn't as well known here as Xavi's.

I'm kept here at spear point for what feels like forever, but in reality is probably only about twenty minutes. A smaller door in the large sparkling gate opens, and I smile when I see Xavi's face. "Let her in, boys, she actually is a friend."

His chuckle reinforces the guard's words from earlier. I guess it was foolish of me to assume that they'd just let me in. I really do need to get out and see more of the world.

I move forward, and once I cross the threshold of the gate, I let out a sigh of relief. At least I'm here now. I'd like to think that the hard part is over, but that would just make me more foolish than I've already been. "I appreciate you coming to see that it was me," I say, remembering Ares' warning about thanking the Fae. Hopefully not saying thank you will be enough.

"You have no fear in minding your words with me, Morgan. But I have to say, yours was not the face I expected to see when the guard told me a pretty, dark-haired girl insisted on seeing me." He chuckles as he starts to walk up the white stone path toward the palace. I fall in line beside him.

"Thank you," I say sincerely before sighing. I offer him a tight smile as I continue, "But a lot has happened since I saw you last."

"I see. I guess we have much to discuss if you came all the way here." He watches me with apt fascination as we climb the gleaming white steps up to the palace before us.

"You could say that. Is there somewhere private we can speak?"

He nods as the ornate doors of the palace open, and he waves me in. "Yes, of course. Does Killian need to be here for this talk?"

I shake my head and bite down on my lower lip. "No, I don't think so. At least not to begin with. Once I'm finished explaining, if you think we need him, then I'll follow your lead."

"Ah, a girl with a good head on her shoulders as well as fire in her heart. I was right, you would have been well suited to this city." He gives me a sad smile before shaking his head and wiping it from his face. "Now then, let's go to my library, we will have peace and privacy there. I'll have some refreshments brought up for us. Talking is thirsty work."

He winks at me, and I can't help but laugh. I feel lighter here than I've felt in days. There's just something about being around him, and being in this place, that brings a sense of peace.

"Yes, yes it is." I smile back at him, and he offers me his arm.

"Shall we?"

I nod, being more than willing to follow him anywhere if he can help me. I hope that I don't lose myself while finding a way to free us all.

Once we finish sorting out refreshments, and I get over gawking over the sheer amount of books he has, we finally sit down at the long, shiny table in the middle of the room. I open my mouth to speak, but Xavi shakes his head quickly.

"That will be all, Lacey. Thank you. Ferry, you can leave too," he calls out, and I hear a small squeak. Then two young girls rush from behind one of the book stacks and run straight out of the doors. "There you are, now we're alone."

With a flick of his wrist, a white shimmer covers the doors and windows. "And now we have the privacy I assume we're going to need. So why don't you get me up to date with what I've missed, and then we can speak about why you're really here."

So I tell him. I tell him about my father's threats, the attempt on Ares' life. I tell him about the Captain and about the plans Caleb and the others came up with.

"I'm assuming you have a plan of your own?" he asks, his eyes dancing with amusement.

I nod sharply, trying not to seem as nervous as I feel. "You could say that."

"So what do you need my help with?"

I take a deep breath, trying to take comfort in the fact that this man basically offered to save my life. That alone should tell me I can trust him. "I'm about to tell you some things that almost no one knows about me."

I pause, and his face turns more serious. I wait a beat and then continue. "I killed my mother."

"What the fuck!" he exclaims, his eyes going wide.

"She was beating me, just another Friday afternoon in the palace. I can't even remember why at this point, the reasons all seem to blur together into general disappointment, but during her beating, one of my powers emerged… Shadow Fire."

He leans back in his chair and runs a hand through his hair. "Well shit."

"Pretty much. Ares helped me clean it up, and no one

ever looked at either of us in regard to her disappearance. Why would they? My brother helped me learn to contain my power. More recently he has been helping me explore it, not just learning to contain it, but to control it as well.

"In doing so, I've learned that I'm capable of more. A lot more. In fact, we haven't found something yet that I can't do. Obviously time has been limited, so we haven't tried all that much, but Ares seems both excited and terrified about this." I take a breath, giving him a moment to take it all in. "So with all this in mind, the reason I'm here is to ask for your help, to ensure my brother lives long enough to take the throne."

"I don't understand," he says, his brow furrowing.

"I know Ares made a bargain with you to take me and my friends and keep us here, safe, until he ascends to the throne. I'm asking you for the same deal. I'll give you whatever it was he offered, but I want you to keep him safe. Him and the ones he loves. Here, in Avaenór. Just until I can kill my father."

"Regicide? You don't do things in half measures do you?" He barks out a laugh, shaking his head. "Do you even know what your brother bargained with?"

"No, and I don't care. Whatever he was willing to sacrifice for me, I'm willing to sacrifice for him tenfold. He's only at risk now because he put everything on the line to help me." Xavi nods at my words and sighs.

"How exactly do you intend to bring down your father?"

"I'm still working on that. But Ares has plenty of friends, and I'm pretty sure I can be just as charming as he is," I tell him, leaving out the whole Chosen One thing that Theodore kept referring to when we were plotting with him. It still all seems a little far fetched to me, even with the markings between me and Caleb.

He looks at me, as if weighing up my worth before nodding his head. "I will accept your offer, Morganna Voux."

"Thank you." I let out a sigh of relief. With Ares safe and out of the way, I can focus on what is important. Clearing the way for Ares to ascend to the throne.

"As for what Ares bargained... it was simply a continued alliance between the Realms once he came to power. I do not want anything from you, but it says a lot about you that you were willing to pay an unknown cost to save the ones who mean the most to you."

"Really?" I sit, my jaw ajar. "Thank you so much."

"Thank you for confirming that your brother should be the one on the throne. You will make a good queen one day. I'm sure once the Prince of the Dead pulls his head out of his ass, he'll see that too… That is, I assume, if you're still going ahead with the marriage?"

"I have little choice," I tell him with a sigh. "For now, I

need my father to feel like I'm not a threat to him. Besides, there's still too much risk to everyone else if I fuck it up."

Xavi nods and reaches over the table to squeeze my hand. "I have a feeling, Morganna Voux, that there is more to your destiny than we're aware of. I'm pretty sure that the Prince of the Dead will come around, and when he does, who knows just what the two of you will be capable of."

NINETEEN

"We should talk."

I wince as I hear the words fall from my lips. Caleb lets out a terse laugh before sitting opposite me. "Never have more ominous words been spoken. What's up?"

I look around the small room that's been allocated to him in the guard quarters. I figured his place was as good as any to have this conversation. The Captain has a heads up that he might go off, so I'm pretty sure he's cleared the space.

"We need to talk about this arranged marriage," I say softly, and he clenches his fists where they sit on top of the table. "I know neither of us is happy about it…"

"That might be the understatement of the fucking

millennia, Mor," he grunts, and I just smile at him. I'm as happy about it as he is, but now that my plan is forming in my mind, I've resigned myself to the fact that there is no way around it.

"It might be." I sigh, prepared for just how badly this conversation is about to go. "But it needs to go ahead."

He stands, and kicks his chair across the room in a fit of rage. I don't even flinch. I know he won't ever hurt me, even if he's so angry he can't see straight. "This is bullshit."

His eyes go black, and his fingers turn into claws as he pulls at his hair before punching the wall. Stone flies through the air from the force of it. Still, I stay seated, not wavering for a moment. I knew he wasn't going to like it, but I also know that deep down he knew it was coming. The shadows that flare from him practically pulse, but he looks just as beautiful to me now as he usually does. I know this display is his love for me driving him to the brink of madness.

"You and I both know that we need my father to keep thinking I'm weak. That I'm not capable of being a threat to him. For the plan you created with Ares to work, we need him lulled into a false sense of security. We can't do that if I try to throw down with a show of power so I don't have to get married." I gulp, leaving out the fact that he's at risk too. It's one of the biggest parts of my reasoning. I won't be the reason he gets hurt—or worse.

"This is bullshit, Mor. There has to be another way," he growls, pacing back and forth in the room. His restless energy hits me like a tsunami, but I try to stay calm. One of us has to be, otherwise everything is going to go to shit.

"If there was another way, one of us would've come up with it already. Nothing changes between us just because I'm marrying him. You are still the one who holds my heart," I say as calmly and honestly as I can. I mean every single word, and while I have my own plan that I'm keeping to myself for now, there's a reason for it. I know they'll all try to stop me. Even though they know what I'm capable of, they want to protect me. They underestimate me, and for once, I want to be the one protecting them.

"I know," he sighs, deflating and sitting back down on the remaining chair that's closest to me. "And I know that we haven't even really talked about what we are... or about this whole chosen bullshit thing that talks about three others being claimed, but I guess we need to." I nod at his words because he isn't wrong. We've been doing everything in our power to tiptoe around it.

"We probably should." I bite my lip, wondering exactly how this is going to go.

"I've never been a jealous guy before you. I've always just kind of gone with what the world throws at me. But there's something about you, Mor… you got under my skin and into my heart. I don't think I've ever loved another person before, not the way I love you. That being said, I know that love doesn't always mean just two people. It's just not how the world works."

He takes a deep breath, and I keep my mouth firmly fucking closed. "The texts talk about you claiming three others, so I'm already open to that deep down, despite my Demon's issues with sharing you. We're good with it. It's just that marrying someone else really isn't how I saw this going down.

"Sharing you with someone neither of us like wasn't on the agenda either, but I realize that there isn't another way around it. Despite me not being able to control myself, I know this has to happen. I know you'll probably have to fuck him at some point, and I'm fine with that too. Sex is sex, just keep me in the loop of what's happening. I don't want to be on the outside of anything."

"I don't have any intention of fucking him," I tell him honestly, reaching for his hand. "I don't intend on being married long enough that it's even a thing. This marriage is purely to make sure my father doesn't have any reason to suspect anything else that's going on. He expects me to be unwilling, but all he knows about me is all he's ever wanted to know. That's the weak little girl who eventually does as she's told. The minute we put the plan into motion, my marriage means nothing to me."

"Okay," he says, squeezing my hand back. "We've got this, Mor. We're stronger than anyone suspects, and this bond between us is unbreakable. You do what you need to to stay alive. That's what matters most to me."

I stand and move to sit in his lap, wrapping my arms around his neck. "I love you."

"I love you too, Mor," he murmurs, his lips against mine. "More than you'll ever know."

This is going to be one hell of a fucked up night.

If I make it out alive, unscathed, and no one I love is dead at the end of it, I'll take it as a win. Because honestly, I'm not confident that any of those things are going to happen. At least not entirely.

I know the Captain will help me get Caleb and Ares the fuck out of there if shit starts to go down, but I'm really hoping that calmer heads prevail. Caleb hasn't made it a secret how pissed off he is about this match. Not that I blame him, not even a little, but hopefully my reassurances will keep him steady today. Talking about all of it with him was probably the shittiest conversation we've ever had, but it needed to be done.

I stare back at my reflection and roll my eyes. They couldn't have made me look less myself if they'd tried. I don't get to wear my standard black tonight. Instead, I'm wearing gold… apparently the color favored by the Prince of the Dead.

I have a cuff on each arm, with a wing that extends around my arm. Chains wrap down my arms, starting at my shoulder and coming to a stop on a ring on each of my index fingers. The high necked, shimmering dress shows almost no other skin, except for the thigh high splits on each side. My shoes are fucking gold too, with more chains that wrap up my legs and attach to the top of the splits at my hips.

Even my eyes look different, lined with black and topped with gold glitter.

The only thing that is even partially me is my black painted lips, and my black and gray crown. But then again, these people don't actually want me. They want what I represent, and I guess dressing me up like this is their way of showing that.

There's even fucking gold cuffs on my ears, which are on display despite my hair being down because of the way it's been pinned back.

I feel like a fucking dress up doll, but I gulp down a deep breath of air and just take it. I can get through tonight. Then I can ensure my brother is safe, and that Caleb is safe, leaving me free to try to find a way to destroy my father without getting us all killed in the process.

"Are you ready?" I turn at the sound of my brother's voice and smile when I see him.

"You're looking better."

He strides across the room and hugs me tightly. "Thanks to you, yes. And Bryce has been helping me sweat out the last of the toxins. I'm certain he enjoyed it a little too much."

"He does seem the type to enjoy it." I laugh with him. "Are you ready for tonight? I know the twins will be here. After Father's threat, are you sure that's a good idea?"

"It will be fine. They're not as breakable as you might think."

"What does that mean?"

"It means that the Duttons' are Morphs." He grins, and my eyes go wide.

"What's their animal?" I ask, excited. I've read all about Morphs. Demons who can shapeshift into creatures. The more powerful the Demon, the more forms they can take.

"Teddy is a Tulane," he tells me, and I get so excited. "Lani is a Phoenix."

"Holy shit, that's so cool." Now Teddy's words to Caleb about not knowing what he was capable of when we were at the cottage make more sense.

"Plus, I wanted them here in case shit gets too fucked up. They'll help me wrestle Caleb to their level if I need to," he says, and I kiss his cheek softly.

"You are the best, big brother."

"I know, now let's take your sparkly ass to this farce of a party, shall we?" I roll my eyes at him, and he laughs even harder.

"I look like something a unicorn shit out."

"Very pretty shit though," he teases as he takes my arm. "Caleb is with Bryce, and Bryce swore to keep an eye on him tonight so he doesn't get into trouble too. Between us all, we should all make it out alive."

"Let's hope the Fates don't fuck with us and that we haven't just jinxed ourselves into oblivion."

I spend the entire night gliding around the room like a fucking sparkly spectacle. I can't even remember all of the faces I see over the course of the evening, but I do at least manage to avoid the Prince of the Dead, so far anyway. Though I'm not sure that's all my doing. He isn't seeking me out either.

No, instead, I spend the night smiling so widely that my cheeks fucking hurt while my father lords his great idea to the whole Realm about how he's making such a strong alliance. Personally I think the Fae Realm would have been the better alliance, but what do I know? I'm just the doll being dragged around the room.

My feet are killing me from these fucking shoes, and I swear I have a headache from the glare of all the sparkly shit on my body. Every time something catches the light, I light up like a glow bug.

I feel a trickle of icy dread run down my spine, and I just know he's looking at me. I turn to find the Prince of Dead scowling at me from across the room. His parents wave me over, and I wish the floor would open up and swallow me whole.

Unfortunately, the fates isn't on my side. No one comes to rescue me from the Favreau family. So I find myself weaving my way across the room until I'm standing before them, realising I don't even know their names.

"Oh, Morganna, you look stunning," Malik's mom gushes before pulling me in for a hug. Malik glares at me even harder. "You're going to fit right in in Kavaraí. Beauty is highly revered in our Realm."

"So is strength of character and backbone, but I doubt those are qualities Morganna holds," Malik hisses, and I just roll my eyes, ignoring his comments.

"I'm sure Kavaraí is a beautiful place," I say to the Queen, making her smile wider despite her asshole son's words.

"It truly is."

"Morgan, there you are." Ares appears, saving me once

more. "Apologies for interrupting. I just need to steal my sister away for a few moments."

"Please do," Malik murmurs before stalking away from us anyway.

"Ignore my son," the King says, and I try not to freeze from shock. I think it's the first time I've actually heard him speak. "He will do his duty, and he will make a good husband. He's not usually so obstinate."

"It's fine," I tell him, waving it off. "I've dealt with plenty of surly men at court. This is nothing new for me."

"Just because it isn't new doesn't make it right." The King frowns down at me, and I worry for a second that he sees more of me than I want him to. It's easy to underestimate the quiet ones. I learned that from Zafar. I won't make that mistake again. "Regardless, you are excused. I'm sure your brother's request is more important than discussing the dishonor my son brings to our family with his actions."

I smile softly at his obvious dismissal. He takes his wife's hand, and they move in the direction that Malik disappeared. I turn to face Ares who doesn't look exactly happy. "What's wrong?"

"Father asked me to find you. It's time for the official announcement." I feel the smile drop from my face. I knew it was coming. It's what this whole night has been about, but that doesn't make me any happier about it.

"Let's go and face the music, I guess. Where's Caleb?" I look around the room for him, but I can't see him.

"I had Bryce take him back to the guard quarters. I figure he's already dealing with enough in regard to all of this. He doesn't need to hear Father droning on about it all either."

I sag in relief, just a little. "Thank you. I know he's struggling with all of this. He just isn't used to this world."

"Let's hope he never becomes used to it," Ares says softly. "This place can ruin a person. Now then, let's go and put you on show. Hopefully after that we can both escape this Gods forsaken party."

I let him lead me across the room to where my father sits on the throne he's had moved to the ballroom. Ours sit prettily beside his, so I do my duty and take my seat beside him. Ares drops regally on the other side of him, and our father stands.

The room falls silent the instant he stands, and I fight the urge to roll my eyes at the level of fear he invokes. On one hand, I get it since I still live with it. He is a giant asshole without a threshold to what he's willing to do to get his way. He's basically a spoiled toddler with too much power, but everyone kisses his ass—some out of fear, some out of blind faith, and so nothing ever changes.

"Thank you, everyone, for joining us to celebrate the stronger allegiance between The Shadow Realm and

Kavaraí. It brings me great joy to officially announce the union of my daughter, Princess Morganna Voux, and Prince Malik Favreau." Applause and cheers sound out around the ballroom so loudly that my ears start ringing.

Malik looks like he wants to kill my father on the spot, and I can't help but smirk over the fact that this might just be the one and only time we've been on the same wavelength. Once he's had us stand together and just fucking pose for the vapid masses, he dismisses everyone back to the party.

Before I have the chance to escape, he grabs my arm and yanks me backward behind the thrones. "You are going to Kavaraí in the morning, and I swear to fucking hell if you fuck this up in any way, you will ask me for your death personally, little girl."

He releases me, practically throwing me from him, and the only thing that keeps me standing is Ares catching me. Father storms away, and I sag against my brother's supportive form.

"Ares, I can't go there. What if something happens to you while I'm gone?"

He pulls me into his arms and hugs me while we're still hidden from the rest of the room. "You have to go, so don't worry about me. I'll make sure that Caleb's fine too. Just focus on keeping yourself alive, and do not trust *anyone* in that place."

TWENTY

"This is fucking bullshit," Caleb grumbles from where he's lying on my bed as I finish packing up my trunks for this stupid trip.

"It is, but it's just another thing we have to get through." I sigh and drop onto the bed next to him, giving up on packing for the time being.

"I know I'm being a little whiny bitch. I'm aware of it. I'm just going to miss you." He wraps his arm around me and pulls me against his chest. I curl my legs over his and snuggle against him.

"I'm going to miss you too. Nothing about this trip is going to be fun. I can already guarantee that I'll want to be back here, exactly at this very moment, every second that I'm gone." He kisses the top of my head and holds me close.

“We’ll survive this and anything else your father throws at us,” he murmurs, and I let out a deep sigh, feeling content despite the shit that just won’t stop coming.

“We will. Just promise me you’ll try to keep your head down while I’m gone. I can’t survive this, any of it, if you’re not there waiting for me at the end of it.”

“I promise. I’m pretty sure that Ares is trying to get me to go to the Duttons’ with him.” I shake against his chest as he chuckles, and I smile while looking up at him.

“That’s a great idea. Do that!”

“I thought you might agree with him. But I’m also pretty sure Bryce will be pissed if I fuck with his guard schedule.”

I roll my eyes and pat his chest. “Trust me, the Captain will get on board. If you get the chance to get away from here, take it. Even if it means you don’t get updates on what’s happening with me. Ares will keep you up to date if anything bad happens, but I honestly don’t think anything will. Malik might be a giant bag of dicks, but his parents seem okay.”

Caleb growls, the vibrations of his chest soothing me. “If he hurts you, I’ll tear his fucking throat out.”

“You won’t need to; I’ll have already done it. But I appreciate the sentiment.” He growls a little again, but I settle against his chest.

"Let's not think about it anymore, let's just enjoy these last moments we have together."

"Oh, princess, I have some much better ideas about how we can enjoy this time together." He grabs my waist and moves me so I'm straddling him, my hands on his shoulders. His hard cock digs into me, and I bite my lip as I grind down onto him.

"I'm definitely down for this sort of enjoyment."

"I'm going to make sure you can feel me the entire time you're away." His words send shivers down my entire body.

"You think you're up to that sort of challenge?"

"Oh, princess, you have no idea just how well I'm going to prove my point." He lifts me and throws me back down onto the bed, covering my body with his.

"I'm pretty sure I'm not going to complain." I laugh softly, and he smothers my laughter with his kiss until I'm a panting and writhing mess beneath him.

Yeah, I'm not going to complain at all.

He lifts up to pull off his t-shirt, and grins down at me before plunging his hand beneath his waistband and pulling out his cock. It's glorious and thick and veiny, just begging to be inside of me. He tucks himself back away with a smirk and turns his focus back to me, but all I can think about is his dick.

He lifts the skirt of my dress and pulls the top down

so it's all gathered around my waist, exposing me to him completely. With his gaze searing a path of lust across my skin, he rises from the bed, pulling me up with him, before tearing my dress off and pushing me against the nearest wall with my back to his front. Instinctively, my ass pushes against his thick, hard cock, unmistakable under his pants.

Reaching down, he unzips himself, all without fully letting go of me. I'm so desperate for his touch, that I whimper even with the minor loss.

His nails dig into the flesh of my hips ad he takes hold of me and drags his name from my lips in a gasping breath, as he plunges deep inside me in one rough and sudden thrust. My hands push against the wall, keeping myself steady as he pounds into me. With one of his hands snaking around my waist and up to my neck, he settles his fingers just below my chin and squeezes just enough to catch my breath with every thrust inside me.

The lack of breath coupled with not being able to see him properly makes everything else seem so fucking heightened. He isn't making love to me right now, he's marking me from the inside, making sure that with every move I make, the only thoughts I'll have will be of him and this very moment. Thoughts of his increasingly hard thrusts, thoughts of his fingers tightening across my throat, thoughts of his nails marring my otherwise smooth skin. I am not going to complain.

He grunts as his dick rubs against my G-spot, feeding something primal inside of me. It's been almost no time at all, and I already feel like I'm going to come apart in his arms.

"Shhh, princess," he grunts in my ear before pulling out and waiting for a short second before slamming back inside me. "Don't think. Just feel. Feel every inch of me ruining you for anyone else. This pussy belongs to me, and you had better remember it. No one can ever make you feel the way my cock makes you feel."

His dirty words finally do it for me.

But more than that, the subtle squeeze of his hand around my neck with every thrust makes my pussy clench around his girth. He grunts and moans behind me.

"Do that again." His command is a mere whisper, and still my body obeys without question.

Clenching my muscles on his next thrust, I revel at the feel of him squeezing my neck in response, making my pussy even wetter.

It's like we're pushing each other closer and closer to the precipice until one of us tips over it completely.

I'm certain I'll be the first to plummet over that edge and lose all control.

Without a doubt, he knows my body better than I do, and every word, every movement is directed toward making me lose control.

"Come for me, Mor. Show me how much you love the way my dick feels inside of you."

I can't help it, his words are my weakness.

I come on a cry, screaming his name as my fingers dig so hard into the wall that I feel it give beneath my grip.

But he doesn't stop there. He thrusts into me twice more before he growls at me, "Don't move."

Through the haze of my orgasm, he spins me around and I feel him getting on his knees. His hands slide down my thighs before he lifts my legs up onto his shoulders and his mouth latches onto my pussy. He feasts on me like I'm his last meal. He worships my pussy like I'm his goddess and his tongue is a fervent prayer.

The sounds of him eating me out, of how much he's enjoying it, push me even closer to coming yet again. "Give it to me, Morgan."

His command, mixed with his fingers plunging into me are enough to make me see stars again.

Only when my legs feel like they're made of goo does he let me down. He climbs back to his feet and grins down at me before moving me over to the bed.

He lies me down and cages me between his arms before kissing me like he can't breathe without my lips on his. He fucks me hard, but he looks at me like I'm the sun his life revolves around. Grunting with every thrust, he tells me I'm the most beautiful woman he's ever met. He tells me that he loves me, that he worships me, that he would do anything for me.

And I believe every single fucking word.

Then, just when I think I'm going to lose my mind, he reaches down and circles my clit with his thumb, hurling me into another orgasm before he spills himself deep inside of me.

Caleb truly knows how to fuck me like I'm his possession yet love me like I'm his queen.

"I love you, and I swear to fuck, Mor, it makes me hard again just knowing you're full of my come."

"Mmmm," is all I can say, because my brain is on hiatus and my body is about to give out.

"Come on, princess, let me take care of you."

Malik arrived at the Shadow Palace to collect me, and after bugging out about the sheer amount of stuff I had to bring with me, he hasn't said another fucking word to me. I don't know how long this trip is meant to last, but I can already tell it's going to be a barrel of fucking laughs.

Not.

My father has been talking at him for about ten minutes, seemingly clueless to the fact that the Prince of the Dead couldn't give two fucks about what he's saying.

"The Hellhounds aren't coming," Malik says, glancing toward them sitting at my feet.

"The fuck they're not. Either they go, or I don't," I challenge him, and he rolls his eyes.

"Morganna, do we need to speak again?" my father asks, his threat clear as fucking day. I swear to the gods if he hurts my puppies while I'm gone, I'm going to paint the walls of this palace with his fucking blood. Malik just smirks at me, and it takes every ounce of sheer willpower I have not to slap it the fuck off of his face.

My father smiles, happy with my silence. One of the stable boys appears and Kaos growls at him as he tries to herd them away from me. I drop down to a crouch and stroke his head, trying not to cry. I don't want to go without them, dammit. "It'll be okay, boy. You guys stay out in the stables and stay out of trouble. I'll be back before you know it."

I keep my voice quiet, touching each of them, sending my thoughts directly to their mind so I don't have to speak again, and eventually they each stand and follow Havoc from the room. Kaos howls before he leaves, and it breaks my fucking heart.

I turn back to the two assholes in my life once the hounds finally leave, and my father simply dismisses my pain before dropping yet another threat. "Well, I'm sure you'll both have fun. Morganna, remember what I told you."

Like I could forget, the fucking asshole. Except all that falls from my mouth is, "I will, Father."

I despise how much I hate him and how afraid I still am of him deep down. I might have all these grand plans, but I'll have to grow a stronger backbone if my plans are ever going to work. If it was anyone else, I wouldn't have any issues, but he's conditioned me to have a fear response to him. It's so ingrained in me, it's taking me a minute to try and un-train my brain.

"Let's go," Malik grunts, and I roll my eyes. He offers me his hand, but he looks like he'd rather cut it off than have me touch him.

Guess what, buddy, me fucking too.

But I take his hand as expected, and my power stirs inside of me at his touch. The power seems more than a little interested in this asshole, so I slam the door on it and keep it shut. There's no way I'll let this asshole in on even a hint of what I'm capable of. "Whenever you're ready."

I hate that he seems to have such a better grip on his powers than I do, but then, I don't even fucking know how old he is. We whisper from the Shadow Realm to Kavaraí before I'm even finished speaking.

When the ground is firm beneath my feet again, I look around at where we are.

A city made of sand.

At least, that's what it looks like. The walls of the palace have that burnt orange, deep red color to them, and the windows and doors are all curved with points at the top. It's beautiful in the most unusual way.

Malik drops my hand the second he can and turns to face me. "I do not want to marry some stupid fucking spoiled princess. So just stay the fuck out of my way. We might not have a choice about the union, but if you stay out of my way, I vow to stay out of yours as well."

Without giving me a chance to respond, he stalks away from me, leaving me alone in a place I don't know.

What a giant fucking asshat.

I make my way up the dusty path, following behind Malik as he disappears into the distance. Sentries line the path, and while none of them even acknowledge my presence, I can still hear the sounds of people outside of the palace walls.

This place is nothing at all like I expected. It's so much brighter than I thought it'd be, and the smells… My mouth waters even though I'm angry. I have no idea where the smells of such deliciousness are coming from, but I'm sure as hell going to find out as soon as I get my bearings in this place.

Once I reach the main entrance of the palace, I turn around and realize I can see over the walls from here. The city stretches out as far as the eye can see. To the left, a huge body of water covers the space, and I can see the docks from here. To the right is nothing but more desert.

I'm not sure how life works here, but this really is a million miles away from what I pictured. I turn back toward the palace and take a deep breath.

Ready or not, here I come.

I enter the building through one of the giant archways, and it's instantly cooler. I hadn't even noticed how hard the sun was beating down on me until I was no longer directly under it. The inside is bright with cream-colored tiles and smooth walls whose color match the tiled floor. Brightly colored art covers the walls, and white marble statues dot the entry room. An entryway that should feel cold and hard somehow feels cozy. It's very bizarre.

Having no idea where Malik went, I work my way further into the palace. There are people rushing around, speaking a language I don't understand, but they all ignore my presence. Everyone looks like they're doing something urgent, so I don't try to stop them. I figure I can find my way eventually, right?

I wander through the halls, unwittingly finding the kitchen, which I am urgently ushered out of by a woman so pale she makes me look tanned. I hurry in the opposite direction and end up back where I started.

Okay, so maybe I can't work this out on my own.

Fuck my life.

I'm going to have to try to speak to someone, but considering I haven't understood one word uttered here since Malik left me, I'm not feeling all too confident.

"Ah, Morganna, there you are." Malik's mom comes to my rescue, and I find myself warming to her more and more. Even if she is marrying me off to her jerk of a son. "Where is Malik?"

"I honestly have no idea," I tell her, trying not to sound as exasperated as I feel.

"That son of mine… I swear to the Gods… I am so sorry. Let me show you to your rooms, have you been wandering around here for too long?" She waves at me to follow her down one of the halls, and I only just manage to keep up with her. She might not be very tall, but damn she's quick.

"Not too long, Your Highness," I respond, cursing myself yet again for the fact that I don't even know her freaking name.

"Oh, please. Call me Mimi—there should be no titles between family." She smiles at me warmly, and it's jarring as shit. She is so different here to how she was that first time I met her. We walk up a few flights of stairs and down another few halls before she opens a door and ushers me through it.

Inside, I find a room with a wall of arches, all looking out over the body of water I saw earlier, covered with a red see-through material. They move in the soft breeze, and I realize there are no windows. Just open spaces. I'm glad I can't die from falling from a great height.

The bed frame is a gold metal, as is all of the other furniture in here. The cold, tiled floor is the same cream color from the entry, and there are red accents everywhere.

I'm sensing a theme.

"I hope this is to your liking. Obviously, once you've married Malik, you will live with him in his quarters should you wish, otherwise these can be your rooms for the time you spend here. Of course, we can change the decor if you wish."

"This is perfect, thank you," I say to her, not wanting to offend her. I only just got here, and while I don't intend on this marriage lasting, I have no idea how long this trip is. I'd really rather not be poisoned because I said the wrong thing and offended her.

"Great, well, I'll leave you here to rest up, and I'll make sure Malik collects you in time for dinner. I've made sure all of my children will be home so that we can officially welcome you to the family."

"That sounds great." I hope the smile on my face isn't as fake as it feels. Because the idea of spending dinner with their entire family sounds like my idea of hell. I just hope the rest of her children are more like her than they are Malik.

"I'm going to go and ensure the final touches are ready for tonight. Please make yourself at home. After all, this will be your home soon enough."

She disappears from the room, closing the door behind her, and I let out a sigh before dropping down onto the bed. Even if this mattress does feel like a cloud, I refuse to let myself get too comfortable here. Ares told me not to trust them, and since I trust him implicitly, I'm not going to let my guard down.

Not even for a moment.

Malik walks me down to the dining room without saying one fucking word to me. I really don't know what his problem is, but I get the feeling that if I ask him, I'm not likely going to get a decent answer either.

So I keep my mouth shut and follow him through the maze that is his home.

One upside is that I get to pay more attention to the actual building. Obviously it's different from the Shadow Palace, but there's something about the place that still feels familiar. Though, there doesn't seem to be an undercurrent of fear the way there is at home. Can't say I miss that.

But I do miss Caleb.

He was basically all I thought of while I was locked

away in my room. I couldn't help but wonder where he was, what he was up to, or worry about what could have possibly gone wrong in the scant few hours since I left.

Unfortunately that last list was long and kept me pacing until the moment Malik appeared at my door.

Once we reach the dinner room, I find a lot more people than I expected sitting around a long table. I lean over to Malik, despite his chilly exterior and whisper, "This is just your family?"

He nods, before stalking off to the seat next to his father, leaving only one chair open. The one between his mom and a girl I'm guessing is his sister. Before Malik can sit, his mother clicks her tongue, and he rolls his eyes, moving to the empty chair and pulling it out for me.

Once I sit and he tucks my chair under the table, his mom shakes her head. "Malik, I raised you with better manners than this."

"You also raised me to be headstrong and make my own decisions before taking my decisions away from me. So I guess we're all having a shitty time right now." He glares at her before dropping into his chair, and his dad slaps him around the back of his head.

"Speak to your mother like that again and see just how far I throw you."

"Sorry, Father. Sorry, Mother," Malik mumbles, glaring down at his place setting.

"Morganna, please forgive your betrothed. I'm sure he will soon see the error of his ways and pull his head from his ass," Malik's dad says to me, and I can't help but laugh a little.

"It's forgiven," I say, trying to stifle the laugh around a sip of water from the filled glass in front of me.

"Let me introduce you to the rest of our family." Mimi smiles. "Next to Malik are his younger brothers Nasí, Shai, and Harlyn. Then there is his older brother Tariq. Next to you are his two sisters, Korrín and Zhanna." They all smile and wave as their names are called, and I don't understand why Malik is the thundercloud over what seems to be a family of sunshine. Even if it is a huge family. As someone from a kinship as small as mine, this is a little overwhelming. I try to take it all in stride regardless.

"Tariq chose a life dedicated to the faith," Mimi explains, and I figure that explains the white tunic and pants he's wearing. He's dressed in a fashion dramatically different from the others. The rest look like they're ready to go to battle, but I have no idea what faith it is Mimi is on about. I didn't even think that was a thing in any realm except the mortal realm. "Korrín is our most promising collector after Malik, but since he is destined for the throne, she will lead the collectors."

The white-haired girl smiles at me. She seems so starkly different from her tanned, dark-haired brothers and sisters. There's a story there, but I'm not about to pry right now. "What is a collector?"

Malik grunts in exasperation. "You see, she doesn't even understand this place. She is not fit to be my queen. She is nothing more than an uneducated, untrained, spoiled brat."

I bite my tongue. Honestly? Fuck him, and the chip on his shoulder. He doesn't know me at all. But it isn't worth arguing about because even though he doesn't realize it, I have no real intentions of being his queen.

"Malik, if you don't stop being a dick and speak to your intended like she's an actual person, Mom and Dad won't be the ones who tear into you. I'll make you fucking bleed," Korrín seethes from beside me, her hands clutching at her knife.

My eyes go wide, and I place my hand over hers. The whole table gasps as I make contact with her, so I pull back. "What? I was just going to tell her I'm used to dealing with jackasses."

"She didn't die…" Tariq says with awe.

"I'm sorry, what?" My heart pounds as I take in what he says. Why would they sit me next to someone who could kill me if I accidentally touched them. What the actual fuck?

"Usually, people who touch me without my permission, at least on bare skin as you did, have a bad habit of dying,"

Korrín says, shrugging. “Sorry, I forgot about gloves. But you’re not dead, so bonus. Guess there’s more to her than you thought, Malik.”

He watches me through narrowed eyes as if he’s trying to work me out.

Good luck, buddy, even I don’t have a clue of who I really am.

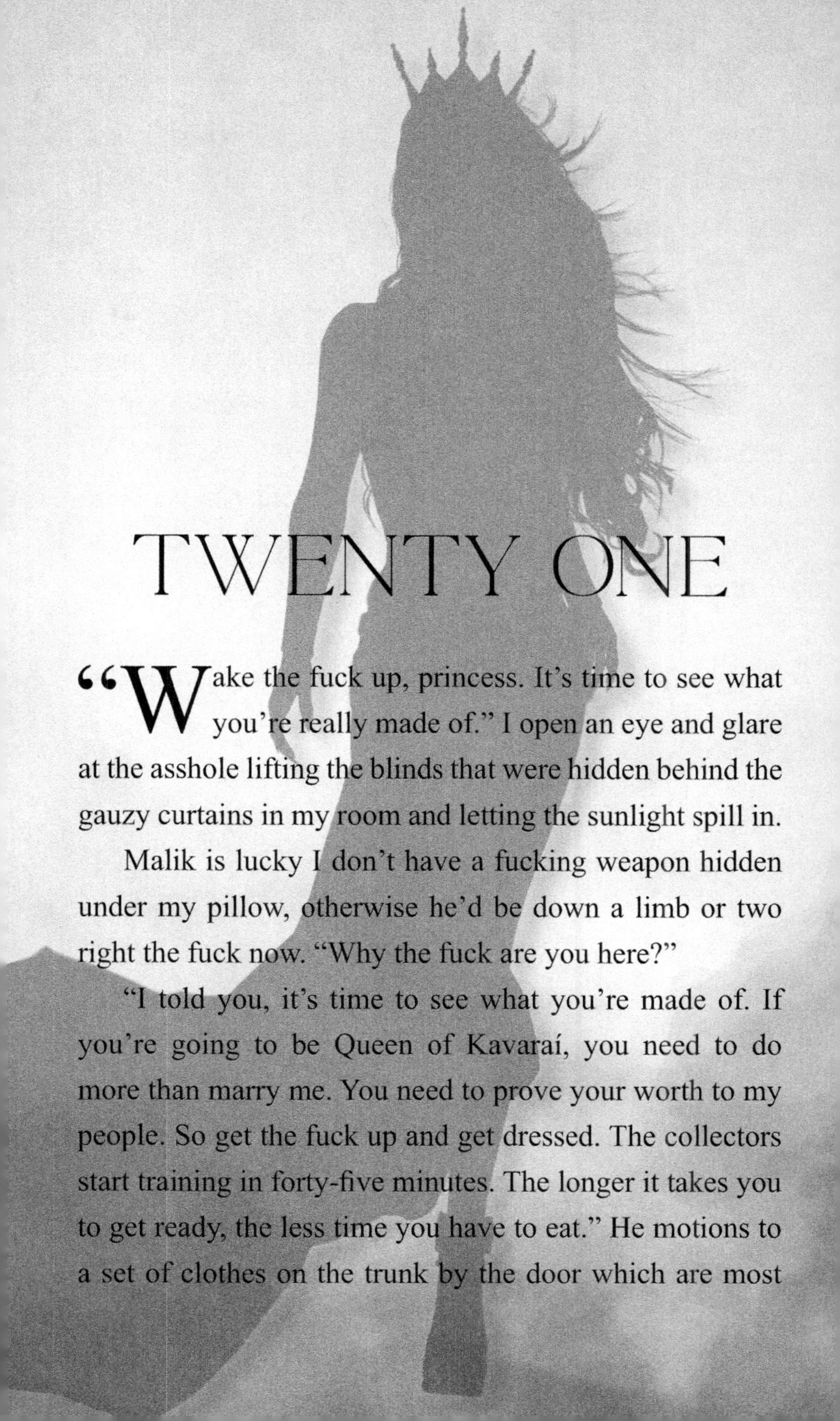

TWENTY ONE

"Wake the fuck up, princess. It's time to see what you're really made of." I open an eye and glare at the asshole lifting the blinds that were hidden behind the gauzy curtains in my room and letting the sunlight spill in.

Malik is lucky I don't have a fucking weapon hidden under my pillow, otherwise he'd be down a limb or two right the fuck now. "Why the fuck are you here?"

"I told you, it's time to see what you're made of. If you're going to be Queen of Kavaraí, you need to do more than marry me. You need to prove your worth to my people. So get the fuck up and get dressed. The collectors start training in forty-five minutes. The longer it takes you to get ready, the less time you have to eat." He motions to a set of clothes on the trunk by the door which are most certainly not mine. "Korrín picked them and said they should fit. So get your ass up. And do not keep me fucking waiting."

He storms from the room even though I've barely even opened my eyes. I grind my teeth together and take a deep breath. I miss my Hellhounds. Kaos would have never let that asshole in my room. I groan as I climb from the bed, thankful I got a shower last night, and take a look at the clothes he brought in for me. It's similar to the outfit Korrín wore last night. It's made of a mix of cotton and leather that look far more complicated than they should be.

I shimmy my way into the pants, which are pretty baggy except for around the waist and ankles where they're super tight. I guess I won't fall over them, at least. I pull on the tank-style top and then work out how the leather wraps work. Once I'm done and slip my feet into the thigh-high leather boots, I kind of feel like a badass. I definitely approve of the collector's uniform if that's what this is.

I'm not sure how much time has passed, so I pull my hair back in a high ponytail and haul ass down to breakfast which I'm hoping is where we ate last night. Malik is already an insufferable dick; I don't need to give him an *actual* reason to bust my ass.

I find my way down, but only Malik and Korrín are at the table. Malik's scowl makes me think I'm late, but Korrín smiles at me as I slide into the chair next to her where I sat yesterday, so I feel a little better.

"That was quicker than I thought it would be, and it seems like you've got everything strapped on right." Korrín laughs. "You're already doing better than Malik did on his first go."

I bite my tongue to stifle the laugh that threatens to spill over because Malik's scowl deepens. "Of all people, Korrín, I would've thought you'd have been on my side with all of this."

"Malik, I am never going to support you being an ass just for the purpose of being an ass. Arranged marriages aren't anything new around here, so pick up your ball sack and get on board. I think our girl here is going to surprise you," she says to him before turning to me. "Now eat up, because today… Well, it's going to test you. You'll be training with the collectors, and I don't take this shit easy on anyone."

"I got this," I say with way more confidence than I feel. I just need to make sure my power is locked all the way down, especially if we're training. My only saving grace is the amount of power training I've been doing lately with Ares and Caleb. Maybe this won't actually kill me off.

I eat my fill because the food here is fucking delicious with an array of different meats, cheeses, and potatoes. It's not at all like the breakfast food I'm used to, but I am so here for it.

Malik smirks when I push my plate away. I know I probably ate too much, but I'm not even sorry.

"Time to see what the ice princess is made of." He stands from the table and storms away. I roll my eyes at his retreating back and turn to Korrín.

"Any idea why he's such an asshole to me?"

She just smiles sadly at me and shrugs a little. "Yes and no, but I'm pretty sure you'll find out soon enough. I wouldn't worry too much. He's actually a good guy when he pulls his head out of his ass."

"Is he in love with someone else?" I ask, almost hopeful, because that could solve a lot of problems.

"If only it were that simple. Come on, let's head out to the training ground. I'm looking forward to seeing the girl that no one usually gets to see. I can feel there's more to you than you let anyone know. I think we're going to get glimpses of her today." She grins at me and stands, so I follow suit.

She's right. There is a lot more to me than what most people see on the surface, but I don't really intend on letting them know that. Korrín can think what she likes, but my main focus is getting back to Caleb and then getting my brother on the throne. But if I can make an ally out of her through all of this, it might just make all of this a little easier.

I tuck away the thought and follow her from the room

and through the sand palace. She takes me out to the stables and sorts out a horse for me. We ride through the desert for what feels like ages before we come across a massive group of warriors lined up with Malik yelling at them at the top of his lungs.

"Time to show us what you've got," Korrín says, taking the reins of my horse. "I'll get your horse sorted out." I look at her like she's lost her mind, but I guess this is what's happening. I dismount and head toward Malik, jutting out my chin and pretending that I'm more confident than I'm feeling at the moment.

Well... This is certainly going to be fun.

These collectors don't fuck around. We've apparently only done the warm-up, and I feel like my lungs are on fucking fire. It doesn't seem as if a single other person is even out of breath, let alone wanting to die the way I am right now. Training with Brandy was a fucking breeze compared to this group. Though, there are a lot less people than I'd have thought there would be.

I guess this is just a specialist group or something. At least I hope so because otherwise, fuck knows what their training would look like.

I bend over and suck in a breath before taking a drink

from the water bottles Korrín hands out to everyone. She moves to the front of the group, taking Malik's place once she's done, looking totally at home. "Okay, let's split up into groups of five and work on our blade handling. We might be chasing the dead, but there are plenty of assholes that will try to stop you. No need to get sloppy."

She winks at me, and I get the feeling that the last bit was more for me than anyone else. I go where I'm herded and accept the curved blade that's offered to me. It's bigger than any of the blades I've worked with before, not quite sword length, but for sure bigger than any daggers I've handled.

I flourish the blade, getting used to its weight and balance the way Ares taught me to. I don't miss the whispers and murmurs of the other collectors, but I don't let myself focus on them. Whispers aren't anything new in my life.

Korrín moves over to my group and pulls me away from them while they pair up. "You're with me. I want to see what's underneath the princess mask."

I grin at her like I'm not terrified of her. But I know if she sees more than I want her to, I am so fucked. "Bring it on."

Her grin matches mine as we move slightly away from the group. "Show me what you're made of," she says, laughing, and drops into a defensive position. I tilt my head from side to side, trying to assess her, but I've barely met her, I have no way to know how she's going to fight. So I draw on everything Ares and Brandy have taught me and attack.

I get lost in the parry of swords and the sound of metal on metal. Holy shit, she's good. My arms burn from the use of the unusual blade, but I refuse to give in. My power dances happily inside of me; but because I have to focus so hard on not letting her best me, I lose the tight grip I've had on it for the past several weeks. It behaves for now, so I leave it be, not wanting to lose focus.

She fakes a right and dives left, but I react too slowly and end up flat on my back, staring up at the clear blue sky.

A hand appears in my face and I take it, jumping back to my feet. It's then that I notice pretty much everyone else had stopped training to watch us.

"Show's over!" Malik yells. "Get back to your own fucking training." Murmurs carry through the air about the sparring, but I push the noise away and turn my focus back on Korrín.

"You fought better than I expected." Korrín grins at me, and I can't help but laugh.

"I get the feeling you were going easy on me."

"Oh I was, but even so, you are more skilled than I thought you'd be from what I've heard about you. Have you trained formally?"

"Gods no. Does my father seem like the type to let his daughter train with the guard?"

"I've never met him, but I'm going to say no," she laughs.

"Yeah, exactly. I've trained mostly with my brother. Nothing official." I shrug making light of it. "I just enjoy a good workout."

She bursts out laughing, and Malik glares over at us.

"Yeah, I don't believe you even a little. But if you're adamant, we can go again."

Her grin lets me know just how much I'm going to regret it, and I groan a little, but fuck it. "Sure, let's do it."

I faceplant on my bed when I finally make it back to my room. My entire body hurts. I'd love to say I gave as good as I got in training today, but I got my fucking ass handed to me. When Korrín kicked my ass the first time and I ate dirt, I caught the look on Malik's face. It might have been the first time I've seen him smile.

Of course he smiled at that. *Jackass.*

"Are you going to sleep, or are you up for some exploring?" I groan as I roll over, finding Malik standing at the end of my bed, arms crossed. Why does he have to look so fucking delicious when he's such an unbearable asshole? The muscles in his arms are fucking insane, especially with those leather bands on them when he folds them over his chest like that.

"I'm up for seeing more of this place," I tell him as I sit up, even managing to smile a little.

"Okay, well get cleaned up. I'll be back after I've showered, and I'll take you out into the city." He doesn't wait for me to answer before he turns and leaves the room, shutting the door as he goes. I'm going to take his civility as a small win. While I have no intention of sticking around with him long enough for it to matter too much, it will be much easier to get through all of this if he isn't being such a dick.

Though, if he's nice, I'm likely to feel even guiltier about fucking him over and dropping his ass the second I can. That said, maybe he'll understand it if he gives me a chance to explain. I shake my head at the thought because it isn't even a possibility yet. I don't like him, let alone trust him. I need to remember the plan. This is all just part of keeping my father lulled into a false sense of security. This is not my life, and it never will be.

That being said, I drag myself from the bed, and grab a quick cold shower before re-dressing. Back in a floor length black dress and some flat sandals, I feel much more myself. I let my hair down and fluff it a little so it's not such a mess. I'm not here to impress anyone, so I figure that's enough.

Just as I'm finished, a knock sounds at my door, and I turn to find Malik standing there waiting for me. I'm not sure if I'm more shocked about the knocking or the lack of scowl on his face. "Ready to go?"

"Yup, let's go see your home." I smile at him, and he doesn't immediately glare back. I'm going to take that as another win. I follow him wordlessly as we leave the sand palace, and the walls beyond it. This time, instead of heading into the desert, we head toward the city that I saw when I first got here.

"Kavaraí is very different to the Shadow Realm," Malik tells me as we walk down the dusty path. "Here, we do not rule with fear and terror. We want the respect and loyalty of our people because we need them as much as they need us. I'm not sure how much you really know about Kavaraí, but everyone knows that we are the Realm of the Dead."

"Honestly, there isn't much written about this Realm, so I don't know much beyond that," I tell him, frowning a little.

"There is a reason for that," he says, nodding. "The Realm of the Dead holds the souls of all of the dead, from every Realm. Though no longer for the mortals or the Angels. They go to the Shadow Realm, or stay in Avalon as I'm sure you know."

I nod at him, not wanting to interrupt him even though no, I didn't know that they no longer held the souls of Angels. I want to learn, though. The Seven Realms have always fascinated me, and it doesn't hurt that this is the most he's talked to me without insulting me. I'm not about to knock it. "The dead don't always want to leave their old lives behind, which is why we have collectors. Some Demons can obviously regenerate if they have enough power, but for example, if they've been sentenced to death of the body, their soul is held here, and they don't always want to come. And there are more than a few people who are willing to help an errant soul.

"Then there are those who like to try to steal souls, trying to collect the souls of their enemies for whatever reason. That is why our collectors are an elite force."

"It's a very fascinating way of life."

"It might not be as glamorous as some, but it's a good life. We take care of the souls here as they should be taken care of, no matter what some people might think," he growls, and I startle.

"I don't know what that means."

He grabs my arm and glares down at me. "Of course you don't. You're a pampered little princess. Let me show you why you're not fit to rule here."

He shakes me before gripping my bicep hard enough to leave a bruise in his fingers' wake. Before I can object, he whispers us from the path to the city.

I have a feeling I'm about to get dropped in the middle of fucking nowhere and left.

I gasp as the surroundings materialize, and I try to work out where the fuck we are.

"This, this right here is why you aren't fit to rule."

"I don't understand," I whisper as I look out over the bleak space. It looks like this used to be another city, but the earth is scorched. The buildings are no more than ruins. It's a bleak landscape, but something about this place just feels wrong.

"Of course you don't. You've been nothing more than a little princess sitting in her ebony fucking tower while the rest of the world crumbles."

"Why don't you explain it to me?" I ask softly, being gentle despite him being such an ass. I think I might finally understand his motivation if he tells me about this place.

"This city is where I was born. It was my home once before…" he trails off, and tugs at his hair. He looks like he's lost to a nightmare inside of his head, but I can't do anything to help him. I think if I tried, he'd likely cut my throat before accepting it.

"Up until about seventy years ago, Kavaraí was the

home of the dead. All of the dead. Until Samiel and Michael decided that the Angel souls, and the mortal souls, weren't being treated with the respect they deserved. Which is total fucking horseshit—we treat all souls with the respect they deserve. Each and every fucking one."

I nod, but stay quiet since he's obviously going through something.

"Avalon declared war on Kavaraí. We'd been fighting for around seventeen years when we thought luck was finally on our side. We captured an Angel, and she was taken prisoner in this city. We were trying to barter with the Archangel, Michael, to pull back his troops in return for the safe passage of the Angel. All we wanted was to discuss what to do with the souls like civil fucking people," he yells to the skies and starts pacing again. "The Angels pulled back, and my uncle decided he didn't want to give up the Angel prisoner until after a deal was made. In doing so, he condemned this entire city."

"I'm sorry," I say quietly, and he pins me with a stare before scowling even harder and looking away.

"Sorry, she says," he mutters and kicks at the ground before turning back to me.

"I don't understand how that decision resulted in all of this, or why this destruction means I'm not fit to rule beside you," I say, trying to capture his attention again, hoping to hear the rest of the story. It's obviously a hard one for him to tell, but I'd really like him to not treat me like a piece of shit every time we're within sight of each other.

"Of course you don't fucking understand, and that's exactly why you're not fit to rule. Do you have any idea the kind of power the Angels wield? You're too fucking weak, and we need to be strong. That's what this particular war showed us. My uncle wasn't strong, and it cost us so much. Too much." He pauses before dropping to the ground, curling his knees in front of him.

"My uncle, in all his idiotic wisdom, underestimated the might of the Angels. We'd held our own for seventeen years; and he figured if we tried, we could win against them if it came to it. So he kept the black-winged Angel as a failsafe. He tortured her, trying to get information about Avalon's weaknesses. I still hear her screams in my nightmares—but they are nothing compared to the screams that came next.

"It turns out the Angels they sent here to invade were just a young group of Death Dealers. They sent in their weakest to fight us, and it almost overwhelmed us. Then after they pulled back and my uncle betrayed them, it only took one of them to ravage this place." He takes a deep breath, and I decide to sit down as he drops his head onto his arms which are resting on his knees.

"One Angel… the Archangel of War. He took it as a personal offense that we'd taken this Angel hostage. And the things my uncle did to her? Let's say it more than pissed him off. In retaliation, he laid waste to the entire city. The scorch marks are where his lightning burned people alive, turning them to dust in seconds. The storm he brought here killed every single fucking soul that was in the city. My uncle included. Nothing grows here now. It hasn't since that day. My father released the souls of the mortals and Angels the next day, and Avalon reclaimed them before making a deal with your father to hold the mortal souls in the Shadow Realm."

I sit there, speechless, trying to take it all in.

One Angel did this? Holy fucking shit.

At least now everything Malik has said and done makes sense. He doesn't want a useless queen. He wants someone who can help protect his people from more devastation, from anything like what happened here. My heart aches for him, and I hate my father a little more for putting him through. How could he do this to either of us?

"This is why your parents wanted to align with my father?" I ask, not expecting him to respond, but he does.

"Pretty much. Your father isn't someone people want to piss off. Even if his powers are useless against some beings, he has a lot of Demons at his beck and call. The savages within the Shadow Army are feared in all Seven Realms. If we have ties with the Shadow Realm, my parents believe that no one will be able to hurt Kavaraí the way it's been hurt before. But they're idiots if they think your father will come to the rescue. We asked for help before, and no one came. No one."

He stands and dusts himself off before glaring down at me again. "That is exactly why I have no interest in marrying you. You're not the Queen Kavaraí needs or the one it deserves. You are nothing but a spoiled Shadow Princess, and there isn't anything you can say or do that will change my mind."

TWENTY TWO

I've been here for four days now, and Malik has ignored my presence ever since he showed me the ruined city. He left me there in his anger, and it wasn't until later that Korrín found me and brought me back to their home, apologizing the entire way for her brother. I told her not to bother, I half get it. He loves his people, and he thinks I'm not good enough to help save them. I can't say I wouldn't be a giant bag of ass if I was in his position too.

I've spent most of my time with her and Zhanna in the library here. It's fucking beautiful in there, and I've made the most of it. There are a lot more history books here than there are back home. The history of the Seven Realms fascinates me in a way not much else does, and I've soaked up as much knowledge as I've been able to.

The boys have been off doing fuck knows what, but I think they're just trying to stay on Malik's good side. Considering the shit he's given his sisters for being nice to me, I can't say I really blame them.

I honestly just can't wait to go home, which is really saying something. The longer I'm here, the more I feel for the plight of these people. I want to know more about the war with Avalon and my father's sudden deal with the Angels to have the mortal souls in the Shadow Realm. I wouldn't put it past him to have started the fucking war in the first place. He's so fucking twisted that it probably seemed like fun for him, and a win-win.

Especially since now Kavaraí is willing to have a tighter alliance with him.

I get the feeling the wedding is just the start of the madness. I don't even want to think about what else might happen.

I sit and eat my breakfast quietly, letting the family's chatter wash over me. I might not like it here, but somehow I feel safer here than I do at home. Even though I spend basically every second worrying about my brother and Caleb.

I really need to take a day and just think about what the fuck my next move will be once Ares is safely with Xavi. My father is going to know I had a hand in it even if he doesn't believe I could've orchestrated it. I'm hoping that I can hide Caleb and I in other parts of the Realm long enough for him to calm down about it.

I have all these big plans about killing my father and placing Ares on the throne, but deep down, my father still fucking terrifies me. I might have the power to kill him, but he's nearly a thousand years old, and he's one of the Shadowed. He's in touch with his powers and the shadows in ways I've never been, and I'm not sure that I'll learn in time to get Ares on the throne without losing my own life.

My hatred for him burrows deep, but I'm not sure if that's greater than my fear of what he's capable of.

I hate being this honest with myself. It makes me feel like a lost fucking child, only just pretending at being an adult. Xavi seemed to have faith in me when I gave him a brief idea of my intentions, but then, he doesn't really know me either.

Gods, most days, I don't even really know me.

I wish I had more time. Time to work on my powers and discover what I am truly capable of. Hell, even more time to find out what this claimed and chosen one bullshit is about because maybe that could give me the edge I need to best my father.

I clasp my fork tighter as my hand starts to shake at the overwhelming mess of it all. I have to believe I can do this, otherwise my father will keep doing what he's doing with zero fucking consequence. I can't keep looking the other way while he plays with his toys in the throne room. I can no longer ignore him literally destroying people and then encasing them in stone to torture them further.

My power stirs inside of my chest as my body fills with dread at the thought of living out my existence that way. I know there are things in life worse than death, and my father is capable of each and every one of them.

He needs to be dethroned, but as strong as Ares is, he doesn't have the power to end our father the way I do. I'm also not sure that in the end he would have the stomach for it. I might not have meant to kill my mother, but I did it. I haven't regretted it once. Not even for a second. Ares will make the best king, but I don't think killing our father is something he's capable of.

"Hey, are you okay?" Korrín asks quietly, nudging me with her shoulder. I look up to see both her and Malik staring at me.

I smile tightly at them both before turning back to face Korrín. "I'm fine, just lost in my own head."

"Looked more fucking terrified than lost," Malik mutters, and my gaze bounces back to him. I'm more shocked that he was paying me any attention than I am that he's actually speaking to me again.

"What reason do I have to be afraid? I'm a witless, weak princess, remember? Protected at all costs." I roll my eyes as the words fall from my mouth. I'm just glad his parents aren't here. I don't feel the need to bite my tongue with his siblings present the same way I do around his parents.

"How could I forget," he snorts, shaking his head. "You're with me today, the others are all busy. So just stay quiet and don't get yourself killed."

"What are we doing?" I ask, trying to find some sliver of joy despite having to spend my day with his cranky ass.

"We're going hunting," he says, and I grin. I look to Korrín who nods, confirming his words.

"I'll be there too," she says, and I grin even wider.

"Yes!" I exclaim, happy to finally be doing something other than reading. Surprisingly, that isn't something I thought I'd ever say.

"Don't get too excited," Malik grumps. "You're not helping. You're just along for the ride." His words don't diminish my excitement at all. I'm totally excited about seeing how this works, though I do feel a small pang of sadness that Caleb isn't here for this. He'd love it too.

I smirk back at Malik who is still frowning at me. I'm not letting him ruin this for me. From Korrín's wicked smile, I get the feeling this is going to be the most fun I've had since I got here.

I gear up in the outfit Korrín gave me on my first full day here for training, and I wait in the stables for Malik. Korrín paces with a grin on her face, strutting one way across the stables and then back the other way, the same way she has since I got here. Her nervous energy mixed with her excitement has me on edge, but I don't hate it.

"I know Malik was being a dick earlier, but we really can't afford for you to get hurt." She hands me a sword and sheath, which she helps me strap on to my back in a mimic of hers. "Do not take risks. If you think you can fight, then fight. Otherwise stick to one of us like glue. We're going to Silvius. Dark Elves are no fucking joke. They're trying to resurrect this asshole, so we need to get in and get the soul before they manage it. The King of Silvius is not happy with this shit happening, so we need to claim this soul and quickly."

"I've never been to Silvius. Prince Callisto was the first Elf I've ever met," I tell her, and she chuckles.

"Your father really did keep you sheltered and tucked away." She shakes her head before checking the strap for the sheath once more. "Don't worry, you'll be free of that place soon, and even if Malik doesn't take you places, I'm always down for having you come explore with me."

I grin at her, trying to hide the sadness in my heart knowing that won't actually happen. "Sounds awesome."

Malik appears in the next second with three other

collectors. “I brought more hands, just in case the Elves decide to be a problem. Plus it’s more help if the princess gets herself kidnapped.”

“You almost sound like you hope that happens,” I snark at him, and he honest-to-Gods smiles.

“Least then you’re not my problem.” He smirks and holds up his hands. I roll my eyes and turn back to Korrín.

“Such a charmer, your brother.” She laughs at me before looking at the others, becoming more serious in an instant.

She explains to the others who the target is and what the expected situation we’re heading into is before asking if anyone has any questions. Everyone stays quiet, and since I’m just along for the ride, I keep my mouth shut too.

Malik moves so he’s standing at my back before whispering in my ear. “Do not get yourself fucking killed, *rainha*. I might not like you, but my people do not need another war.”

Before I even get a chance to respond, we whisper away. When the world reconstructs, we’re in the thick of the forests of Silvius. It’s pitch black here, and I’m suddenly glad for my enhanced eyesight. I’ve read of the monsters that live in these forests, and I really don’t fancy being anyone or anything’s dinner today.

If I didn’t know better, I’d say Malik’s words almost sounded like he cared, but I know deep down that it’s about his people rather than about me.

I follow them through the trees, ducking and weaving through the branches and under the bush. I try to stay silent, but it's almost impossible, for me anyway. It eventually gets to the point that Malik stops, huffing like I'm doing it on purpose and makes me climb on his back. If it wasn't for the fear that I'd get someone else hurt with my noisy ass, I'd have flat out refused. Instead, I climb up and feel humiliated. *What an asshole.*

Korrín looks at me, trying to apologize for him with her eyes, but I shake my head. She is not her brother's keeper.

The group keeps moving, and Malik moves as if my ass isn't even on his back. I have to duck every now and then to avoid branches, but otherwise we move seamlessly through the forest.

Firelight flickers in the distance, and Malik finally lets me down onto my own feet. I'd thank him if I didn't think he'd throw it back in my face.

Korrín starts making hand gestures, and I assume that she's communicating the plan she went over with them before we left since we can now see the group of Elves in the distance. The others start to move, so I take a step. Malik grabs my arm. "You're staying here."

"Why even bring me then?" I hiss, and he shakes me, gripping my arm tighter.

"Because my mother insisted. Now stay the fuck here." He doesn't bother saying another word before he blends into the darkness. So I stay where I am, pissed off and humiliated yet again, while the others move to capture this soul from the Dark Elves.

I don't know much about the politics of this Realm, at least not current ones, but from what I've managed to work out from the conversations today, the Dark Elves are trying to overthrow the royal family. After meeting the Prince, I can't say that isn't for the best, he was a special kind of cruel and creepy. Just because someone is a royal, doesn't mean they're fit to lead. Just look at my father.

Shouts start up in the distance, and I try to focus on everything that's going on, but I can't see. I move closer, trying to stay out of sight and notice just how many Elves there are. There must have been others hiding in the trees that we didn't see before.

Shit, they're overwhelmed.

I bite my lip, hesitating over what to do. Do I wait and see if they can get out of this on their own, or do I try to help?

My power stirs in my chest, and I know that I can help. It feels almost instinctual, in a way that my power never has before... other than the time I killed my mother.

I move toward them, staying as quiet as I can, not that it matters. All fucking hell has broken loose in the clearing.

I see one of the collectors on their knees, the tip of a sword at the back of their neck. Shit. Shit. Shit.

I get closer and find a discarded bow and quiver. I pick it up and nock an arrow, like I've done a thousand times before, and let it fly.

Woah, Elven bows are the shit.

My arrow flies true and through the throat of the Elf who had the collector captive. I let loose a few more arrows, each one landing true and disabling the intended target. I move closer still and watch as Korrín collects the soul, the white, smoky substance captured and swirling in a glowing glass-like box. It's weird as fuck to watch. I've never seen a soul like that before, but then again, I've never been around collectors or Elves before either.

Every day is a school day these days. The last of the Elves are quickly disabled, and I turn my attention back to Korrín when Malik shouts her name.

Just as she looks down at the soul, an Elf appears behind her, sword lifted. I let loose my last arrow, taking him out before he pushes the blade through her throat.

All eyes turn to me, and Korrín belts out a laugh. "Guess it's a good thing we brought you along, otherwise I'd be toast. What was your body count?"

I shrug, not wanting to brag about my twelve arrows and twelve disabled Elves.

She just turns to Malik and grins. "Told you there was

more to her."

Since the hunt with the collectors, Malik has been almost nice to me. It's been weird as fuck, but apparently saving his sister means that he's starting to soften toward me. That or Korrín's badgering is wearing him down about the fact that there's more to me than there seems.

Personally, I'm just hoping it's the fact I killed the Elf. I so don't need him thinking that there's more to me than meets the eye. I'm also glad I didn't have to use my power, especially since it's been a little erratic after I let it have some breathing space when I thought I might need to use it. It keeps getting excited when Malik is near me, and I keep shutting it down. I don't know why it's so curious about him, but nope. I don't trust him.

Even if he is being nice. Maybe less so *because* he's being nice.

I've been left to my own devices today, so I decided to finally go and explore the main city that's situated just outside of the palace walls. It's literally a whole different world here. No one takes my money. Apparently word of saving Korrín has gotten around, and so all I hear is that I would dishonor the people of Kavaraí by not accepting their gifts. I've had more sent up to the palace than I feel comfortable with, and I'm going to find a way to pay these people for their wares if it kills me, especially after seeing some of the devastation they've been through.

I won't lie, though, all of the food I've tasted has been absolutely divine. I've refused full servings of everything because I physically can't eat that much food, but the few bites of each dish are so fucking good. From the spicy, to the tart, to the sweet. I haven't eaten something yet that I don't like. I've noticed more people speak in my language today too. Whether that's because they understand that I don't know what they're saying or because these people actually just speak the same language as me, I don't know.

I tuck the question away to try and remember to ask Malik or Korrín later.

I've found small gifts for Ares and Caleb as I've wandered too. A ring of black metal for Caleb that I hope fits and a jacket for Ares. It's black, with red lining and stitching, and it is all kinds of beautiful. I just know he'll love it.

My mind wanders back to them and home the entire day. I feel like I've been away far too long. And while I know that if anything had gone wrong, someone would have gotten word to me, I still can't help the pit of dread sitting in the bottom of my stomach.

When the sun starts to set, I make the walk back up to the sand palace, enamored with this land and the beauty it holds. Especially at sunset. The way the sun paints the sky with pinks and purples is unlike anything I've ever seen.

The air grows much colder once the sun is down, so I hurry back to the palace to get out of the chill. When I reach the main entry hall, I find Malik and his father, Kharim, shouting at one another. I hover just outside the door because this is not a fight I want to be a part of.

They're speaking the language I don't know, the one I heard others in the palace using, so I don't feel bad for hovering, but once I've heard my name more than a few times, I change my mind and walk into the hall. Malik spots me and throws his hands in the air before walking in the opposite direction.

"Is everything okay?" I ask Kharim as I walk over to where he's standing.

"Yes, it's fine. No one had any idea where you were, and we were going to send out the guard to try and find you."

"I'm so sorry, I didn't think to tell anyone where I was going. I've just been exploring the city," I tell him, feeling really quite guilty. I didn't think anyone would really notice I was gone to be honest.

"You are fine, my son just doesn't quite know what to make of you. He is not used to such headstrong women I think, despite his older sister. The girls here have never really fought him about anything. It is good that you do not bow to him." He grins at me and places his arm around my shoulders. "Now that you're back, let's go find some sweets, shall we? I've been craving a pie all day."

I laugh softly at his words. It's so funny to see this side of the King of the Dead. I get the feeling not too many people get to see the softer side of him.

"I have eaten so much down in the markets today," I tell him, rubbing my stomach.

"Pssh, there is always space for sweets." He winks, and he is so full of joy I can't make myself deny him.

"You're right, there is always space." I grin at him, and he squeezes me into his side.

"That's my girl! I have just the sweet for you!" He lets me go, and I follow him through the halls, hating myself a little for the fact that I've been lying to them all, and that I'm going to just abandon these people when my father is out of the way.

After eating so many sweets with Kharim that I feel like I'm going to be sick, we head toward the family room. When I spot Malik running down a hall looking for us, my stomach drops. "You need to come, quickly."

He turns and runs back in the opposite direction. I look up to Kharim who frowns, but takes my hand. "I know where he's going."

He whispers us to a room I've never seen before, but it looks like a study. He moves behind the desk, and a second later, Malik walks in the door. "We have a visitor."

Seconds later, Teddy strolls through the door, and my eyes go wide. He's pissed and that fucking terrifies me.

"What's wrong?"

"Your father threw a tantrum. We managed to get Caleb out before he was found. He's back at the farm, but the King has your brother locked down." My heart sinks while Malik and his father both turn to look at me.

"I think we're missing something," Kharim says, and I nod, dropping into the chair opposite him. "Why don't you tell us exactly who Caleb is, and why your father has your brother?"

"I need to get back, I just wanted to let you know, Morgan. We'll keep Caleb safe, but your father's making all sorts of threats about him if this wedding doesn't go as planned." I stand and hug him quickly.

"Thank you for keeping me up to date." I sigh, and he nods before disappearing in a cloud of mist. I take my seat again, and my power flares. I rein it back in, but I know that Malik and his father both felt it because their shock is written all over their faces.

I sit and tell them about Caleb, leaving out the whole claiming thing, but Kharim just looks sad for me. I guess with arranged marriages being a thing here, this is more common than I'd have thought. Then I explain about my father's threats should the marriage not go ahead.

"You did not know about the wedding until it was announced?" Kharim asks, and I shake my head.

"I had my suspicions as my father isn't exactly discreet about some things and talk of me being 'sold off' was all over the Realm. I know that you are all great people, and the alliance is advantageous for you all too, so I have no intentions of not going ahead with the wedding, but I am afraid for my brother and Caleb."

Malik doesn't say another word. Instead, he stands and leaves. I get it, he doesn't want this marriage either, but there's nothing fun about hearing about someone else being forced to marry you either.

"Do not worry about him. As I said before, my son has trouble expressing his emotions in the correct manner. You must go home, and I will make arrangements to bring the wedding forward. I assume you would like your lover to come here with you after the marriage? And that he won't be a problem?"

"I didn't even realize that was an option," I say, sitting back in my chair, just sort of blinking at him. "But if it's a serious option on the table, then yes please."

"Royal consorts aren't exactly an uncommon thing. Especially with arranged marriages. As long as you hold up your end of the terms, I will ensure your lover is safe here."

"Thank you," I say, sagging down in my chair. "For everything."

"Of course, while I require your father's allegiance, I am not exactly… approving of his methods with certain things. But power is power, and after the tragedies we've suffered, we need a powerful ally," he says with a nod. "Now, I assume you would like to head home sooner rather than later to check on your brother?"

"Please, if that's okay?"

"Of course, head to your room and pack your things. I'll have Korrín take you home within the hour."

"Thank you," I blurt, and he nods once more before dismissing me.

Yet again, guilt racks me that I intend on abandoning these people, but then a new idea takes root, and I smile.

Maybe not all hope is lost.

For any of us.

TWENTY THREE

I've been home for three days, and I haven't seen my brother or Caleb once since I got back. I'm trying to not be pissed off about it, but I'm failing. Being away from here, I'd almost forgotten how lonely it is at the Shadow Palace. At least Kaos hasn't left my side since I got back.

None of the pack has really, and I am not even a little sad about it. My father has taunted me at every opportunity about Ares, and it's making me physically ill. I hope his taunts are to fuck with me and not what he's actually done to my brother. The thought of Ares at the mercy of my father and The Carver makes my stomach roll.

I finish pinning the bright white pearls into my dark hair and stare back at the person in the mirror. I don't look anything like myself. I've never wanted to do anything less in my entire life. But not knowing where Ares is or what my father has really done to him, all I can do is see this through.

The only thing that keeps me going is knowing that Caleb is safe with the Duttons' right now. I know he'll be with them at the wedding, I just hope that Father brings Ares to the wedding too. Only then can I put my plan into action. I already know Xavi will be here, Father lorded that over me too. Little does he know that I'm over the moon he's coming.

It's all just down to timing.

I need to get Ares out of here. If anything happens to him because he tried to help me, I'll never forgive myself.

Xavi and Killian will keep him safe. Their Realm is the only one other than Avalon strong enough to actually go up against my father. It's the only place he'll truly be safe. At least while my father lives.

I just hope it's not too late already.

I smooth down my dress and take a step backward, taking in the full view of myself on my wedding day. This isn't exactly what I pictured as a little girl when I envisioned my wedding. But then again, who pictures plots of murder, my heart breaking for my brother, and fear for us all. Marrying a man who I'm pretty sure hates me, even if he was less cold toward me by the time I left Kavaraí.

Yeah, that's not what I imagined at all.

I can't even say it'd be different if my mom was still alive. Because if she was, this would probably be even worse.

I take a deep breath and look out at the setting sun.

My time is nearly up.

"At least I'll always have you, right boy?" I say to Kaos as I scratch the space between his ears, and he whimpers at me like he knows just how much I hate all of this. "It's okay, you've kept me safe this far. I promise I can keep myself alive through this bit."

I hope.

A knock sounds at the door, and I let out a sigh.

I guess it's time for me to get married and make my father's dreams come true. I let out a dry bark of a laugh and my bedroom door opens. Amelia grins at me from the doorway.

"How are you here?" I gasp, feeling happiness for the first time in days. She rushes in the room and hugs me tightly. I practically crush her in return and try not to cry.

"There is no way I wouldn't be here for you today. Don't worry, Dad has me locked down, but I wanted you to know I was here. I have your back, however you need me."

"Amelia Harris, I freaking love you," I gush before releasing her.

"I know," she grins, winking at me. "And I love you right back. Now go marry the Prince of the Dead, and we'll catch up later."

I walk down the center aisle of the throne room. It's pretty much the last place I would've ever picked to get married, but just like everything else with this wedding, it was my father's choice. At least the sentient statues are gone.

I stand out like a freaking beacon in my white dress—it's a stark contrast against the black of this room. My face is covered by a veil, so at least I don't have to pretend to smile to the masses here. I recognize all of the ruling families of the Realms and a few other faces in the sea of my father's sycophants as I walk toward Malik.

He's in a black and gold tunic and pants. Even the buckles are gold. Gods, this whole thing is such a farce.

I spot the Elvish and Mer princes next before seeing Xavi and Killian. They at least give me a sad smile each. Caleb is sat with the Duttons', and I hate that he's here. I guess that was my father's doing too. My power jumps in my chest at the sight of them, and I desperately want to escape with them alongside Ares today, but we won't ever be truly safe while Father still lives.

I look over to the right to see Malik's family sitting and grinning at me. To them I offer a true smile. Despite everything, they gave me nothing but kindness while I was with them in Kavaraí. Even if they act differently here with my father, I know the truth of who they are, and I cling to that. It's one of the few things that keeps me placing one foot in front of the other as I walk toward my twisted fate.

My father sits on his throne, just behind where Malik stands. I'm almost thankful to find Malik scowling at me, that much, at least, I know is a truth from him.

When I reach Malik, I turn and scan the room, finally finding my brother. He walks from the back of the room to sit on his throne beside Father, and though he's trying to hide it, I can still see his limp. He looks thinner and very nearly broken. My heart breaks from seeing him, especially like this, but Malik takes my hand and pulls my attention back to him before he lifts my veil.

He squeezes my hand, but I'd be stupid to think it's anything but a warning not to fuck this up. Even if he doesn't want to marry me, he doesn't want to piss off his parents either.

Our officiant clears his throat and begins addressing the room. I shut it out, all of it. None of this is for me. This entire day is about my father, and just one look at his smug, smiling face tells the world that. He's very pleased with himself, and it only serves to piss me off further.

I take a deep breath and unclench my jaw so that Ares doesn't pay for me not putting on a good enough show. Because even without him saying the words, I know that is my father's intention.

"Morganna Voux, Princess of the Shadow Realm, do you willingly enter this joining of souls with Malik Favreau, Prince of the Dead?" The officiant's words bring me back to the wedding, and I nod.

"I do," I say loud and clear, so that no one perceives me as anything but the willing and compliant little girl my father portrays me as.

The officiant nods and repeats the words back to Malik, and he agrees as clearly as I did.

"Then with your agreement, may your souls be bound together in this marriage. I now pronounce you husband and wife." The crowd cheers and claps while I try not to cry in anger. Of course they're happy about it. They don't care that neither of us truly consented to this or that we were forced into it.

Why wouldn't they cheer?

"Now ladies and gentlemen, the viewing of the consummation of the marriage will commence shortly. If you make your way to the ballroom, the married couple and the viewing party will join you after."

What the actual fuck?!

I did not agree to this, not even a fucking little bit.

The procession leaves the room with most of Malik's family going with them. Only a few people are left other than my father and Malik's parents, and I don't recognize any of them.

"Did you know?" I hiss at Malik, and he just shrugs at me.

He fucking *shrugs!*

"Let's get this done, shall we?" my father says, standing with a clap of his hands. I glare at him, and he just grins back at me.

No fucking chance.

"They can't be serious about this," I hiss to Malik as we're led down one of the halls in my father's wing of the palace.

"Apparently they are," he quips, side-eyeing me. His parents and my father trail behind us along with a group of other faces I don't care to name. I try to think of any way to get out of this.

There is no way in hell I'm fucking this guy, and I'm sure as hell not doing it in front of a room full of people. I look back again, and I'm just grateful that Ares heard my father's words and got Caleb the fuck out of the palace. I don't know where they went, but I just hope it's real far from here.

The guards ahead open a set of double doors ahead of us, and my jaw nearly hits the fucking floor. I can't believe they think this is okay. Even from here, I can see the gold four-poster bed inlaid with gems, the red sheets, and the sheer curtains that surround it. It's fucking ridiculous. All of it. I skid to a stop on the spot, spinning to look at my father before going anywhere near that room. "You can't make us do this! We're married, that should be enough."

"Do you really want to question my orders, Morganna? Or do you forget so easily the consequences of not doing what you are told?" His eyes dance with laughter because he fucking knows he has me pushed into a corner. He knows I won't let him hurt Caleb.

I turn back on my heel and grab Malik's arm, pulling him into the bedroom and slamming the doors closed before anyone else can get in. Turning the key in the lock, I lean back against the door and take a deep breath. I know we don't have long, so I need to speak to Malik alone and quickly. This was always going to happen, and I'm not exactly shy about having sex with him. It's the audience I'm fucking opposed to, but fuck them.

"I guess this is happening." I sigh, and he shakes his head.

"I have no issue with fucking my bride. Would I rather not have her dad watch? Sure. I'm looking forward to that part about as much as having my mom in the room. But this is a standard custom at home." He shrugs and drops onto the bed.

"Well, at least we're on the same page I guess, but just

FYI, that's a custom that's going to go if you expect me to rule beside you, because it's fucked up."

"Agreed." He nods, and I laugh.

"Well, that's two things we've managed to agree on. At least the marriage is off to a good start," I joke, and his eyes sparkle.

"I am aware you love another, Morganna. I will flat out refuse to do this though, if you do not consent." I kinda want to kiss him for that alone.

"I consent, you're my husband. Even if I did get married against my will. I'm not shy about sex."

"Well, I guess you better hold onto that thought," he says as fists bang against the door. I move to stand beside him as he opens the door and grins at my father. "Sorry everyone, I just needed a minute with my wife. Let's get this done, shall we?"

"About time," my father grunts as he saunters into the room with Malik's parents entering behind him. They move to the seats on the far side of the room, and I can't help but cringe at how the room is laid out. It's like a fucking sex theatre, and all I want to do is gag.

Malik takes my hand and places his other hand under my chin, bringing my gaze to his dark eyes. "Forget about them," he murmurs as presses his lips against mine. There's a spark when his lips touch mine, but up until a few moments ago, this guy has been nothing but a giant asshole to me. I'm not about to forget that, but at least he is trying to help me through this. He guides me to the bed as he kisses me, and it's not until he pulls back that I realize he's positioned us so one of the sheer curtains hides us partially and my back is to everyone else.

Maybe he's not as big of an asshole as he's made himself out to be to this point. "Eyes on me," he commands, and I look back up at him, his dark skin glistening in the candlelight as he takes off his jacket and shirt. His calloused hands reach forward and pull me to stand, and he turns me to face away from the bed before starting to undo the strings of the corset on my dress.

Once he has me stripped down to nothing he throws me back on the bed, my back to our audience. He grasps my throat and leans forward until our noses are almost touching. "You're probably not going to enjoy this. I'm nothing like the other boys you've known."

Well, that's not ominous or anything.

If he thinks I'm going to cower to him and his words, he clearly doesn't know who he just married.

Bringing both my hands up to his wrists, I stare at him like I don't give a fuck just to show him just how unaffected I am. It's all bravado, of course. This isn't exactly how I saw today going.

Why does he have to be such a fucking dick?

Before I have time to register the movement, he

leans down, one hand grabbing both of my forearms and whispers menacingly in my ear.

"Do. Not. Fucking touch me. Ever. This isn't one of your story books where people fall in love and have a happily ever after, Morganna. We marry, we fuck until you've given me an heir, and then you shut the fuck up while I rule. That's it. The next time you touch me in our bed, I'll make sure you never forget it. Trust me, you don't want that."

No matter how afraid he thinks I might be of him and his outdated traditions, he has no idea who the fuck I really am. I refuse to give him the satisfaction of seeing me even a little afraid of his threats. And here I thought he was being somewhat decent. I guess not. Full asshole mode, engaged.

His words do nothing but make me more curious than ever, and I want to push every fucking button he has just to see how far he'll go. "Consider me warned. And don't worry, you're doing me a favor. At least this way I won't have to pretend to enjoy it." His dark eyes blaze with simmering rage. Good.

Fuck him and his fucking crown. I have my own, dammit.

As his gaze flickers to the restless onlookers, he gives them a smirk and then releases my throat long enough to remove his tunic. I have questions about the scar on his chest, but now is definitely not the time. I don't want to even hint that I might have an interest in him. I thought our time in Kavaraí had maybe changed things between us, but today has shown me that I was very fucking wrong.

I also don't want to enjoy the view but damn, it's hard to ignore the cut lines of his chest, the ribbed valleys of his abs, and the distinct 'V' that dips into the hem of his pants.

Pants that he's now unbuttoning.

Looking at him feels like a betrayal to Caleb, so I avert my gaze, but he's having none of that. His hand goes back to my throat, and the squeeze of his thumb and middle fingers are a bit tighter than before until I look back at him.

"Eyes on me. You watch as your husband takes you for the first time." I fight the strong urge to roll my eyes at his theatrics but manage to keep myself under control. That would be a response, and I can feel how much he wants one from me.

Our first order of business once he's crowned King will definitely be the removal of these medieval practices. No one should have to suffer sex in front of their parents. Especially with assholes like this. Fuck it, arranged marriages are out too.

"Yes, sir," I drip with sarcasm, my eyes narrowed as his mouth curves into a deadly smile.

Fuck, he likes that. Well, I won't be saying that to him ever again.

Asshole.

Darting my gaze to his crotch, I notice he hasn't even taken his pants off. His dick is out for all our spectators to see but only because he's taken it out from the vee of his opening.

Great, I don't even get that much from him.

I bet he can't even make me fucking orgasm. Of course, I'm going to have to suffer through this with absolutely zero pay off. Yay fucking me.

I barely finish that thought when his cock slams inside me without even a hint of preamble.

"Bet you I can."

My gasp is a mixture of surprise from the girth and invasion of him, and the fact that I apparently didn't just think those words.

"Even if I do, it's just physical. It doesn't mean a damn thing."

"On that we agree."

And then he fucks me like he hates me. One hand choking out most of my air and only leaving enough to keep me conscious, the other on my hip where I know I'll find bruises in the morning. I don't give him the satisfaction of showing any type of pleasure... or pain. In fact, I'm actively refraining from enjoying his hard dick pumping in and out of me.

The fact that I'm wet can't be helped; it's the mechanics of it all. At least that's what I'm going to tell myself because it definitely isn't about this asshole.

Curling my fingers in the bedspread, I let my mind wander to Caleb, but it's like Malik has a sixth sense, and he draws my attention back to him.

"You don't fucking think of another, Morganna. I demand respect," he hisses at me, loud enough so only I can hear.

Respect this, asshole.

Maybe I've said that aloud too. I'm going to guess so from the sheer hatred rolling from him.

The problem, I'm learning, is that his cock is too fucking talented. Not only is he creating delicious friction against my clit but the head of his cock is hitting my G-spot, over and over again.

By the time I see a thin sheen of sweat gather on his chest, I realize I'm panting, feeling the telltale signs of my impending orgasm.

The bastard knows it, too.

Speeding up his punishing thrusts, he grunts every time he bottoms out, and by the time his mouth lowers to my nipple and bites it enough to draw a drop of blood, I'm crying out into the room as wave after wave of unwanted pleasure courses through my entire body.

I squeeze my eyes shut to block out the view of him and bite my bottom lip to quiet my heavy breaths when I feel him pull out, still hard and angry.

Behind me, I can hear a light applause for my performance but the bastard hasn't come yet.

As though I weigh less than a feather, Malik picks me up and turns me onto my stomach, putting me on display for all of those viewing. My face heats with embarrassment—or maybe it's white-hot rage toward my heartless husband—as he leans in and murmurs, "Told you I'd make you come."

My jaw sets, my eyes narrow, and instead of falling away like a withering rose, I position myself so that my ass is right where he needs it. The faster he comes, the quicker I can get the fuck away from him.

Still half dressed, Malik places his hand back on my throat and pulls my head back so that I'm looking straight up at the dark red hue of the canopy bed. His mouth is at my ear again, his tongue darting out to flick my earlobe when I hear the devilish tone of his laugh.

"One day, you might even learn to like a little rough fucking, wife. Or maybe not. Personally, I don't give a fuck." Then he slams back inside me from behind and fucks me like an animal possessed. My back arches as far back as I can physically bend, and I can feel the skin at my hip breaking from his digging nails with every deep thrust inside me. It doesn't feel like he's just fucking me, it's like he's punishing me. Like any of this was my fucking choice.

The way he holds me like nothing more than a

possession belonging to his fucking throne makes my blood boil.

What he doesn't know is that I will melt that fucking throne and make a fucking crown out of it.

Once again, his skilled cock rouses a fire inside me I'm not willing to acknowledge.

"Don't move," he growls before releasing my throat. He brings his hand to my clit and flicks the hard nub enough to release another moment of pleasure from my core but not quite enough to make me orgasm.

Yet.

It's when he pushes inside me practically to the hilt that I feel the hard pinch of his thumb and forefinger, and then I hear the grunt as he gets close to orgasm and I, again, explode onto his cock. I'm so slick, I can hear the slapping of our skin as he resumes his punishing pistoning and it pisses me off that he's worked my body so well. He fucks me in sync with my cresting climax, before planting his hands on either of my hips and stilling while he comes inside of me with a shout.

This time, the applause is loud and unwanted. A job well done by the future king.

Fuck the future king.

Before he releases me, he murmurs out a 'thank you', and I don't know if he's talking to me or our audience.

In a moment of uncharacteristic kindness, Malik covers

my naked body with one of the sheets before he tucks himself in and walks to the bathroom. Seconds later, he's back with a warm cloth, surprising me, and for a moment, I think that maybe he's going to look after me.

Of course, he fucking doesn't.

Dropping the cloth at the side of my head, he winks and walks away with the rest of the watching court, laughing as they leave me in my fury.

TWENTY FOUR

It's been three days since I was married, and I haven't seen my husband since. Something about a deal he made with my father, keeping me at the Shadow Palace until he's ready to have me at his side. I don't know what sort of bullshit that is, but if I don't have to be around him, I'm not sad about it.

What pisses me off is that my father has some sort of magical fucking chain on Ares, which means Xavi couldn't take him to Avaenór without causing him a potentially lethal injury. I'm still so mad about it I could fucking spit.

I don't know how my father is always two steps ahead of us. I'm pretty sure he doesn't have a seer, but it's pissing me off nonetheless. All I need is one clear opportunity to get Ares free of all this. I hate that he's still here, basically chained to my father.

I've tried to speak to the Duttons' and Brandy about it, but no one seems to have any idea how I can free Ares without my father lifting whatever bind he's put on him.

The only upside to these few days is that Caleb is back with me. As soon as the wedding bullshit was over, Teddy brought him back to me. Though the Captain has kept him so stupid busy that I've not had any real time alone with him yet. I almost want to nut punch Bryce for that, but all eyes have been on me since the wedding.

Honestly, I'm still pretty pissed about that too, but I'm trying to not freak out about too much stuff right now. I feel like I'm juggling so many fucking balls that even a little too much rage will cause everything to come crashing to the ground around me. I've never felt more useless in my life.

So instead, I've spent the last few days in my room, trying to work out what else my power is capable of. Without a teacher or a guide, it's been pretty fucking slow going, but I refuse to just sit around and mope. I need to do something with myself.

Which is exactly why I find myself stomping over to the guard quarters. The Captain has had my claimed for too long now. Today, I want him to myself. I want to get the fuck away from here, even if it is just for a few hours.

I knock on the Captain's door, and laughter sounds

out from behind it before it opens. When it does swing open, I find Caleb and the Captain practically crying with laughter. I close my eyes and take a deep breath. I can't be pissed about their happiness just because my life is falling a-fucking-part.

"Mor!" Caleb says, jumping to his feet as I breeze past the Captain and into the room. "I've missed you."

I clamp down on the 'looks like it' that threatens to spill from my lips. I'm such a cranky fucking bitch right now.

"We were just having a break between rounds," the Captain offers, and Caleb smiles guiltily, making me feel like an even bigger bitch than I already did.

"I'm glad you're having fun. But I'm here to steal you away," I say to Caleb, and the Captain opens his mouth, but I shake my head. "Nope, not today, Captain. Not fucking today. I need you to keep an eye on my brother, but I need a sliver of joy. Just a tiny fucking sliver. So I'm stealing him away, and you're going to make sure my brother stays alive while I do."

The Captain just smirks at me and salutes. "Yes, ma'am."

Usually I'd be snappy about the smarmy-ass way he speaks to me, but I just don't have any space left in me for anything else at the moment. My whole world is crumbling, and I just fucking can't.

“Where are we going?” Caleb asks, wrapping his arms around me as if sensing I’m moments away from losing my shit, and I sink into his embrace.

“Far the fuck away,” I murmur, feeling safe and at peace for the first time in weeks. He’s been gone too long. Even my power feels calmer now that he’s touching me.

“We can do that,” he says quietly. The Captain coughs, reminding me he’s here, and I stiffen again.

“Thank you for all of your help so far, Captain,” I say, offering him a tight smile before turning back to Caleb. I take his hand and whisper him away to Level Seven, to the nest of the Tulane. No one will think to look for us here, and that’s exactly what I need.

Respite from the rest of the world.

“Do you want to fly?” he asks, and I shake my head. He drops to the ground and pulls me down with him to sit in his lap. “Talk to me, Mor. What’s going on in that head of yours?”

For a second, I hesitate. I don’t really want to burden him with any of this, but then I remember that he’s in this with me, whether I like it or not. I know he won’t leave my side, regardless of what I say or do, so I purge all of the craziness inside of my head.

The worry about Ares. My foiled plans of getting him to Avaenór. My frustration at my father, and his seemingly knowing ways. My fear of not being able to bring him down, my worry about my lack of ability to do what's needed. My deep-seated fury about the wedding, and everything that followed it. My humiliation and shame about the consummation.

And he just sits, rubbing my back as I unload on him until I'm spent.

"Mor, you don't have to carry this alone. We're in this together, always. Keeping me in the dark about so much… It's not a surprise you look like you're about to break. I already knew about the wedding, and everything after. And I already told you I was fine with whatever you had to do. Him, I'm pissed at because he was such a fucking dick about it, he definitely could've gone about it differently." His eyes start to bleed to black before he gets a grip of himself and continues with what he was saying.

"I've heard rumors about the Kavaraí people's ways before, so while I hoped you wouldn't be put through that, I was prepared for it. It was not a betrayal to me, so wipe that shit from your mind. As for the rest, we'll find a way together. I'm here with you now. You don't need to do this alone. Any of it, ever again."

I lay my head on his shoulder and just let him hold me as tears trickle down my face. I don't deserve him at all. Not even a little. But I'm going to spend the rest of my life trying to be worthy of him.

A flash of light pulls Caleb to his feet before he crouches

in front of me. I peer over his shoulder to see the fucking Angel sister of his.

"Sorry, am I interrupting?" she asks with a guilty smile, and I roll my eyes.

"You!"

"Me?" she asks hesitantly.

"Yes, you," I growl, so not ready to deal with this cryptic bitch today, I have enough going on. "You show up here, drop bombs, and then disappear for fucking weeks on end. And then I find out about the war between Avalon and Kavaraí and the brutality of Angels. You have some fucking explaining to do about why you're really here."

"Mor," Caleb says, his arms circling my waist. "Maybe wait to see what she has to say before we lose our shit?"

"Fine," I grumble, sinking into his touch.

"Okay, so yeah. I do have to apologize for dropping that nugget of information and dashing, but there's so much going on in the mortal realm right now... and in Avalon. Sometimes protecting the mortal realm is exhausting. But you guys do deserve an explanation." She sits down on the ground, her wings disappearing as she does so, and I let Caleb pull me to the ground and sit in his lap. "Let me start with introducing myself, I guess. My name is Amantara, and I'm a Shadow Walker…

"So, like I said before, you're my brother. It took me a long time to work out why I am what I am since they're so rare to my kind. So, after much persuasion, I had a friend on the Archangel council finally look into my bloodlines, but nothing made sense until he traced my blood to a Demon. I've been following that trail for what feels like forever, but instead of leading me to my father, it led me to you. After speaking to my friend on the council, we worked out that our father must be dead, which is why I couldn't sense him via the blood, but that you must be my brother, and that's why it brought me to you."

She takes a deep breath, and I let the information sink in. Caleb doesn't react at all, and I'm not sure if that's good or bad, but I stay quiet while she continues to speak.

"I don't mean you any harm. I've just had a really shitty experience when it comes to family, and I wanted to reach out to see if maybe we could build a friendship or something. I don't know." She wrings out her hands and her discomfort is obvious in the way she shifts around where she's sitting.

"Is that all?" Caleb asks, his voice quiet.

"Pretty much," she says with half a shrug. "I just… I've never really belonged at home in Avalon, so I wondered if I could find somewhere else, or someone else to belong with."

"I get that, and I felt the same way until I found Mor," Caleb says softly. "I can't offer you much, but I'm open to seeing where this goes. You should know that shit in our lives isn't simple though."

"Nothing in any of the Realms is simple. I know that better than most, but if you're open to at least getting to know me, I'm happy with that. I was so excited when I found out I had a brother, but then Leviathan reminded me that you might not be open to getting to know an Angel. In fact, he wasn't exactly thrilled about me continuing to come here, but bully for him; I'm a Shadow Walker, so I can be here just as well as I can be in Avalon."

I look to Caleb, who looks just as confused as I do.

"Oh, right. So yeah, Angels in the Shadow Realm… as a rule, not so fun. It hurts physically to be here, and technically our powers are lessened, but let's keep that between you and I, shall we? Call it an offering as a celebration to our new friendship. Also, we probably shouldn't broadcast the whole sibling thing. I don't know how Demons will take it, but let's just say if the Angels found out… well yeah, so not worth that headache." She grins, and I can't help but laugh. Maybe them being siblings explains why I was drawn to them both so strongly at first.

I stay quiet while she and Caleb talk, getting to know little things about one another. The longer we're here, the more I realize that I'm going to like her. She's like a breath of fresh air.

"Shoot, I need to go. Celestial bell is being rung and all that. I'll be back when I can! And if you need me, just draw this symbol in the ground in your blood. It will call to me." She hands a piece of paper over to Caleb before disappearing again, and I just laugh.

"She is definitely something."

He grins back at me and nods. "Yup, she is, and she's my family."

When I get back to the Shadow Palace, Caleb heads back to the guard quarters to check in with the Captain, and I find Ares waiting for me in my room.

"Thank fuck, are you okay?" I rush over to him, wanting to hug him but afraid to hurt him. He pulls me into his arms and holds me so tightly I think I might cry.

"I am now," he mutters as he clings to me, and I cling right the fuck back.

"I am so sorry he's doing this to you because of me. I just need to lift the hold he has on you, and then I can get you out of here," I tell him, not letting him go. I explain to him the deal I made with Xavi, and it's only when I feel one of his tears hit my cheek, I realize that he's crying.

"Mor, you can't do that. Do you know what he'll do to you if he finds out what you did? Or even just in retaliation for me escaping? I can't leave here without you."

"We can't leave him here, Ares. We'll never be safe

while he lives. I'm working on a plan for that too. I just need you to be safe. I can't do what I need to if I'm afraid of what he'll do to you."

"I won't let you take this on, Mor. This is not your responsibility."

"Ares," I sigh and pull back from his arms. "You aren't letting me do anything. I am a grown-ass woman. It is my turn to look after you. You've literally saved me my entire life. Now let me save you, please."

He sags and drops down onto my bed, tears still streaming down his face. "I don't want you to have to deal with him alone."

"I won't be alone. I've been making some friends of my own. Plus, you'll be happy for the first time in what, two hundred years? Xavi's safety extends to Lani and Teddy too. The thought of you being happy like that will make me happier than you can possibly imagine. So if you know of a way to lift this bind from you, I need you to tell me."

His head drops and shakes it. "If I had a clue, I'd tell you, but I don't."

He sounds so resigned that it breaks my heart. "I will find a way, Ares. I just need you to stay alive long enough for me to do it, okay?"

He nods at me, and I hug him again. I hate how far my father has broken him.

"Thank you, Morgan," he whispers, and my heart

breaks all over again. Maybe he won't be fit to rule after all of this, but with some time away to heal, I have every confidence he'll be the best King the Realm has ever known. "You give me such hope."

I smile at him and drop down onto the bed beside him. "You've given me that my entire life. It's about time I repay you."

We sit there in silence for a few minutes, and I just enjoy being with him. My power reaches out toward him, and he gasps, but I don't let go of his hand. I trust the power inside of me because of him, especially when I see some of the glow come back to his skin and his hair doesn't seem so lifeless anymore. He sucks in a breath and smiles. "Mor, how did you do that?"

I shrug because I simply don't know. I'm not even exactly sure what I did, but he looks as if I healed him.

"You just gifted me some of your power and healed me in the process." He looks at me in awe, and I can't help but blush a little.

"I mean, what's the good in having all this power if I can't help you?" I shrug it off because it's awesome that I can do it, but I've never been that great at taking praise.

"Shit, I just remembered why Father sent me up here." My heart sinks at his words, but I don't say anything. "I don't want to spoil this moment, especially when what you just did is so monumental, and you're doing so much for me, but your husband is coming for dinner, so your presence is required. I understand that a few others will be joining us too. I just don't know who."

I sigh, feeling the small grasp on happiness I had slip away.

"Of course, I guess I should get ready."

"I'll wait and walk you down," he says, smiling sadly at me. It doesn't take me long to change in my bathroom. By the time I walk back into my room, Ares looks even healthier than he did when I left him. Hopefully Father doesn't pay enough attention to notice it or at least not question it since we have guests for dinner.

We head down, and in the dining room I find Malik, his parents, my father, Xavi, and Killian. It's an interesting choice of dinner guests, all things considered. I say a brief hello to the Fae, in the hopes that my father doesn't know about my plans with Xavi, and move to say hello to my in-laws. Malik ignores my existence again while he speaks to my brother and the two Fae.

We all move to the table, and I remain basically silent throughout the meal, only speaking when asked a question.

It's not until the talk of war starts that I even pay attention.

"Why not just attack Avalon?" Kharim asks, and my father just scoffs.

"Their defenses are too much for us currently. With

Leviathan as their Archangel of War, and Michael leading the charge, that would be enough to make anyone hesitate, but they have a Shadow Walker among them. An Angel who can wield Shadow Fire." I blink, realizing they're talking about Caleb's sister.

Fuck my life, this just got twisted. And Leviathan, the friend she spoke of, is the one who laid waste to Kavaraí.

Holy fucking shit.

"We know all about her," Malik spits. "She is the one we held prisoner, and her fire was useless against us, but to you all, well you know how lethal that is."

"That we do," my father nods. "Which is exactly why I've opened portals to the mortal realm. We all know how much the Angels love to protect them. So I figure the best way to coax them out of their floating cities is to attack their precious mortals. Michael won't be able to ignore it for long. Then, when we're on a level playing field, you will have your revenge. Even the God of War would be proud of the strategy I've put together."

He smiles like the predator he is. This isn't the first time I've heard him refer to how alike he is to the God of War, and it's not the first time I have to stop myself from rolling my eyes at his theatrics. "We will make them pay in blood, the same way you did."

Shit, fuck, shit.

This is not going to end well.

Well, that dinner made for a fucking shit show of a night. I'm just glad to be back in my room with Caleb. It's the first time we've had any alone time since the wedding. I know he knows what happened… but we haven't discussed it properly, not really.

He said he'd be okay with everything, but I still feel like I betrayed him. Like I cheated on him, despite the fact that Malik is technically my husband.

When the door finally closes on my bedroom, I find myself pushed against the door with Caleb's lips on mine like a man possessed. "Did he kiss you here?"

"No," I breathe as he moves his lips down my neck, nipping me just a little as he kisses me.

"What about here?"

"No, he didn't kiss me at all."

Caleb snorts before pulling down the top of my dress and moving his lips to my lace-covered nipple. "Amateur."

"Did he make you come?" he asks, and I bite down on my lip, not wanting to answer even though he asked. His lips stop, and I let out a moan. "Did he make you come?"

I nod at his repeated question, his tone more demanding. "Yes, I tried not to give him the satisfaction, but…"

"Oh, sweetheart, you don't have to explain anything

to me. Too right you should've come. What's the fun in fucking someone you hate if you don't at least get a good orgasm out of it?" He smirks at me, and I can't get over how well he's taking this. "But you better believe I'm going to make you come harder and better than he did. You won't even remember his name when I'm done with you."

With a bite on my pebbled nipple, Caleb undresses me as he goes down on his knees, peppering open-mouthed kisses down my body until he reaches my lace-covered pussy. The only warning I get before he punctures my panties and rips them apart is a smirk and a wink. I would protest, but really, I don't give a fuck about the underwear as long as he keeps making my body sing with his touch.

"Did he eat your pussy?"

My hands at my side, fingers trying to find purchase so I can stay upright, I look down at him—his disheveled hair and demanding eyes stare back at me—and I shake my head. "No. There was nothing like that. Oh, Gods, don't stop!" His tongue alternates between flicking my clit and lapping up my arousal as it runs down the inside of my thighs.

"Hang on, beautiful."

I suddenly find myself with one thigh on his shoulder as his mouth attacks my pussy like a starving animal. The noises he makes are filthy and hot, and my vision is pinpointed on only one thing; Caleb's mouth. Teeth nipping at me and tongue spearing deep inside me, he's washing away every touch from my husband's cock.

It's when he adds a finger, then two, that I doubt my ability to stand for much longer if he continues his delicious assault.

"Caleb, oh Gods, I can't—"

He cuts me off, but I don't care, because I don't really know what I want to say except that the feelings he's provoking are all-consuming. Not just because he's fucking me with his mouth and fingers but because it's him. Simply him.

"You will. You will fucking come on my tongue, Mor. Now."

With one hand buried in the strands of his hair, I push my hips in rhythm with his feasting mouth. When he sucks my clit like he wants to rip it right off, I feel the electric volts of my orgasm consume me completely. Shaking and grunting, I follow the high of my climax as Caleb continues to fuck me with his face and hands.

He's gorgeous on any given day, but he's undeniably beautiful while he's eating my pussy.

Before I can even come down from my high, Caleb picks me up like I'm his new bride and playfully throws me onto the bed. My brain is fuzzy from my all-consuming orgasm, so it takes me a second to register the look he's giving me.

"Caleb?"

"I'm going to erase every single one of his touches. I'm going to make sure that the only thing your body remembers is me, my mouth, and my cock."

I don't have time to compute any of what he's saying before he has me on all fours and his cock slams inside me like a man possessed.

I take a second to adjust while cursing at how perfect he feels inside me, Caleb brings his hand to my hair and wraps the long strands around his palm, pulling my face back so he can see me.

"You may be his wife, Mor, but mark my words, you are fucking mine. Always."

"Yours, always." I repeat the words more for him than for me. I know this, I don't need reminding, but I get the feeling Caleb needs to hear it. It's the very least I can do to make up for the shitty situation he's in just because we're in love.

His other hand is on my tit, squeezing and tweaking my nipple as he fucks me like his life depends on it.

"Mine. All fucking mine."

Every word is punctuated with a thrust, and I can feel his words and his determination in every inch of my pussy.

I can't speak. My body is being used like a rag doll, and I'm okay with that. In fact, I love it. His desperation is addictive. His need for me is an aphrodisiac in and of itself.

Sliding his hand down my stomach, he reaches my clit and circles it in time with his cock before he brings my ear to his mouth and commands, "Come all over my dick, Mor."

And I do. I cry out almost like I'm in pain. His cock is so deep inside me, I can feel him throughout my entire body. Swirling with my soul. And definitely in my heart.

Shaking uncontrollably, I think Caleb is about to let it all go. With his mouth at my shoulder, he sinks his teeth into the flesh where my neck meets my collarbone and breaks the skin enough to make me gasp.

I come again. Longer and more intensely this time, and I feel my entire being transcending my immortal body. I've never had this kind of experience before, and the overload of pleasure almost takes me out.

Then he's gone, and I'm turned onto my back and facing him, his cock still hard despite his unrelenting fucking.

Bringing my thighs up to my chest, I watch in awe as he gathers my cum, scoops it up, and slides it down to my darkest entrance.

I pant at the idea of him breaching my ass. I'm scared but also curious.

"Did he fuck you, here?" He's not speaking. He growls the words as his finger slowly pushes inside of me, with my juices coating the digit.

"No," is all I manage to say.

Caleb grunts, and little by little his finger disappears inside my ass, and I writhe in unprecedented pleasure.

"Caleb?"

"Shh, baby. I'll take care of you. This too will be mine. All your firsts will be mine. Your mouth, your pussy, your ass. All fucking mine."

I want that too. I want all of my most memorable moments to be with him.

Relaxing as much as I possibly can, I give him the green light to do as he pleases with my body.

That's when he adds more fingers, scissoring gently and preparing me for what I'm sure will be the experience of a lifetime.

As he prepares me, he leans forward and laps at my pussy, keeping me on the edge and primed for another orgasm. I don't know how he does it, how he keeps pulling them out of me, but he does. It's like it's his superpower.

By the time he decides I'm ready for him, his cock looks almost angry and impatient.

Despite my trepidation, I trust Caleb to always look out for me. Always.

"Ready, baby?"

I nod.

"Words, Mor."

"Yes," I utter, and he smirks down at me before looking

back to my pussy.

"So fucking pretty." I watch, rapt, as he pushes his dick inside my pussy, thrusting once, twice, and then pulling out before he brings the head of his cock to my ass and slowly begins to push inside me. He moves slowly, groaning as he does until finally, he has his thumb circling my clit and his cock nearly buried to the hilt.

"Breathe, baby. Breathe, nice and slow."

I do as he says, clutching the comforter like my life depends on it. The pinching pain soon gives way to a kind of fullness I've never experienced before. It's sometimes uncomfortable, but mostly it's fucking delicious.

Caleb clearly sees the moment the pain is gone and the pleasure kicks in. Because that's when he leans down and covers my mouth with his. He kisses me like his life depends on our kiss. All the while, his cock slides out and then back into my ass.

I'm so utterly consumed by his kiss that I forget to breathe altogether, but there isn't any more pain. Only pleasure. From his mouth, from his thumb, from his dick.

"My ass," he whispers against my mouth. His thumb works double time before he plunges two fingers into my pussy and fucks me in tandem with his cock.

"Fuck, Caleb!"

"I got you, baby."

Curling his fingers just perfectly over my G-spot, I feel

my—fuck, I have no idea how many orgasms he's pulled from me at this point—orgasm building intensely as he makes his need to come known with every curse spilling from between his lips.

"Fuck, Mor, I'm going to come so fucking hard. I need you to fucking come for me again, baby."

My entire body tenses as I feel wave after wave of intense pleasure travelling throughout my veins. With my head thrown back and my back arched as far as it will go, I scream into the space between my four walls just as Caleb swallows my cries and feeds me his.

He follows me over the edge and holds me until we both come back down.

This, right now with him... It's all I need to survive this life.

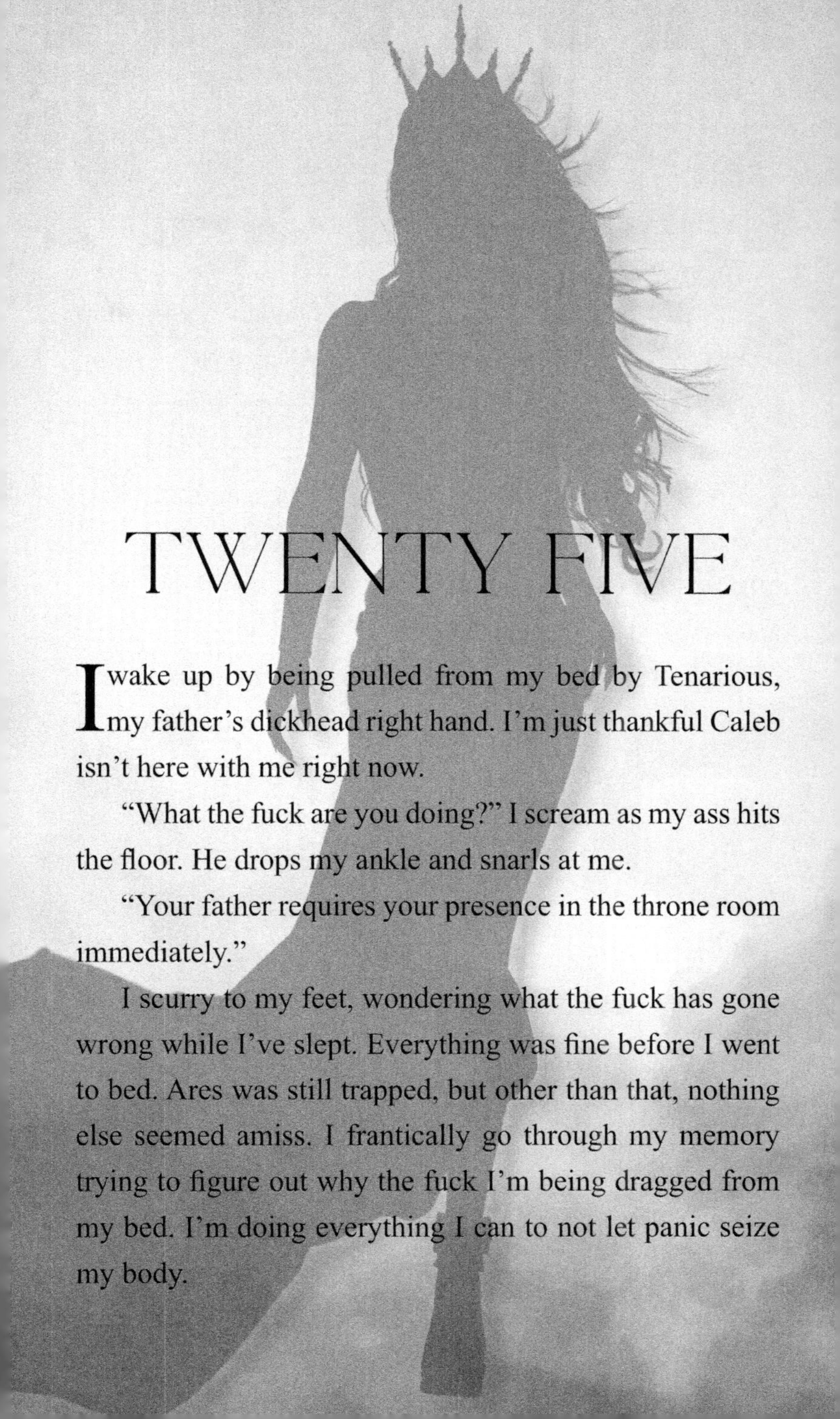

TWENTY FIVE

I wake up by being pulled from my bed by Tenarious, my father's dickhead right hand. I'm just thankful Caleb isn't here with me right now.

"What the fuck are you doing?" I scream as my ass hits the floor. He drops my ankle and snarls at me.

"Your father requires your presence in the throne room immediately."

I scurry to my feet, wondering what the fuck has gone wrong while I've slept. Everything was fine before I went to bed. Ares was still trapped, but other than that, nothing else seemed amiss. I frantically go through my memory trying to figure out why the fuck I'm being dragged from my bed. I'm doing everything I can to not let panic seize my body.

"Now!" Tenarious yells, making me jump. I'm still half fucking asleep. I do not have the wits about me to deal with him or my father right this second.

"Can I not get dressed?"

"No!" he bellows, so I grab my robe and follow him from the room. I clasp my hands together, trying to stop them from shaking. My mind instantly goes to the worst-case scenario.

My bare fleet slap against the polished floors as I rush behind him, and I realize it's the only noise in the otherwise silent palace. My heartbeat sounds in my ears, and I swear I can't fucking breathe. My blood feels like it's on fire beneath my skin, burning through my veins.

It doesn't take long until we reach the throne room, and I find my worst fucking nightmare waiting for me there.

Ares is on his knees before my father.

Teddy and Lani are both here, held by two of my father's sycophants in cuffs of shadow, and my heart drops.

What the fuck is going on?

"You thought I'd never find out?" My father roars and smacks Ares around the face with the back of his hand. Blood flies from his mouth, and I cry out for him.

"Oh good, you're here. Just in time to hear what your brother did. All these years he's had us fooled," my father rants, but he isn't making any sense. Ares looks at me, before glancing over to Teddy and Lani. I know exactly what he's asking, so I nod, my heart sinking.

"Tell your sister what you did!"

Ares rises up on his knees and spits blood at my father's feet. "I didn't do a fucking thing."

"Liar!" My father's roar echoes around the throne room, and I feel my knees start to shake. "He killed your mother!"

My heart sinks, and I drop to my knees. This can't be happening.

I can't let him punish Ares for something I did. I start to open my mouth, but Ares pins me with a stare and shakes his head.

No. This can't be happening. I need to contact Xavi. The risk is worth it. We need to get him away from here. I rack my brain trying to think of how the fuck to get all of us out of here in one piece since we're so fucking far apart in this room. I could get to Ares, but he'd never forgive me if I left the twins here, even if it was to save him.

"For this, you will be punished, and once I'm done with you, I'll torture the ones you love in front of you. Just fucking because. You took from me, and now I am going to take from you."

He yanks Ares to his feet and then touches his forehead.

"No!" My screams tear through the room as I watch my brother turn to stone. I drop to my knees as tears fall down my face. I will find a way to free him if it is the last thing I do. This is all my fucking fault.

I can't even hear Teddy and Lani through my own grief. But when my father turns and smirks at me, I know this isn't over yet. Tenarious grabs my bicep and yanks me to my knees.

"Better yet…" my father says, watching me as he speaks. Before I realize what's happening, his dark mist encases the stone.

My screams ring out, and my father's eyes go wide as Shadow Fire bursts from me in his direction. He disappears before the flames touch him, but Tenarious and my father's other goons are all gone. The flames disappear, and Teddy and Lani drop to the ground hugging each other in their grief.

Tears fall down my face as I move toward my brother's encased body, his soul destroyed by my father's mists.

I fall to my knees at his feet, no longer caring that my father knows about my power. Instead, I make a vow to avenge my brother.

My father might think he's the God of War reborn, but before I'm done, I'll see him on his knees.

GLOSSARY

Airon - *Air-on*

Amantara - *Ah-man-tar-ra*

Ares - *Air-ees*

Avaenór - *A-vah-nore*

Avalon - *A-vah-lon*

Bryce - *B-rice*

Callisto Desai - *Cal-ee-stow D-sai*

Dàgaan - *Day-gah-an*

Einar - *Ay-nar*

Emane Embers - *Ee-mane Em-bears*

Eteryia - *Et-tear-ry-a*

Kaos - *Chaos*

Kavaraì - *Ka-va-rahi*

Kharim - *Ka-reem*

Korrìn - *Ko-reen*

Malik - *Ma-leek*

Voux - *V-o*

Nasí - *Na-sai*

Neva - *Ney-va*

Rainha - *Rain-a*

Samiel - *Sam-i-el*

Shai - *Sh-ay*

Tariq - *Ta-reek*

Tenarious - *Ten-r-re-ous*

Trevalan - *Trey-vell-an*

Tulane - *Too-lane*

Xavi Allaire - *Za-vee A-lair*

Zafar - *Zaa-far*

Zhanna - *Z-ana*

ACKNOWLEDGEMENTS

Well… so that happened.

Before you all start shouting at me, I'd first like to say I wrote three alternate endings to this book, and they SUCKED. So I was true to the characters and this happened.

But this is the Seven Realms Saga… so anything is possible.

Now… back to why we're here. This book literally took a village. There were so many people behind the scenes helping get me through that I need to thank.

First to my bubble. Jenna. Cassie. KC. You guys are amazing, I love you, please never leave me ahaha.

To my amazing beta team. Zoe, Lisa, Steph, Megan, you slayed me while you were reading this one.

To Sarah, Christine & Sam - you guys made this one sparkle and shine, just like always. Thank you so freaking much.

To Lisa, my wonderful PA who does so many things so I can focus like 90% of my time on actually writing. You're a legend.

To Cat for the stunning cover on this book, you continue to amazing me with your genius.

To Steph, Blake & Claire for giving me the chance to

live out my dreams.

To my husband, and his xbox, for giving me the space I needed to get this book done.

And finally, to my readers. We've been in this series for a year now and you're still here. I love you for that. If you're starting with this book, thank you for giving it a chance. I hope everyone loves Morgan now as much as they did earlier in the series, if not more.

Pretty sure I've rambled on for long enough now, and I'm pretty sure I've missed someone, because I'm a menace, but just thank you to everyone who has helped me with this book, this series, and getting to this point in my writing career. I wouldn't be here, living my dream, without you.

ABOUT THE AUTHOR

Sloane Murphy is the author of the international bestselling series, The Immortal Chronicles, as well as a range of other paranormal and contemporary romance. Sloane lives in Peterborough, England, with her husband & fur baby and over the years, she has developed an unhealthy appreciation for cheesy YA Films, cupcakes and bad pop music. She adores fairy tales, ballet and all things supernatural, drinks far too much coffee, and watches an ungodly amount of Netflix. When she's not busy writing, she can be found exploring the world with her husband and chocolate Labrador.

If you would like to send Sloane an email, you can reach her at sloane@authorsloanemurphy.com

Want to sign up for her mailing list? You can sign up HERE

Or come join her reader group on Facebook, Sloanes Little Monsters

facebook.com/sloanemurphybooks

twitter.com/SloaneMurphyBks

instagram.com/sloanemurphybooks

bookbub.com/authors/sloane-murphy

ALSO BY SLOANE MURPHY

THE SEVEN REALMS SAGA

The Shadow Walkers Saga

(Reverse Harem Paranormal Romance)

A Crown of Blood and Bone

A Crown of Smoke and Ash

A Crown of Shadows and Secrets

A Crown of Thorns and Lies

A Crown of Fire and Wrath

A Crown of Pride and Ruin

The Shadow Weaver Series

(Menage Paranormal Romance)

Witch's Curse

Hunter's Heart

Demon's Blessing

The Shadow Queen Series

(Reverse Harem Paranormal Romance)

The Shadow Queen

Conquest

War

Famine

Death

THE IMMORTAL CHRONICLES SERIES

(YA Paranormal Romance. Complete Series)

Descent

Crash

Soar

Rapture

BLACK WATER ACADEMY SERIES

(Upper YA/NA Paranormal Romance. Reverse Harem)

Marked

Chosen

Hunted

DARK FAE DUET

(Paranormal Romance. Dark Fantasy)

Summer Princess

Winter King

OTHER AUTHORS AT HUDSON INDIE INK

Paranormal Romance/Urban Fantasy

Stephanie Hudson

Xen Randell

C. L. Monaghan

Sorcha Dawn

Sci-fi/Fantasy

Devin Hanson

Crime/Action

Blake Hudson

Mike Gomes

Contemporary Romance

Gemma Weir

Elodie Colt

Ann B. Harrison

Printed in Great Britain
by Amazon

79493211R00249